Robert White

Robert White is an Amazon best selling crime fiction author. His novels regularly appear in the top ten downloads in the Crime and Action and Adventure genres.

Robert is an ex cop, who captures the brutality of northern British streets in his work.

He combines believable characters, slick plots and vivid dialogue to immerse the reader in his fast paced story-lines.

He was born in Leeds, England, the illegitimate son of a jazz musician and a factory girl.

He hated school, leaving at age sixteen.

After joining Lancashire Constabulary in 1980, he served for fifteen years, his specialism being Tactical Firearms. Robert then spent four years in the Middle East before returning to the UK in 2000.

He now lives in Lancashire with his wife Nicola, and his two terrible terriers Flash and Tia.

Novels

Rick Fuller Thrillers:

THE FIX
THE FIRE
THE FALL

THE FOLLOWER
THE FELLOWSHIP
THE FIGHTER

Det Sgt Striker Thrillers:

UNREST
SIX
DARK TRIAD

Stand-alone novels:

DIRTY
BREAKING BONES

MADE TO BE BROKEN

A Rick Fuller Thriller
Book Seven
(The Politics of Murder Pt 1)

By

Robert White

www.robertwhiteauthor.co.uk

ISBN: 9798715248459

For my wife Nicola

Acknowledgements

I've lived in the shoes of Richard Edward Fuller and his co-conspirators for the last eight years. The first Fuller novel, The Fix, was intended to be a standalone story. I had no desire to write a series. As a new and eager author, my objective was to spread my wings in as many directions as possible and not tie myself to one or two characters. But Fuller refused to lie down. Somehow, with the release of each adventure, this misfit, anti-hero grabbed the imagination of ever more readers, leaving them clamouring for yet another instalment.

It was seven years later, as I was writing book six, The Fighter, that I began to feel that the storyline had run its course, and with that in mind, I sat down with my wife, my biggest fan and fiercest critic and discussed my ideas.

Nicola agreed that I had two options. End the series at book six and allow Rick his happy ever after or break his heart and tell his story in a different way.

So here we are.

Made to be Broken has been a challenge to write. New characters have emerged, and, for the first time, the story is told in the third person. Changing the format of anything popular is a risk, but I think it was one worth taking.

So, once again, I have my wife to thank for her good advice. A Special Forces veteran that I only ever knew as 'Hugh,' for bringing me the character of Des Cogan and my small but illustrious team of Beards, Debbie and Vassil who do all the behind the scenes work.

Stay safe in these difficult times.

Robert White.

"What Darwin was too polite to say, my friends, is that we came
to rule the earth not because we were the smartest,
or even the meanest, but because we have always been the
craziest, most murderous motherfuckers in the jungle."

Stephen King

ONE

Jomtien Beach, Pattaya, Thailand

The rain was torrential. It pounded the road and clattered the thin tin roofs of the bars, soaking everything and everyone.

He walked steadily in the deluge, his clothes sticking to his skin, accentuating his tall muscular frame. He didn't bow his head or even squint his eyes. He enjoyed the rain.

Some days, it was the only way he ever felt clean.

He dipped his head under the corrugated roof of the Cha Cha Saloon, the rain, and the early hour ensuring he found his usual place at the bar. A place to stand, then lean and sometimes even fall.

Resting his elbows onto the tired timber plinth, he nodded at the attractive Thai waitress. As he did so, droplets of water spilled from his hair and beard and splattered the bar top. He examined them for a moment, before wiping them away with his hand.

It had been almost a year since he'd visited a barber. Almost a year since the funeral. Almost a year drunk.

The bar girl slid an empty glass over to him. One cube of ice, just the way he liked it. Then came the bottle of Mekhong. The tourists all called it whiskey, but he knew better. It was distilled from ninety five percent molasses and five percent rice, so more of a rum.

It was cheap, did the job and got him to sleep at night.

Sleep was one thing, the nightmares, quite another. In the daytime hours, his hatred towards another living being was unrelenting, matched only by his own self-loathing. Yet in the small hours, it was his dreams that tore him apart. For years, he'd endured nightmares featuring a different participant. Now he had another visitor, starring in yet another horrific tableau, his tortured mind forcing him to relive each shocking moment before a sharp intake of unwanted cruel breath wrenched him, sweating and breathless into consciousness and the reality of his empty existence.

Yes, a year. A year of pain, revulsion and crushing guilt.

He brushed his hair back from his face, wiped his wet hand on his even wetter jeans and cracked the bottle.

He liked the sound it made. A new bottle, a new way down the hole.

"You want a towel, Sir?" asked the girl behind the bar.

He shook his head, emptied his glass in one grimacing gulp, and poured another. He'd be dry soon enough. After all, it was thirty six degrees out there.

Twisting his lithe body, he inspected the sparse crowd.

The usual four bar girls were sitting together, eating. It was a Thai pastime. He figured that they ate, almost as much as they copulated. One thing simply helped pay for the other.

He'd never partaken with the whores himself. He'd been tempted a couple of times, especially after a bottle of his favourite tipple, but no, that would only further fuel his culpability, and he didn't think he could stand that.

He again refilled his glass and asked for more ice. The barmaid dropped in another cube and another big smile.

"You going to eat something today handsome man?"

He shrugged. "Maybe later."

Food was no longer a pleasure to him. Indeed, he couldn't think of a single gratifying pastime in his life, other than the Mekhong, that was. He still ran, still worked his muscles to exhaustion most days and would still fight if he had to, yet he felt, well, he felt nothing at all.

The rain was easing and with that, the punters began to arrive. Ageing men, from the obese to the anorexic, sloped in and found a table. They hailed from all countries, all races. Their only binding connection being the pursuit of young sweet meat.

At one point in his life, such things would have revolted him, but this last year, he couldn't find it within himself to be angry about such small matters. Life was a shit sandwich, ask anyone.

The band began to set up, guitars were tuned, drums struck. A bar girl he hadn't seen before approached him and offered him her body. Short time, the equivalent of twenty five pounds.

He bought her a drink and sent her away.

He was halfway down the bottle, the band had played for an hour and the place was finally full. Tourists from the four corners of the globe, mixing with the punters, all finding the mixture of sun, fun, and sleaze, irresistible.

His hair had dried and had curled at the neck. He'd never worn it long before, maybe a little when under cover in Ireland, but he'd hated it even back then. He'd always been a short back and sides kind of guy. Clean shaven, clean living.

Well once. Not now. Not anymore.

Catching his reflection in the sweat streaked mirrors behind the optics, he noticed he looked tanned but tired. The star shaped scar on his cheek standing out against his sallow skin. He touched it wistfully, something he'd done hundreds of times since Stephan Goldsmith had shot him in the mouth causing the injury.

There was a split second when his brain forced him back there, to that very moment, to that night on those deserted moors, back to his former life, dragging him ever downwards, twirling, twisting, first to the mean streets of Manchester, then to Ireland, to Greece, to Albania. He knew all those places well, just as he did his old enemies, the ones that had dared remain in his head. Those foes that gambled he would be off guard, that the Mekhong had worked its spell. But not so today. Not just yet. This day, he was too strong. He scowled, held the bridge of his nose between thumb and finger and forced those ancient images away.

He had to chase them back down their hole, because... because she would be in there, she would be one of those images, and the pain that he would feel, just by seeing her in his mind's eye, even for the briefest time, would be just too great.

Half a bottle became three quarters, and he began to feel the alcohol numb-
ing his senses. He stretched, cricked his neck, scratched his beard.

"Hello," said a voice. An English, female voice.

He turned and examined the speaker. She was young, twenty, twenty
five tops. Pretty, no, very pretty. A brunette, with pale expressive eyes that
he couldn't quite decide on the colour of. Blue, grey?

Whatever.

She looked like a backpacker, all cut off denims, skinny vest, lots of
handmade bangles. Pattaya was full of them. Students on gap years, spending Mummy's cash.

He did his best to focus.

"Do I know you?"

The girl smiled to reveal perfect teeth. "I don't think so. I'm Harriet.
Harriet Casey."

He turned back to the bar.

"You're correct, I don't know you. So go away."

Even in his inebriated state, he realised that she hadn't moved. His rude-
ness hadn't had the desired effect.

He had a second go.

"You still here?"

The girl pursed her lips gripped her hair with both hands and pulled it
into a ponytail.

"Another glass," she said to the bar girl. "And another bottle."

Then she turned to him and gave him a look that he couldn't read at all.

"We need a chat, Mr Fuller. A long chat."

The girl grabbed the fresh Mekhong by the neck, then with the same hand
lifted her clean glass, two fingered, by its lip. It was a practised movement,
something she'd done many times before. She nodded to a corner table.

"Over there," she said. "That will do."

He refused to budge. Examined her again. Yes, he thought, her eyes were
definitely blue.

"Why did you call me, Fuller?" he asked.

She narrowed her gaze, her tone suddenly querulous, impatient.

"Because that's your name," she said, dropping her bottle and glass back onto the bar with an irked clunk.

Harriet pushed her hand into the back pocket of her shorts and pulled out her mobile telephone. She quickly scrolled some content before finding what she was looking for, before sliding the set across the bar. He eyed it suspiciously.

The screen displayed a scanned copy of a black and white photograph. At some point in its life, it had been folded down the middle, a deep white score cutting the image in half, as if it had been creased for some considerable time.

"There," she announced. "You, four years ago, Manchester, Richard Edward Fuller. Ex Special Air Service, widowed, no dependants, no permanent address, no ... Well, other than an extremely healthy bank balance, which looking at this establishment, and the brand of your preferred spirit, you are keen to hold onto, no... anything at all, actually."

He peered at the shot. It had been taken early 2006, outside his apartment on the Manchester Docklands by an old flame, Tanya Richards. She, like any other woman he'd taken to his heart or bed was dead. Shot on a nondescript road outside Amsterdam. The mental image of her corpse made him dizzy as he fought to stop his brain filling with other damaging memories.

"Where did you get that?" he asked.

She ignored his question and tapped the screen with a clear varnished nail.

"This is you though, isn't it?"

She looked into his eyes and tried to read what was there. Failing miserably, Casey blew out a long breath. There was a hint of weariness in her tone.

"Can we stop fucking about... please?"

She collected her phone and pushed it back in her pocket, picked up her bottle and glass and once again gestured towards the same table.

"And I really would prefer to sit. It's been an awfully long day, and I need a drink."

Unmoved by the girl's request, he pushed his hair behind his ears and emptied the remnants of his bottle into his glass. Slowly he scrutinised Casey again, her raven hair, that early confidence, that piqued insolent tone taking him back to yet another place.

"You remind me of Sellers," he said, a hint of a slur in his voice and still no nearer moving from his chosen spot. "Not quite as posh. But just as pretty."

The girl shook her head, her defiance turning to disappointment.

"Well, I don't know who that is, Mr Fuller, and quite frankly, I don't give a shit if you think I'm pretty. I was told that it would be worth my while travelling halfway around the world to find you, that you could help me… no, would help me. But it seems that some of the information I was given was incorrect. You're nothing more than a washed up mean drunk."

He snorted.

"And just who gave you this… information?" he said, downing his drink and dropping his glass just a little too heavily on the bar.

The girl swallowed nervously. There was a delay in her answer he found suspicious. Moments later, he knew why.

"Uncle Damien," she said. "Well, he's actually Daddy's uncle, not mine, but I've always called… "

Fuller twisted his head, eyes suddenly clear, teeth bared. "Damien Cartwright?" he snapped.

The girl seemed shocked by his sudden show of aggression. "Erm… yes, he…"

"And he told you where to find me?"

She nodded. "To a point."

Harriet Casey once again tried to read those chocolate eyes. They were full of hatred and suspicion, yet she couldn't look away. He frightened her, frightened her a lot.

Fuller picked up her bottle and turned.

"Bring some ice," he said.

He sat heavily, his knee knocking the table, rattling the two empty glasses she had put there. He ignored, or just didn't notice his lack of coordination, cracked the new bottle and poured.

Casey sat gingerly. What Fuller couldn't see, mustn't see, at least for now, were the bruises to her lower back, the injuries so professionally inflicted by the man she had escaped from in Frankfurt.

There was blood in her urine, her kidneys were damaged, but there was no time for the hospital. She'd called an old university friend, a med student. He'd said it was possible that they would heal themselves.

She hoped he was right.

"So, how is the old bastard?" growled Fuller.

Harriet wore a puzzled expression. "I'm sorry?"

Fuller snorted again and took a large gulp of Mekhong. "I thought I was the drunk. You need to keep up. Cartwright of course, your MI6 chum."

"He's not my chum, he's my..."

"Great Uncle, yes, I got that. So, like I asked, how is the old fucker?"

She watched him miss the lip of the table with his elbow and almost fall on his face.

"He's not too well, actually. He's got... look, Fuller, maybe you should have a coffee or something?"

This time he made the table with both elbows. He slid his powerful frame across the surface, his face just inches from hers. There was that look in his eyes again. Eyes that could have been so beautiful, tarnished by loathing, repugnance, bitterness.

Damien Cartwright had explained to her that Fuller was a damaged individual, but she wasn't expecting this level of mental anguish.

"I've known you less than ten minutes, and already you're pissing me off," he sneered, grabbing for the bottle and missing.

She poured him a drink and handed him his glass.

He scoffed but took it.

"Suppose you want thanks for that eh?" He took a slurp. "What are you, some kind of travelling nun?"

She filled her own glass for the second time, took a swig and re discovered her undoubted courage.

Casey eyed him. "I've been called a few things, Fuller, but never that." She turned and looked out from under the tin canopy to the road outside. "Where do you live?"

"Why?" he slurred. "You offering to carry me home?"

"No, you can still walk. But I think the conversation we need to have is pointless right now and I need a bed for the night."

He sat back in his chair and looked her up and down.

"How do you know I'll keep my hands to myself?"

Harriet lifted her backpack from between her feet and unzipped the top. Resting neatly on a perfectly folded towel was a M1911 semi auto. She patted it lovingly.

"I have holiday insurance," she said.

Fuller gave a wry smile, blew air down his nose and let his heavy lids fall for a moment. Opening them, he said, "A nun with a gun. Well isn't this my fuckin' lucky day?"

"I'm tired, Fuller," said Harriet. "That, and what I have to tell you, will be best said once, before you find the bottle again. So, if you don't mind…"

He ran his tongue across his teeth and took another large swig of amber liquid. Dropping his glass, he sniffed loudly.

"Come on then," he said. "It's not far." He gestured towards Harriet's rucksack. "Have you fired that yet?"

Casey jutted her chin.

"Maybe."

Fuller gave another snort. "If you bought it here, it's probably from the Vietnam war. If you came by it in Europe, the Provos bought a shed load of them in the 1970's. Old, but effective in the right hands."

"Fascinating, Fuller. But like I said…"

He ignored her and continued his questioning on one of his favourite subjects. "What load are you using? .45 ACP?"

She nodded.

"Full metal jacket or hollow point?"

"Hollow."

He drunkenly pointed at her, like a child pretending to have a gun. He made a clicking sound with his tongue.

"This nun likes to make a mess," he said.

Harriet didn't allow her gaze to falter.

"It's a dangerous world out there, Fuller. Lots of men who think they are too big and clever."

He stood unsteadily, nodded at the Thai girl behind the bar and made to leave.

Harriet cocked her head.

"I have a tab," he said. "I'm a regular."

"No shit Sherlock," said Harriet.

* * *

Fuller's apartment was above a laundry on Soi 9. Not exactly unusual as the small streets off the Jomtien beach road were littered with them. Those, and massage parlours, both genuine and offering 'extra' services. Entry to his modest abode, was gained via a narrow concrete staircase.

He stood on the small square landing at the top and fumbled for his keys.

Harriet waited, three treads down, wary and suddenly unsure that she'd made the right decision.

Fuller didn't appear to notice her reticence and there was a noticeable click as he turned the lock and pushed open the door.

Casey trod into the flat two steps behind him.

The room was simply furnished. A sofa, a small TV, a round metal table, two chairs. She'd expected a mess. After all, from what she'd seen, Fuller was either an alcoholic or certainly alcohol dependant and neither of those kinds of men were noted for their tidiness.

Not so.

The room smelled of bleach and was immaculate.

He staggered the half a dozen steps it took to cross the living space and pushed open a door that led to a small kitchen.

"Help yourself to whatever you can find," he said, "Bathroom's off to the right."

He then managed a few more strides to a second door that led to a solitary bedroom, reached inside the jamb and clicked on the light.

As with the rest of the apartment, the room appeared spotless, the bed made to the exacting standards you might expect of a military man.

"I changed the sheets this morning," he said. "You take the bed, I'm good on the sofa."

At that he walked past her, brushing by with his shoulder. Harriet didn't know if it was intentional, or just the Mekhong doing its job.

He sat heavily and yanked off a pair of Timberlands, then stood, and pulled his t shirt over his head. Casey couldn't take her eyes from his body, the mat of hair on his chest running down his stomach past his navel did little to hide the numerous scars that littered his torso.

Casey had scars too. Not so many as Fuller. But they were there, some visible, and just like his, some not.

"You don't wax, then," she said.

Fuller unbuttoned his jeans.

"Go to bed," he said. "I wake up early."

* * *

Casey opened her eyes. She could hear a shower running. It took her a second or two to realise where she was. Sitting up, she reached to the bedside cabinet for her SLP.

Of course, it wasn't there.

The pain in her back had eased slightly, but even so, as she swung her legs from the bed, her kidneys complained bitterly.

Stepping into the small lounge area, the mystery of her missing firearm was solved. It sat on the small round metal table, stripped to its working parts, magazine and ammunition missing.

She heard movement behind her, just as Fuller appeared wrapped in a towel, hair dripping.

"I always feel nervous when I have an armed house guest," he said. "Especially one associated with The Firm."

Harriet felt suddenly vulnerable. She wore just the skimpy vest she'd arrived in and a pair of panties that did little to hide her modesty.

Fuller didn't appear to notice.

"Why don't you get dressed and we can go eat?" he said.

"When do I get my gun back?" she asked, her petulance at being outdone so easily showing in her tone.

"When I get to know you better," he said.

Harriet showered and changed. As she pulled her t-shirt over her head, Fuller stepped into the bedroom.

"Don't you ever knock?" she said, further irritation creeping into her voice.

He gestured at the damage to her lower back. "Those look sore," he said.

"I'm getting there, Fuller. Don't concern yourself."

"You pissing blood?" he asked

"Was."

"I know someone, someone local, discreet. We'll go after breakfast."

"I'll be fine, and…"

He dropped her pistol onto the bed, fully loaded.

"No you won't. You need that looked at. I'll wait outside. Don't be long, I'm hungry."

They walked in the oppressive heat. It wasn't so much the temperature of the day, but the humidity. By the time they sat in The Pirate's Bar on the beach road, both were wet with sweat.

Fuller ordered for the pair of them and they sat in silence as both devoured two American breakfasts and coffee.

Finally.

"Do you remember anything from last night?" she asked.

Fuller wiped his mouth on a napkin. "Everything."

She looked impressed.

"When's the last time you went a day without a drink?"

"Three hundred and forty three days ago."

She raised her brows. "Nothing like being precise."

"Change the subject," he said. "Let's talk about you, Casey. What brings you here and why?"

She took a deep breath.

"You, Fuller. You bring me here. Uncle Damien says you are the best dark ops agent he's ever seen. And as he is rather keen to keep his great niece alive, he sent me to you."

Fuller shook his head.

"Look sweetheart, I feel like dog shit every day. My hands shake in the mornings. I puke a lot and I have nightmares that are so real, that sometimes I don't know if I'm asleep or awake. So, no matter what little adventure you have in mind, or why Cartwright has made the decision to send you to me, you are not dealing with the man that left the UK a year ago. You were right, last night, Casey. I'm nothing but a washed up, mean drunk."

"Maybe you should throw some more self-pity in there, Fuller," she said quietly.

That hurt him, and it showed. She saw his dark brown eyes flash. There was still life in there. Still a quick brain working inside a very capable body.

"Don't be clever, Casey," he said, and found something of interest to look at across the road.

Directly opposite the bar, sandwiched between the beach and the road, was a small free gym. It had a mixture of indoor and outdoor fitness machines and was popular with the locals as well as the holidaymakers. Jomtien, a district of Pattaya, attracted visitors from dozens of countries, including many Russians, and it was just one of the plethora of Muscovites pumping iron not twenty yards away that had distracted Fuller from his conversation.

"The guy on the shoulder press, shaved head, Ray Bans… you seen him before, Casey?"

Harriet eyed the guy. He was a big bull of a man. Lots of muscle, red speedos, flip flops.

"Not my type," she said finishing her coffee.

Fuller scanned the promenade, left and right.

"How about the guy in the shocking Hawaiian number standing by the beachwear stall?"

Casey shook her head. "What are you seeing that I'm not, Fuller?"

He clocked a third man, off to his right sitting on a metal bench. White chinos, black silk shirt, who, just like the other two, had a tiny covert comms set in his right ear.

Fuller checked the alley that ran off to his left and back towards the centre of Jomtien. It looked clear.

"Tell me you brought your pistol with you," he said.

Casey pulled her hair back into a ponytail.

"I never leave home without it," she said.

TWO

Loch Lomond, Scotland.

The car was too far away for him to hear the engine note. The first thing he noticed was the glint of the sun on its windscreen as it made its way gingerly along the narrow track that mirrored the landscape of the loch. The vehicle's destination, however, was never in doubt. After all, there was only one house at the end of the lane… his.

He was grateful for the sun. As he lay back against the hull of his small boat, it warmed his bones. Even though the temperature was less than ten degrees the fact that the sky was blue, and the sun shone, cheered him. It had been a hard winter in more ways than one. Lots of rain, grey sky, cold wind.

The harsh Scottish weather had mirrored his life the past year. He had hoped for a new start, the beginning of something fresh, positive. Yet instead it had turned into a time for awkward silences where the past was never mentioned for fear of remembering ones that had been so special. Ones that, in the cold light of day, could never be replaced.

The car, which he now recognised as a BMW, was struggling with the rutted track. As it grew closer, he could hear the scrapes from the underside of the vehicle as it bottomed out.

He pulled his small metal pipe from his jacket and tapped it out on the side of the boat. Filling the bowl with fresh makings, he pressed the fragrant mixture in place with his thumb, before lighting it and drawing the smoke deep into his lungs. As he exhaled, there were further metallic scrapes emanating from the approaching saloon.

"That sounds expensive," he muttered to himself.

Two further drags on his pipe saw it empty and he stowed it before checking his fishing gear. Reeling in the line, he saw that the bait had been taken, yet the wily fish had escaped to fight another day.

He turned to his dog, Bruce.

"Looks like beans on toast again, son," he said.

The dog whimpered.

Bruce was a new addition in his life. He'd never had a pet, not even as a kid. And in his later years, the way he'd lived, he'd hardly been in a position to care for himself, let alone an animal. He'd bought the dog for Kaya. The speech therapist had said it would be good for him, a stimulus, and animals are non-judgemental, so they say.

The Collie had turned out to be too boisterous for the lad. The animal's somewhat comical features of one ear pointing upwards to the heavens, and the other flopping against his skull, had done little to endear him to Grace either. However, Bruce's banishment to the cottage on the loch, rather than the far more salubrious surroundings of Hillside, was made a certainty when Bruce ate a third pair of Grace's shoes.

Despite the dog's shortcomings, he liked the animal. He was company on the cold nights, someone to talk to. Something to take his mind off the old days.

Once again, he eyed the approaching car.

"And who d'you suppose this is the now?" he said, checking the direction of Bruce's gaze.

The dog cocked his head, looked across the shimmering water and let out a low growl.

Des Cogan rooted in his Bergen and removed a Browning 9mm.

"That's just what I was thinking, son."

The car finally made it to the front of the cottage and a lone male stepped out of the driver's side. He walked to the front door and knocked. Of course, there was no reply.

From Cogan's position on the loch, he could see that his visitor was a young, slender, well-dressed man and he stood at the gate of the house, turning full circle, his hands on hips, seemingly perplexed as to what to do next.

Cogan was probably two hundred yards offshore. He gave Bruce another look.

"What ye think eh pal? Ye think we should see what the wee boy wants?"

Bruce whimpered and hopped from foot to foot.

"Come on then," he said, starting the small outboard. "It has to be more interesting than beans on toast eh?"

The noise of the boat's motor drew the man's gaze. Cogan watched him shield his eyes against the low sun in an attempt to see who was aboard the tiny vessel. Des rested his Browning on the bench next to him.

Better safe than sorry.

As Des piloted the boat towards the shore, his visitor took it upon himself to walk closer to the water's edge to greet him. The incessant rain over the last days had ensured that the loch side was slippery and, in places, ankle deep in mud, most definitely unsuited to a shiny two piece and brown brogues. The young man wobbled, lost his footing and fell on his backside.

Des could just make out the tirade of expletives coming from him as he scrambled to his feet. The Scot picked up his sidearm and slipped it back in the top of his Bergen. Bruce gave him a confused look.

"The fella disnea look too dangerous fe here, now, does he?"

The Collie gave a muffled bark, unconvinced.

Des gave him a reassuring pat on the head.

"I'm beginning to think ye have trust issues, pal."

By the time he'd steered to land, his visitor had scrambled back to his car and was attempting to scrape mud from his suit trousers. Bruce jumped from the boat before Des could tie up and was running around the well-dressed visitor, grumbling, but wagging his tail.

"Could you take the dog away, please," shouted the suit in some of the best Queen's English Cogan had heard since Victoria Sellers had left for Dubai.

"He'll no bother ye," he replied. "He's just a bit daft is all."

The man stepped back against his car, unconvinced. "That is as maybe, sir, however, I'm allergic to dogs, of all types and temperaments. Friendly or otherwise."

Des called Bruce away and held him by the collar.

"Thank you," said the man.

"That's ne bother," he replied, inspecting his company further. "So, my mate, by the look of ye, I'd say yer here by accident. Are ye lost? Yer certainly no dressed fer fishing or hunting eh? Have ye never heard? It rains in Scotland fe time to time."

The man continued to wipe mud from his suit. "No such thing as bad weather, just the wrong clothes, that's what they say, isn't it, Mr Cogan?"

Des cocked his head, lowered his voice. There was instantly menace there.

"So you're no here by accident at all then eh? You knowing my name and all."

"No, sir. Not a chance meeting, mishap, or wrong turn, I'm afraid."

"Afraid? What are ye afraid of son?"

His visitor managed a thin smile. He was young, fresh faced and handsome in an angular kind of way.

"Just a figure of speech, sir. I'm not actually afraid, as in frightened."

Cogan reached into the top of his Bergen, pulled the Browning from the top and clicked off the safety.

"Well ye fuckin' should be pal."

The guy threw up his arms. Cogan thought the movement almost comical. This was not a man used to having a gun pointed at him.

"Oh... erm... don't do that... I mean... please... my motives are purely peaceful, sir. There is no need for firearms, I assure you."

"Peaceful? Now that's a new one."

"Yes. Mr Cogan, I simply bring a message."

"A message, ye say? What kindae message, and who might it be from?"

The man glanced over his shoulder towards the small cottage, then back at Cogan. He had a look of pure misery about him.

"Might we go inside, sir? I'm rather wet and wretched, and this may take some time to discuss."

Bruce gave a confirmatory woof.

Cogan nodded, reapplied the safety to his weapon and pushed it into the waistband of his trousers.

"Give me a minute to put this boy away so he disnea bother ye. I'll find ye some dry trackies. They willnea match ye posh jacket though."

The man nodded. "Thank you, Mr Cogan that would be splendid."

The small house was warm and cosy. Cogan dropped his Bergen under the staircase, locked a very disconcerted Bruce in the kitchen and found a pair of dry tracksuit bottoms for his caller.

"Bathroom is at the top of the stairs," he offered. "If ye bring yer suit trousers down with ye, we'll see if we can clean them up some."

"Thank you again, Mr Cogan," said the younger man, his pale cheeks flushing from the change in temperature. "I'll just be a moment."

Cogan dropped more wood on the smouldering fire and the dry logs instantly crackled into life. He held his calloused hands to the flames, rubbed them together briefly, then sat in his favourite chair to await his guest.

The man was indeed just moments. As he dipped his head to enter the tiny lounge, Des could barely prevent himself from laughing. He had indeed changed his trousers, yet, in his wisdom, had decided to keep on his shirt, tie, jacket and brogues. Being a good foot taller than the Scot, the joggers barely reached his ankles.

He read Cogan's thoughts.

"I look ridiculous, don't I?"

The Scot stifled a smile.

"At least yer arse is dry eh, son?

"I suppose," said the man, resignedly.

Cogan pointed to a clothes airer close to the fireplace. "Hang yer pants on there, pal, get them dry eh? Then take a seat."

The man did as he was asked. Finally, the unlikely pair sat face to face.

"Ye want to begin with yer name there, son?" asked Cogan. "Then, more importantly, who sent yees?"

The man nodded, leaned forwards, and clasped his hands together. "I'm Casey, sir. Warren Casey."

"That's a start there, Warren."

"Yes, erm… sorry… of course."

"So why are ye here? I mean, this place, the now. Talking to an old soldier like me?"

"It's my sister, Mr Cogan. She's… well, she's in a spot of bother."

Cogan looked puzzled, yet he let his curiosity get the better of him.

"Go on," he said.

Warren nodded gratefully.

"Thank you, well… Harriet, that's her name, well, she was always a bit on the adventurous side you see, and when she left Uni, she decided, well actually, we both decided, to take up jobs within the Security Services."

Des wasn't convinced.

"You? You work fer MI6? The Firm?"

Warren blew out his red cheeks.

"I'm… I'm strictly an analyst, Mr Cogan. I'm sure it's obvious that field work would not be my forte."

Cogan nodded.

"I gathered that there, son. But no yer wee sister eh?"

"No, not Harriet. She loved the idea of being at the sharp end. Pretty soon, we'd gone our separate ways, so to speak. I remained at GCHQ, I'm a translator, languages are my specialism, whereas she went to work for… Uncle Damien."

Cogan sat up in his chair.

"Damien? Fer fuck's sake, not Damien Cartwright?"

Warren nodded.

"And he sent you to me?"

Another nod.

"Why? I'm retired. Long retired. There must be dozens of field agents out there that can help yer wee sister."

"I realise what you are saying, sir, but… "

"What aren't ye telling me son?"

Warren took a deep breath.

"Uncle Damien is sick, Mr Cogan. He has colonic cancer. He no longer has any influence within the Service. He hasn't been operational for nine months or so. When he became ill, Harriet was allocated a new handler, a chap called Abrahams. I am reliably informed that her new supervisor, dispatched her and two other field agents to Germany to recover an item that the Russian ambassador was secretly attempting to transport to the UK, to Liverpool, if my memory serves me. And before you ask, I have no idea what that item was, or indeed if the team managed to prevent its transportation. What I do know, however, is that Harriet's comrades are dead and that she barely managed to escape Germany with her life. She's on the run, Mr Cogan."

"So send out the cavalry to collect her."

Warren gave Des a look he knew only too well.

The Scot let the information sink in.

"She was working dark?"

"She's on her own, sir. She's what they call… deniable."

Cogan blew air down his nose, shook his head.

"Nothing ever fucking changes eh?" he muttered.

"So I'm led to believe, sir."

"So yer wee sister called Cartwright, and he sent ye here, to me?"

"In a nutshell, Sir, yes. He dispatched me here, and her to Thailand."

"Thailand? Is that not kindae in the wrong direction?"

"On first examination, Mr Cogan, yes. However, my Great Uncle may be seriously ill, but he still has a sharp mind and there is always method in his perceived madness. Now, I am led to understand that Harriet has succeeded in making it to Pattaya. I also believe she is now in contact with another former agent, who resides there. The very reason for her long trek to the Far East."

"And who might that be?"

"A man called Fuller, Sir. Richard Fuller."

THREE

Fazakerley, Liverpool.

Having just completed eleven months of a two year sentence at HMP Alt-course, Jack Shenton stood on the pavement outside the prison gates, technically a free man. This was because during his stay at Her Majesties' pleasure, he had turned the ripe old age of eighteen, making him an adult, and despite the plethora of checks and balances he would endure for the next year or so, he was theoretically free.

Altcourse, a Category B prison situated in Fazakerley, Liverpool was unusual in that it held both young offenders and adult male prisoners alike. Even more so, that it housed them together.

This bright idea, no doubt dreamt up by some bloated shareholder over a two hundred quid a plate dinner, was not just ill-advised, it was plain dangerous. The practice ensured that aspiring young cons who were keen to further their criminal careers, could draw upon the wealth of experience of the older 'wiser' lags, whereas those eager to simply do their time and, heaven forbid, rehabilitate, were subjected to all manner of abuse that the weary G4S guards seemed unable or unwilling to prevent.

The prison had boasted seven main wings, bizarrely all named after fences of the Grand National steeplechase course. Each of these jauntily termed blocks housed between sixty and ninety prisoners of varying viciousness.

Jack had been landed with Beechers, a wing designed to house short term inmates.

The prison itself was noisy, unruly, and in places, downright treacherous. Drugs were rife, as was the smuggling of mobile phones that the prisoners used to fuel the trade.

G4S' solution to this problem was to give well behaved inmates at Alt-course access to satellite television. Presumably, the idea being that if you stopped dealing in drugs, you could watch The Gangs of London on catch up.

Any thoughts of deterrent measures had long since been discarded by the privately run prison. Deterrents meant punishment, which in turn meant discipline, which needed manpower, which required money. And that, of course, would decrease the profits and bonuses of the same share-holder who had made the decision to put all and sundry in the same blocks in the first place.

During his incarceration, Jack had found any help with his personal securi-ty in short supply, and due to the fact that he considered anyone who took or dealt in drugs to be pathetic losers, the lad had aroused suspicion from most of the cons.

This was just one of the reasons his undoubted prowess for punching people unconscious had come in exceedingly handy the last eleven months.

Despite his relatively diminutive stature, weighing in at just ten stone, Jack had power in both hands. He'd been taught by one of the best in the business and was more than capable of dispatching men approaching dou-ble his weight.

This talent, should anyone choose to describe it as such, ensured that the 'faces' of Beechers wing quickly learned to give the deceptively quiet and un-assuming Shenton, a wide birth.

However, as much as his ability to box had come to his aid inside prison, now, as the February rain fell, soaking him to the skin, Jack bemoaned his fighting prowess. He knew that people on the outside, gangsters who ran 'lemon' on the estates around where Jack lived, would be waiting for him, waiting to take their revenge for what he'd done.

He rummaged in his jeans and found the travel warrant issued to him by the prison. This free pass was designed to ensure that he made it across Liverpool, to a bed and breakfast, allocated by the probation service as his new, but temporary residence.

Jack Shenton was a Scouser. Born in Croxteth, he had never known his father, and his errant mother had long since given up her somewhat shoddy attempts at parenting, preferring both a child free environment and to earn her money lying on her back, or any other position, for that matter.

This meant that before his untimely internment, Jack had lived the life of what had become known as a sofa surfer. Up until Jack had made the age of fourteen, Social Services had done their best to keep him out of the clutches of unscrupulous groomers, quick to seek out young boys who found themselves tossed out on the streets of the city. But Jack quickly found that what the government referred to as 'Social Care,' was equally as dangerous as street living, and had made the decision to fend for himself.

His local boxing gym had been his saviour, as had his trainer Danny Blatchford. Danny had been an all forces champion middleweight, before turning pro and lifting both the British and European crowns. Danny had taken Jack to his heart and his home, the son he'd never had.

Yet just weeks before the incident that would see him jailed, things had taken a turn for the worse. Blatchford had been killed in a freak motorcycle accident, and Jack had once again found himself alone and on the streets.

The lad shivered, the cold rain and his dark thoughts causing the involuntary reaction. He pushed the travel warrant back into his pocket, squared his broad shoulders and began the short walk to the bus stop.

Jack had travelled no more than fifteen paces when a silver M5 BMW pulled up alongside him. The driver's window made a hissing sound as it opened to reveal, Julian Nix, drug dealer, gangster and all round evil bastard of the parish. He lolled on the heated leather seat, picking his teeth with a long manicured nail. The rumours about Nix and his methods had rattled around Liverpool, just as the gossip had about the Krays in London in the sixties. Except, in this case, the talk was that Nix was connected to an organisation known as The Brothers Circle, Bratski Krug, a Russian led Mafia group. Just how the born and bred Liverpudlian had become embroiled in such a tight knit crew, was a mystery, however, Julian's shadowy connections to international drug traffickers and people smugglers were of little consequence to young Shenton. He was far more concerned with saving his own skin. Right here, right now.

"Alright there, Jack, lad?" said Nix, finding a joint and lighting it, his dark eyes peering over even darker glasses.

Jack instantly checked the street ahead for any evidence of another vehicle that may contain more of Julian's crew.

Sure enough, not fifty yards away, with two fat alloys firmly on the kerb, burbled an Audi A4. He clocked two faces up front and presumed by the way that the car was sitting, there would be at least another two in the back.

He dipped his head and peered into the Beamer so he could look into the face of the man that had vowed to kill him the moment he was released from jail.

"Jules," he said, nodding his recognition. "This your idea of a coming out party?"

Despite being ten years Jack's senior, Nix was of similar size and build to the lad, wiry framed, with jet black metreshair and pale skin. Always immaculately dressed, the gangster was rarely seen out in public without his trademark suit and tie. Although no one would ever mention it to his face, the notorious Liverpudlian criminal had a somewhat unhealthy fascination with Johnny Depp and copied the American star's look whenever he could. If Johnny wore a goatee and soul chip in his latest film, Julian would quickly follow his lead. Silver suit on the red carpet? Jules would have his tailor running up a copy in double quick time.

However, of more concern to Jack was that, not only did Nix love Depp's style, but the guy was also as insane as the star's infamous character, Captain Jack Sparrow.

"This isn't a party, Jack, lad," said Jules. "This is a wake. I made you a promise."

Nix cocked his head.

"And a promise is a special thing. A man who fails to keep such assurances, could never be considered a gentleman." He ran the backs of both hands down his lapels. "And as you can see, I am indeed a gentleman."

"Your Steven came at me with a blade," said Jack flatly, as the rain ran down his face and into his eyes.

Nix tutted, flicked his joint out of the window and resumed his teeth picking activities.

"And you were, policeman, judge and hanging jury were you not?"

And therein lay the problem.

Some eighteen months previously, Jack had been visiting his then girl-friend, in Old Swan. He had left her house and was walking to catch the 68A bus back to Croxteth. As he passed the Masons Arms pub, he couldn't help but notice a group of young men dishing out a shocking beating to a guy who was lying face down on the tarmac between two parked cars.

Now, Old Swan was not an area noted for quiet suburban living, and Jack had spent long enough on the streets of Liverpool to grasp the fact that it was unwise to interfere when the likes of the Nix gang were deliv-ering some summary justice to a rival street dealer who had strayed onto their turf.

That said, four onto one, especially when the one was already semi-con-scious, is never fair, and Jack, for all his shortcomings, was nothing but.

He'd shouted over from what he'd considered a safe distance.

"Come on lads. He looks like he's had enough, eh?" Then, pointing up-wards towards the pub exterior added, "And this gaff is all camara'd up."

Two of the four looked up towards him. They were dressed in trademark gangster black tracksuits, hoods pulled tight around their faces. One had added a black scarf across his mouth for added discretion.

"Fuck off, la," said scarf. "Or you'll get some."

All four resumed their task of kicking and stamping on the immobile youth beneath them. Jack stupidly stood his ground.

"I'll call the Bizzy's," he shouted, knowing this to be a lie even before it came from his mouth. After all, Jack had spent much of his youth dodging Merseyside police officers.

However, that stopped proceedings. Not because the gang were in any way concerned that the local cops would come careering around the corner within seconds, but more so, because some arrogant and obviously insane kid had dared to suggest he'd even make the call.

All four instantly lost interest in the moaning lad at their feet. One, stepped forwards, pushed back his hood from his shaved head and pulled a knife from his pocket.

"Well look here," he sneered, heading for Jack, wild eyed. "It's a fuckin' grass."

Jack had already decided to do one. To turn on the spot and show the group a clean pair of heels. But the best laid plans and all that.

As he spun his body, some superior being with no sense of humour decided that Jack's ability to mimic Cruyff at his best should falter, and, rather than sprinting away, widening his stride as he disappeared into the night, he found himself scrambling on all fours on the pavement.

Jack had just seconds to get to his feet before the knifeman and the three other members of his crew would be upon him.

Lifting himself, he swiftly straightened his body, instantly finding his natural fighter's balance, yet before he could raise his fists, the man was at him, slashing and lunging, face contorted with hatred. Jack stepped away, leaning back as if avoiding a wayward haymaker.

The knifeman slashed again, grunting as he flashed the blade in a wide arc, hoping to open Jack's cheek, maybe even his throat.

"Cut the fucker," shouted one of his crew. "Go on, Stevie lad, slice the cunt."

The knifeman spat at his feet, then looked Jack in the eye and sneered.

He made to lunge again, pushing the blade towards Jack's face. But now the teen fighter was set, left hand loose at his waist, right cocked under his chin, shoulders rounded. He waited for the thrust and simply rolled his torso at the waist, causing the man to miss by more than a foot, something he'd done hundreds of times to avoid the thousands of punches thrown at him in the gym.

And now the knifeman was off balance, right arm outstretched to reveal his torso.

Jack dropped his left shoulder, knees bent. As he twisted his body, he delivered a peach of a left hook to the knifeman's ribs and followed it with a second, almost identical blow a few inches higher, just under his armpit.

The two shots were delivered with speed, power and accuracy, cracking ribs, knocking the wind from his attacker. The whole street could have heard the cries of pain.

Jack saw the man's legs buckle. He knew he had him right there and then, knew the fight was over, but… but boxers are not taught mercy. They are trained to finish their opponent. And after all, Jack needed to dissuade the other three fools currently looking on wide mouthed, not to try their hand too.

The right cross was textbook. Everything was perfect. Stance, delivery, follow-through. Jack felt the contact all the way down his forearm.

Steven Nix was dead before he hit the concrete.

One punch too many.

The judge had been sympathetic and had given Jack two years.

However, the man's brother, the man sitting in front of him this very moment, gangster, Julian Nix had vowed revenge, and his only penalty… was death.

FOUR

Jomtien Beach, Thailand.

Rick was calculating the odds. He spoke to Harriet with a fixed smile, to all intents and purposes, carrying on a normal casual breakfast conversation.

Yet, his objective was anything but normal. He was mentally planning the demise of the three men currently watching his every move, three men that he suspected to be members of the elite Russian security agency, Spetsnaz.

Fuller knew all about these boys. Spetsnaz, an umbrella term for Special Forces in the Russian language, were controlled by the main military intelligence service GRU, and were highly trained and capable soldiers. Just why they were interested in his newly acquired young guest he still had no clue. That said, when it came to dealing with Damien Cartwright, when had he ever known the full story?

He sniffed and began to wish he'd not had that last couple of shots of Mekong the night before.

"Looks to me like you've attracted some unwelcome company," he said, the smile still etched on his face. "The big boy pumping iron doesn't look much of a sprinter, so hopefully, I just need to dissuade the other two from following you." He glanced over his shoulder. "Make like you're going to pee. The loo is at the back. Don't go inside, swing to your right last minute, and take the alley. It runs for about a hundred metres. Turn right at the end which takes you to the main Thappraya Road junction. Directly opposite there is a bike taxi stand. Jump one and ask for Walking Street. Offer them double to get you there quick time. Don't mess about, get on your toes, don't look back and for Christ's sake, don't start shooting unless your life depends on it. The cops here are worse than these Russian fuckers. Once you get to Walking Street, find Hot Tuna bar, grab yourself a cold beer, and order one for me."

Harriet glanced across the road at the guy in the red speedos, still working his huge shoulders.

"Did I tell you to start people watching?" spat Fuller.

She looked at him, wide eyed.

"Sorry, no, but..."

"Then do as I just told you."

Harriet swallowed hard and stood. She winced, her kidneys instantly reminding her that they'd recently taken a serious beating.

"Please tell me you can run," said Fuller.

She glared at him.

"I can run, Fuller... can you?"

He stood, took in air through his nose and pushed a wad of Bhatt under the ashtray.

"I don't need to, sweetheart. You do. Now... why the fuck are you still here?"

She gave him a sweet but fake smile and made to leave.

"I'll make sure your Chang is cold, Fuller. Don't get hurt, you're out of practice."

* * *

He cricked his neck and watched Harriet walk towards the back of the restaurant. The girl was right. He was out of practice. The long, lonely nights of hard drinking had dulled his senses. Okay, he'd hit the gym most days, ate right, but there was no escaping the fact that he was pushing fifty and had drowned his sorrows in cheap whiskey every night for a year.

Add those unwelcome stats to the fact that the three boys across the street all looked young, fit and switched on, he considered he may be up against it.

He'd studied Spetsnaz over the years, their training methods, their combat missions. And make no mistake, they were both capable and uncompromising. Not only did they train hard and select well, but they were prepared to use just about any weapon or tactics available to achieve their goal.

Take the seizure of the Dubrovka Theatre for instance. In October 2002, a group of Chechen Islamist militants stormed the place and took more than eight hundred hostages, demanding the withdrawal of Russian forces from their country.

In order to end the siege, Spetsnaz would have had to fight through more than thirty meters of corridor and attack a well-defended staircase, before they could reach the hall where the hostages were held.

Not an easy day at the office.

So, these boys decided to pump an undisclosed chemical agent into the building's ventilation system before mounting their attack.

All the Islamists were killed during the ensuing battle with no casualties among Spetsnaz. However around a hundred and fifty of the hostages, including nine foreigners, died. Not due to friendly fire, or militant bullets, but because of choking to death on the stuff the boys had pumped into the gaff.

Spetsnaz didn't give a flying photograph.

That said, neither did Richard Edward Fuller.

As Casey made her exit, he casually strode across the street towards his first target, the man dressed in the black silk shirt. The Russian sat on a metal bench, legs coolly crossed, head supposedly buried in the Bangkok Post. Yet as Fuller began to close, he noticed him touch his right ear. No doubt the boy dressed in the awful Hawaiian shirt at the beachwear stall had tipped his pal the wink that their target was on the move and that Fuller was closing. In his peripheral vision, he noticed the bull of a man in the red Speedos lift his massive frame from the resistance machine and roll his shoulders.

Fuller felt his skin prickle, a sure sign his adrenaline levels were rising. His vision sharpened, the air seemed fresher, and all around him began to slow. It was an almost dreamlike state, something he'd experienced all his adult life. Something he missed almost as much as he missed Lauren North.

He quickened his pace slightly. Not so much as to trigger any alarm bells, but enough to cause black shirt to misjudge the moment of his arrival.

And when it came, it was as devastating as it was unexpected.

Fuller was three strides away before the guy reacted, dropping his paper, standing, half turning his body. As he stood, he reached behind his back, raising the tail of his shirt, but he was a split second too late.

Fuller lifted his left leg and smashed his heel into black shirt's kneecap. Rick felt the connection instantly, the huge downward force causing massive trauma to the joint, rendering the guy useless.

Black shirt's leg collapsed under him and he screamed in agony gripping his ruined knee with both hands.

Fuller didn't break stride as he reached down and stripped the Russian of the weapon he'd been about to draw.

It was a Glock 19, so no safety to disengage. Purely from the weight in his hand, Fuller knew it was fully loaded.

He gave the boy a cursory glance before shooting him in the head. The entrance wound, just above his left eye was clean, but the exit was a mess. Blood and bone splattered the sun bleached tiled promenade. Obviously, unlike Casey, the Spetsnaz boys preferred full metal jacket ammunition.

It took a few seconds for the screaming to start, but once the beach lovers of Pattaya realised just what was happening, they began to run in all directions, grabbing loved ones and diving for cover.

Red Speedos began to lumber towards Fuller. He'd picked up a shoulder bag from somewhere and had his right hand stuffed inside it. Rick lifted the Glock, exhaled slowly and dropped the guy with a double tap to his massive chest.

The street was now total pandemonium, and in all the chaos, Fuller had lost sight of Hawaiian man.

He felt the air displace by his right ear as a round passed him, then heard the crack of a weapon.

Sure enough the player was walking straight towards him, gun raised.

Fuller dove to his right, rolled and came up in the kneel behind a concrete planter.

Once again, he formed his sight picture, controlled his breathing and squeezed the trigger.

Before the man hit the floor, Rick's thoughts had turned to his escape.

He didn't run at first. Instead he strode towards the dead Spetsnaz operative.

Fuller wiped the smoking Glock on his shirt, dropping it by the Russian's twitching corpse. Then he sprinted towards the beachwear stall, pushed past the terrified owner and grabbed at a rail of t shirts.

Seconds later, he was pounding the path he had given Harriet to follow, along the alley and towards the main road, tearing his own shirt from his body and pulling on the first of three different coloured tops he had just acquired.

Twenty minutes later, he strolled into Hot Tuna, where Casey was nursing a cold Chang.

As he sat, she eyed his t shirt. It was too small and had the words, 'I Love Thailand' emblazoned across the chest.

"And I had you down as a Ralph Lauren kind of guy," she said.

Fuller wrinkled his nose.

"I like to support the local economy. Now, where's my beer, and just why are Spetsnaz chasing you?"

FIVE

Loch Lomond, Scotland

Des watched from his doorway as Warren Casey turned around his BMW. The somewhat delicate young man was no expert behind the wheel, and it took him five or six attempts. Then, as the German flagship trundled slowly down the deeply furrowed track away from the Scot's tiny cottage, Bruce nuzzled into Cogan's knee and whimpered.

Des stroked his head.

"Sorry, pal, but ye'll have to go back to Hillside fer a spell. Looks like I'm going to get a wee bit of exercise."

An hour later, Cogan had packed his carry on and locked up the tiny cottage. Finding his car keys, he pushed the mobile phone, or 'burner,' that Casey had given him, into his jeans, let Bruce into the rear seat and fired up the engine. All he knew, was that he was bound for Liverpool and that Cartwright would call him on the disposable phone once he was there.

Of course he realised that young Warren hadn't told him the whole story. Now, that was not to say that the boy was lying, or in any way deceptive. The probability was that he too was as much in the dark as the Scot. Damien Cartwright was the true messenger. The real question was just why the old spy had gone to the trouble of turning to two men who, let's face it, were at the end of their usefulness as field agents.

Some things you couldn't change, and one of those was your best by date. Cogan, like Fuller was nearing his half-century. All his old injuries, both physical and mental had taken their toll on him and, if he were a betting man, he would wager that his oldest and dearest friend, had not been in the best state of mind the last year either.

Yes, they had been up there with the best. But that was then.

Now?

So, the big question was why him? And why Rick? Was it because Cartwright had lost all his power at MI6 and couldn't ask for their agents help in saving his niece's skin? Or was it because the dark ops job Miss Harriet Casey had been involved in was just too hot to handle and he needed people that wouldn't ask questions? People he could trust? That had always been the problem with the spy game. Just because someone worked alongside you, drove to the same office every day, even visited your home, didn't mean shit when the bullets started flying. In the espionage business, your so-called best pal was just as likely to shoot you in the back as kill your enemy.

By the job's very nature, deception was king.

Either way, the moment young Warren had mentioned Rick Fuller's name, it had given Des the shivers.

As he drove, there was the merest hint of a smile on the Scot's face. Back in 2006, Fuller had been shot and Des had presumed him dead. Then, days later, there had been the revelation that he was alive, lying in a coma at Leeds General Hospital, being cared for by Lauren North.

Now, four years on, it was almost as if his old chum had been resurrected all over again.

Nonetheless, the Scot's smile was short lived. As he drew closer to Hillside Cottage he began to shift in his seat. Never a man to shirk any conflict or responsibility, Cogan was as tough a character as anyone could wish to meet. However, dealing with women was simply not his forte.

As Des pulled his car up outside the house he had bought for his wife, Ann, he couldn't help but think that it had been a place of the best and worst of times.

Walking down the path with Bruce at his heels, Cogan couldn't help but recall Ann's last days there, and the terrible toll they had taken on him.

He did his best to clear his mind of those final hours, but they refused to budge. Stubborn, determined memories he'd done his best to forget. He felt for his pipe, deciding on a quick smoke before stepping into the fray. As he lit the mixture, he could still picture Ann lying in the front room of the house, her hair all but gone, her agony all consuming.

Swallowing down his emotions and tapping his pipe out on the heel of his boot, Cogan considered that maybe it was more than simply the memory of JJ Yakim that had prevented he and Grace from making a go of things. Maybe Ann had never been far enough from his thoughts too.

He knew that Grace would understand that he had no choice but to go to the aid of his lifelong friend. But Des leaving Scotland, leaving her and the boy, was more than that. It was confirmation of what they had both known for almost a year. Confirmation that they could never be a couple, never form a normal relationship.

JJ … and others, would always be there between them and they knew it.

No, this unexpected call to arms was for the best.

Kaya was progressing well, Grace had settled in her new home and with Cogan out of the way for a while, she would have the freedom to spread her wings a little.

Finally, he pushed open the front door and Bruce ran inside to find the boy.

Hearing the arrival, Grace stepped out of the kitchen and into the hall. She wiped her hands on a tea towel.

"Hiya, Des. I wasn't expecting you. I thought you were fishing all day today?"

"Awe, nothing seems to be biting, except the midges," he offered, managing a brief smile.

It was a brave attempt at casual conversation, but he'd never been too good at delivering bad news, especially when a woman was involved.

On the other hand, Grace had lived with a fighting man all her adult life, and now, at twenty eight, the petite attractive blonde was an expert at instantly seeing through to the truth.

She opened her mouth to speak, just as Kaya and Bruce barrelled into the hall, the boy laughing uncontrollably as the pair rolled on the floor, the Collie doing his best to lick Kaya's face.

"Kaya," snapped Grace. "Take Bruce out into the garden, please."

The boy looked up at his mother, then over to Des. He had his father's eyes, dark and brooding.

"Hi, Des," he said.

"Hello, son," offered the Scot. "Just do as yer mother askes eh. We need a wee chat."

Kaya picked himself up, grabbed Bruce by the collar and did as he was told.

"He's a good kid," said Des quietly.

"Tell me something I don't know," said Grace.

Des nodded. No time like the present. "I have to go away," he said.

"I'd figured that already," said Grace. "I've seen the look too many times."

Des nodded and took a stride closer. Grace stepped back, held up both hands.

"Please, Des. Don't make it any harder." She gestured over her shoulder. "What do I tell Kaya? Will you be back?"

Cogan thought about that for a second too long.

"So that's a no then?" said Grace, wrinkling her nose, the first signs of tears forming.

He hadn't expected this. Tears. After all, he and Grace hadn't occupied Hillside together for over three months. They had agreed, hadn't they? Agreed that things weren't working. That it was best for all concerned, including the boy, that they keep things platonic. So tears were not on Cogan's list of possibilities this day.

"Awe come on Hen," he said. "Dinnea start the greetin' on me now."

Grace was tough. After all, she hailed from Irish travelling stock and had married a Turkish knife fighter. Even so, the tears were genuine.

"I know what we said, Des," she whispered. "Me and you. I know it isn't going to work. But the boy needs a man in his life. I didn't think I'd ever hear me say such a thing, but he does. You're not his Daddy and never will be. We all know as much. But he looks up to you, just as he did JJ. So you can't just walk in and out like this."

Cogan bowed his head a moment, then looked up into Grace's eyes.

"It's Rick," he said. "He needs me."

Grace snorted her derision.

"And you go running."

"That's not fair, Hen, and you know it."

"No? I'll tell you what isn't fair, Des… This… You walking in here, dropping off your stupid dog with your bags already packed, and stepping out of the door, leaving Kaya and me, not knowing if you'll ever come back."

"Of course I'll be back."

"Unless you take a bullet… like JJ."

He stepped closer again. She backed further away.

"Just go," she said.

"Not like this, Hen."

Grace glared at him, her tears suddenly dry.

"There is no other way, Des. I've had my fill of waiting for a man to come home. Had enough of praying that the phone wouldn't ring with bad news." She softened slightly. "Look, what you've done for me, for us, is more than any man need have done. You've kept your promise to JJ. We are safe, we have this wonderful home and I know you care for us both."

"I do," he said.

Grace stepped forwards and held a delicate finger to his lips.

"Don't say anymore, Des, please. Just do as I ask. Turn around and go to Rick Fuller. It's where you belong. It's who you are, who you'll always be.

Cogan looked into her eyes. He could feel his heart beating in his chest. He wanted to hold her, to tell her he'd be back, to tell her… what exactly?

Instead he nodded, gave her a flicker of a smile, turned and was gone.

SIX

Fazakerley, Liverpool.

Julian Nix leaned over and opened the BMW's passenger door.

"Get in, la," he said.

The rain was now incessant, and drips fell from Jack's nose. He was drenched. However, water wasn't going to torture and kill him, Nix was.

"I think I'll walk, Jules," he said. "No offence, like."

The gangster shrugged.

"You could choose that path. You may even escape for a brief while. But I'd find you again. How long do you think you could hide for? A day? Two? You have nowhere to go, son. No one to help you. No friends, no family."

Jack shot a look down the street towards the parked Audi. The two men he'd clocked sitting up front had stepped out and were sauntering towards him. A second pair, that he'd always suspected were in the back, were climbing from the car, one carrying what looked suspiciously like a machine pistol.

Jack was trapped.

However, Shenton had always been a fighter. He'd never backed away from a contest and had no intention of starting this day. If he'd learned anything at all in his short life, it was that nothing was ever gained without courage. He sniffed loudly, wiped his wet hands on his jeans, and played the game the only way he knew how.

"I thought you'd have more bottle, Jules," he said gesturing towards the approaching henchmen. "I actually thought you'd do your own dirty work for once. Y'know, not having to rely on them Russians and all that."

Nix curled his lip.

"You trying to goad me, son?"

Jack took two strides backwards. He stood in the centre of the pavement, arms outstretched, eyes narrowed, the rain battering his face.

"Call it what you want, pal. Why don't you step out here and find out?" He glanced again at the four men approaching. "Or are you sending these girls to do a man's job?"

Nix's eyes flashed.

"I heard you were a crazy motherfucker. Now, stop making it worse for yourself, and get in."

Jack figured there was nothing worse than doing as Nix suggested. He had nothing to lose.

"And I heard you were soft as shit, just like your dead brother."

That did it.

Nix was out of the car, tearing his sunglasses from his face, teeth bared. He launched himself at Jack, head down, aiming to knock him over with his shoulder, but Shenton was too quick, too lithe, and too wily. He stepped left and Nix charged into nothing but thin air. As the older man sailed past him, Jack swivelled his body and hooked him to the kidney. It wasn't the best of connections, but his second shot to the back of Nix's head was enough to put him off balance and send him flailing to the floor.

As he hit the deck, Jack saw that the gangster had lost something in the process, it had fallen from his jacket and it clattered along the rain soaked pavement. It was something extremely valuable.

A semi-automatic pistol.

Now, eighteen year old Jack Shenton had never even held a gun, let alone fired one. And even in the shockingly dangerous scenario he found himself in, he had no desire to start shooting people and risk going straight back where he'd just come from. However, desperate times meant desperate measures.

He grabbed the weapon with his right hand, then the collar of Julian Nix's jacket with his left. A split second later, Julian found himself with the muzzle of a Colt Defender 45ACP in his ear.

Of course, Jack had no way of knowing that the Defender had what was known as a beaver tail safety. Basically this meant that by simply gripping the weapon in your hand and applying pressure to the trigger, the gun would fire.

That said, this snippet of information was not lost on Mr Nix and as Jack lifted him to his knees, the gun firmly pushed in his neck, he held up a hand towards his approaching men.

"Steady on there, lads. Let's not be hasty, eh?"

The four Russians stopped in their tracks and gave each other a look that told Jack they had no clue what to do next, so he helped them out.

"Which one of you bozos has the keys to the Audi?" he asked.

One man mountain glared at Jack as he produced a fob.

"Chuck it," said Jack.

The guy didn't move. He looked to his boss for guidance.

Nix rolled his eyes.

"It's fuckin' preferable to a bullet in my head numb nuts," he spat.

The guy threw the key.

"Now fuck off back to the car, all of yers" said Shenton, growing in confidence. "Me and Jules here are going for a ride."

The men glared menacingly but did as they were told. Jack lifted Nix to his feet, steering him back to his BMW, gun at his head.

Shenton slid in behind the gangster and tapped the barrel of the Colt on his skull as a gentle reminder of his presence.

"Get me to the Mersey," he said. "You're going for a swim."

"You must be fuckin' joking," sneered Julian. "You'll be dead before you reach Toxteth."

Jack quickly drew the pistol away from Nix's head and with a flick of his wrist cracked him across the back of his skull with the barrel. Julian cried out as blood poured down the back of his neck, dripping onto the collar of his pure white shirt.

Jack returned the muzzle to its original position.

"Do I sound like a funny guy to you, pal? No? So shut the fuck up. Now, there's a coach park on Riverside Drive. That will do nicely."

"You think you can get away with this, Shenton?" said Nix. "My guys will find you within hours."

Jack shrugged.

"They can try."

Nix glared into the rear view.

"You do know I'm an Avtoritet? And because of that, you do know what the Russians will do to you? To your family?"

An Avtoritet or Authority, is like a captain in charge of a small group of men, similar to a Capo in the Italian-American Mafia. Except Julian Nix's boss, his Godfather, the man in overall charge of the massive criminal enterprise known as The Brothers Circle, would be called, Pakhan, or Papa.

Yet none of this mattered to Jack. Mystery men with foreign names, mafias and gangsters were all secondary to the here and now. This was a straight contest. This was a him or me moment.

Could he pull this off? He wasn't sure. However, one thing he was absolutely certain of, was that if Julian Nix had his way, Jack would be dead before the day was out. The young lad's options were, to say the least, limited.

Jack leaned forwards and whispered in Julian's ear.

"Like you said, Jules. I don't have any family… Take Upper Parliament Street then the Dingle Road."

Despite the gangster's predicament, Nix was like a broken record, issuing threats every few seconds. What he was going to do to Jack, to anyone who knew him. Shenton considered swiping him with the gun again, but figured it may make him crash the car, so he bit his tongue and waited for his moment. Finally, they pulled into the large coach park. Other than two ageing empty vehicles they were alone, and the BMW was able to drive right to the water's edge.

"Out," said Jack, prodding Nix with the barrel of the Colt.

For a moment, he didn't move, and Jack thought he would have to shoot the gangster after all. But a second prod and some pressure on the trigger did the trick and he finally did as he was told. Seconds later, both men were out of the car and back in the torrential rain.

"Empty your pockets," said Jack. "And take off your shoes."

Nix stood by the low concrete wall that ran the length of the coach park. He peered over at the fast moving black water that ran on the other side.

"Not a chance son. My boys will be on their way right now."

Shenton shrugged.

"I've never fired a gun," he said. "But I reckon I could hit you pretty much anywhere I wanted from here." He pointed the weapon and closed one eye. "Maybe I should start with your bollocks."

"You really haven't thought this through, have you son?" said Nix, dropping the contents of his trouser pockets onto the tarmac. "The Russians consider me family, they'll… "

"Yeah, so you said pal… now, shoes," said Jack, eyes as cold as the rain on his face.

"Fuck you," spat Nix kicking off his loafers. "Why not just shoot me, eh? Go on, do it." He curled his lip. "You haven't the guts, have you? You never meant to kill my Stevie. It was bad luck is all. And worse luck that he was who he was. You're no killer, you ain't got it in you."

Shenton stepped forwards. It was a swift movement, the pistol in his outstretched right hand never wavering from its target. Nix couldn't take his eyes from the gun, which proved to be his greatest error.

Jack twisted his body at the last second, lifted his left hand and pushed Nix firmly in the chest. The gangster was wide eyed with surprise. He grabbed at Shenton in the hope of steadying himself, but Jack had once again used his talents as a boxer and was inches out of reach. Nix was falling. He began to windmill his arms in an attempt to keep his balance, but it was to no avail. The low wall was behind him at knee height and the weight of his upper body pivoted him over.

Jack stood and watched Nix drop until he hit the ice cold black water, disappearing into the depths. Seconds later, Julian breached the surface, coughing and spluttering. The current was vicious, and it began to drag him out towards the open sea. If he remained afloat long enough, it would pull him past the newly built waterfront bars, shops and restaurants. But Jack knew that wouldn't happen. He knew the cold would take him. Within seconds Nix would fall into shock, into hypothermia. Too cold to beg for help, too cold to even breathe.

Shenton watched as the gangster began to sink into the murky depths of the river. Julian waved his arms once, twice. There was a weak shout. Jack thought he heard him call for his mother, then, seconds later, he was gone.

Shenton took in air through his nose. He thought he may be sick. Punching Julian's brother, Steven and discovering that he had taken his life by accident had been bad enough, but this? This was a different matter. People could say that he had no choice, that it was kill or be killed, but at that very moment, Jack realised something about himself that, luckily, few men ever have to grasp. He could kill in cold blood.

He picked up the wallet, some small change, and a set of keys Nix had thrown to the floor. Then found Julian's loafers, before placing everything neatly on the wall where he had fallen.

Shenton turned, wiped rain from his face and strode to the BMW. He dropped his soaking wet frame into the driver's seat, rested the Colt on the dash, had a quick root in the glove box, then popped the boot.

The lad had no idea what he was looking for, but as he peered into the trunk, with the rain battering his shoulders, he somehow realised that he had discovered something valuable. Lying on the beautifully carpeted interior, was an aluminium briefcase.

Jack snapped the catches open and lifted the lid. Sitting inside were ten bundles of cash and what appeared to be a silver coloured laptop. He'd never seen so much money in all his life. Shenton picked up one bundle, looked furtively around, and flicked through the notes.

"Fuck me," he muttered.

Giving little thought to the small computer, he dropped the bundle back in the case, closed the lid and lifted it out.

As he passed the BMW's driver's door, he reached inside and grabbed the Colt.

Jack Shenton knew he was on borrowed time. He knew that the Police would find Julian Nix sooner rather than later and then the Russians would come for him.

However, he also knew the city like the back of his hand, had money, a gun and nothing to lose.

"Bring it on," he said as he strode away.

SEVEN

Hot Tuna Bar, Walking Street, Pattaya

Harriet Casey watched as Fuller downed his bottle of Chang in one long series of gulps. He dropped the empty bottle on the table then waved to the waiter for another.

"Thirsty?" she asked.

"Curious," he said. "That and running out of patience. Talk to me about Spetsnaz."

Casey waited for the waiter to deliver Fuller's beer. She watched him walk away, took a deep breath.

"Those guys were not Spetsnaz."

"Looked like it to me."

"Well, looks can be deceiving, Fuller. They may have once been connected to the Russian Special Forces, but not anymore."

"Then who were they?"

"Were?"

Fuller downed half his second beer.

"Yeah, past tense, Casey. They're probably being rolled into body bags as we speak."

Harriet pushed her hair behind her ears and shook her head.

"Jesus H Christ, Fuller. I figured you'd just…"

"Just what? Ask them nicely to go away and stop bothering you? Now, who the fuck were they?"

Casey squirmed in her seat.

"That's classified, I'm afraid."

Rick snorted and waved at the waiter again.

"Mekhong," he shouted. "A bottle."

Casey screwed up her face.

"Really, Fuller? Jesus, it's not even twelve."

Rick shot a hand across the table and gripped Casey's wrist. She tried to pull away, but he was way too strong. There was a look on his face she hadn't seen before. Cold, soulless.

"Now you listen in, sweetheart," he hissed. "Three men are dead because of you. Hold that thought for a moment. Yeah, I disposed of them, but it was down to you. They are dead because of what you've done, or what you are about to do. Now, me and your dear Uncle Damien as you so sweetly call him, go way back and I know just how the old bastard works. I've also heard that phrase you've just spouted many times before, 'classified.' It's the same as, 'need to know basis.' The men in suits, the people that work alongside the likes of you, they love all that shit. It makes them feel important, feel like Billy big bollocks. But they're not. They can't do shit without people like me. I used to tolerate the suits because I had to, I was under orders. Then I put up with the sly fuckers because I was earning the big bucks for my trouble. Now, correct me if I'm wrong, but as I'm no longer at Her Majesties' service and I've yet to see you put any green and crinkly on the table, I presume that you and Cartwright expect me to work free gratis. So, right now you have two options. One, keep up this charade and I'll stay here, get drunk and call you a cab, or you can tell me everything and I'll change my order to water."

He released her wrist and sent the waiter and Mekhong back to the bar.

"Now, what's it to be, darlin', because I'm notoriously quick tempered."

Casey rubbed some feeling back into her hand as she glowered at him. Her beautiful blue eyes flashed as she spoke.

"Ten days ago, I was dispatched to Germany, to Frankfurt. I was working as part of a three man covert ops team. The purpose of that operation was to prevent the Russian Ambassador to the UK from delivering a package to one of his countrymen in Liverpool. The intel suggested that Alexander Solonik was using his diplomatic bag to move sensitive materials across the EU. On this occasion, the item was a computer program loaded onto a memory stick, and our orders were that it was not to reach its intended recipient. Not under any circumstances."

"And who was that recipient?"

She shook her head.

"We weren't given that information. Our orders were to recover the goods and deliver them back to our handler."

He glared at her.

"It's the truth, Fuller. We weren't told his identity."

He rubbed his chin. Nodded.

"Okay, but why you? I mean, I can see you're a resourceful young woman, and you're tougher than you look, but you can't buy experience. Black ops teams are usually made up of old hands, even mercenaries like me. What are you, twenty two? Twenty three?"

She gave Fuller a look that appeared tinged with embarrassment, yet she jutted her chin as she spoke. A vain attempt to hide her awkwardness.

"The old hands, as you call them are dead, Fuller. Look, it was the oldest trick in the book. A honey trap. Solonik had a liking for a particular type of girl. Young, dark hair, blue eyes, petite frame." She raised perfectly plucked brows. "Need I spell it out?"

"Yes, you do. Go on."

She paused. Shook her head.

"The ambassador was staying at the Grandhotel Hessischer Hof in town. He'd been visiting Frankfurt trade fair. Well, that was his official reason for being in the country. Our information was that he would be handed the program whilst at the fair, return to his rooms, and then fly to Liverpool John Lennon the next day with the stick in his diplomatic bag. Our handler had been given strict instructions from the top that the Ambassador couldn't be touched once on British soil, therefore, we had to take our chance whilst he was still in Frankfurt."

"And?"

"It wasn't too difficult. Solonik liked to party. His security were just as bad. Lots of vodka, lots of whores. I made myself comfortable in the hotel bar and he came on to me the first night, three nights before he was due to collect the program."

"And you slept with him to obtain it?"

Those eyes flashed.

"No. There was no need."

"But you would have done?"

There was that look again, that defiant discomfort.

"Like I said, Fuller, there was no need."

She took a swig of her beer and wiped her mouth with the back of her hand. It was an action that didn't quite fit her persona. She was indeed an anomaly. The public school accent, the fine features. As unlikely a spy as he'd ever met. Fuller pushed the point.

"You didn't answer my question. Would you have had sex with him to get what you wanted?"

"Are you interested in my morals or what actually happened, Fuller?"

He sniffed.

"Fair one."

She gave him a thin knowing smile.

"As with all men, Solonik liked a challenge. I played hard to get. By the time he was in possession of the goods, I knew I could get in close."

"And you did."

"Yes. We ended up in his room. He was drunk, as usual. I helped him out even more with a sedative in his vodka. After a fumble on the sofa, he fell unconscious and I walked away with the stick."

"Sounds all too easy."

"It was. The Ambassador's security were one thing. We hadn't counted on the recipient's insurance policy."

"Spetsnaz."

"No. Like I told you, not Spetsnaz. The Brothers Circle."

Fuller sat back in his seat.

"The Brothers Circle? Are you telling me they really exist? There were some rumours a few years back that some former Russian Mafioso has pulled together a loose sort of transitional criminal gang that were operating in Europe and the Middle East. But there was never any proof. I heard it was bollocks."

Casey turned down her mouth.

"Well it isn't. They do exist and they are in the UK as we speak. The main hierarchy work out of Dubai, but this program was manufactured in Kiev and was destined for British soil. It was to be married up with a specific computer that is in the possession of the Brothers in Liverpool."

"So what is this program then? What makes it so valuable?"

Harriet pursed her lips.

"How many friends do you have on Facebook, Fuller?" she asked.

Rick blew air down his nose.

"I have one friend in the whole world, and he isn't on social media. Surprise surprise, neither am I."

"Jesus," muttered Casey. "How do you stay in touch with the world?"

"Just tell me why this thing is worth killing for eh?"

She took another long breath.

"Political interference," she said.

"What, electoral tampering?"

"Sort of. For a number of years now, the Russians and others have been spreading disinformation via social media platforms. These stories, fake news, whatever you want to call them are designed to destabilise political regimes. More recently, the ways in which these hackers work has become more complex and far more effective. So much so, that MI6 believe, they have the power to influence our electoral system."

"What? You mean how people vote?"

"Exactly how people vote. Look, just say that you have a criminal who owns nightclubs or is involved in property development. Now, let's presume that the particular borough of a city where he operates is currently in the political hands of an MP who has serious ecological or religious beliefs. With him or her in power, he has no chance of obtaining planning permission for his multi-million pound investment or a licence for his new lap dancing bar. But what if he had the ability to oust this guy at the next local election and install a friendly candidate, who is already in his pocket?"

"And this program enables him to do that?"

"Apparently so. This program phishes social media for potential floating voters then floods their newsfeed with negative stories about the current council or a particular local issue, say immigration or homelessness. Okay, initially, it may only influence a couple of thousand people in each borough, but in some cases, for instance, some of the Northern wards, the majorities are extremely small, just a few hundred. And this new program is apparently very clever. It can influence massive campaigns. Maybe even national elections or referendums. The CIA believe a similar program may even have been used to help elect a president."

Fuller narrowed his eyes.

"But why go to all the trouble of getting this particular stick back? Why don't the Russians just make another copy of the program?"

Casey shook her head.

"Our intel was that it couldn't be done. Apparently, the encryption deliberately prevents copying. We can't even open it. The program will only work when it is married up with the machine in the possession of their man in Liverpool. And there-in lies the issue."

Fuller scratched his head.

"I've heard about these programs before, Casey. I'm sure they're written by spotty kids who never leave their bedrooms, they're two a penny. What's so valuable about this one? There has to be something else."

Casey ignored Fuller's doubts and waved at the waiter.

"Two waters, please," she said.

"I'll take a beer," said Fuller. "I'm still not convinced."

Casey pulled her face.

"Listen to me, Fuller. As I said, our orders were specific… to deliver the program back to our handler."

"So you're telling me that he knows where the computer is that opens it."

"I'm not party to that information, Fuller, but as a result of what happened after we took possession of the program, Uncle Damien thinks not. Not yet anyway."

"Does he now?"

"Yes. It's another reason he sent me to you. He knew you would protect me but feels that the MI6 department working on this mission have been… economical with the truth. He needs someone he can trust."

"Well, who'd believe such a thing," snorted Fuller.

"Exactly… So, he wants us to find the machine before they do and…"

"He wants me to go to Liverpool? With you? Not a chance."

Casey checked her watch.

"There's a flight, Bangkok via Dubai to Manchester leaving in two hours. We can meet our other contact by lunchtime tomorrow. He will help us find the computer that matches this program."

"And just who is this contact?"

"Oh, I believe you know him," smiled Casey. "Cogan, Desmond Cogan… want that water now?"

EIGHT

The Adelphi Hotel, Liverpool

Cogan stepped inside the lobby a little weary. He'd decided to leave his car in Scotland and had taken the train. Including the changes, the journey had lasted just under four and a half hours. However it had been the words of Grace Yakim that had weighed heavy on him as he'd negotiated the cold and blustery stations at Preston and Ormskirk. He'd found himself mentally scrutinising their conversation in great detail, and no matter which way he looked at it, the result always came out the same.

Shite.

The Adelphi was situated in the heart of the city. It had begun life in the 1860's and was one of a handful of flagship hotels that had once housed visitors awaiting the arrival or departure of ocean liners from the nearby Liverpool dock, famously including the doomed Titanic. It had hosted many celebrated guests over the years too, notably, Winston Churchill, Frank Sinatra and Judy Garland. Of course, this wasn't of any interest to Des. In fact, he considered the establishment a little too posh for his liking. Nevertheless, as it had been Cartwright that had organised his digs, and Cogan wasn't about to pick up the tab, he couldn't complain.

As he strode towards the reception desk with his carry on slung over his shoulder, he considered that maybe he should have brought some smarter clothes. That said, the establishment had accommodated Bob Dylan and The Rolling Stones in their heyday, so maybe he could get away with his Levis, plain white 't' and trusty leather.

He shrugged off any thought of fashion shopping, took the final steps to the desk and subconsciously felt in his pocket for his pipe.

The very pretty receptionist eyed him appreciatively and gave him a warm smile.

"Good evening, Sir, do you have a reservation?"

Despite his weathered features, Cogan was a ruggedly handsome man who had devoted the majority of his life to the military, spending thousands of lonely hours, lying in holes in the ground, battered by the wind and rain, or roasting under an unrelenting sun. Those thankless days of solitary service to Queen and country, those hundreds of covert surveillance operations, hidden in freezing ditches or dug into blistering desert trenches, had caused irreparable damage to his skin. The leather like appearance of his face was accentuated by deep wrinkles around his sharp blue eyes. Eyes that had scanned too many horizons and witnessed more suffering than was good for any man. His salt and pepper hair was always cropped short and as he spoke, he scratched the top of his head with a heavily calloused hand.

"Aye, I reckon I have," he said. "I wouldnea be here otherwise eh? Name's Cogan, Desmond Cogan."

The girl tapped some keys, looked up from her screen and gave him another beam.

"Yes, here we are, Sir. You're in 422," she handed over an electronic card key. "Jenny's Restaurant serves a full English breakfast each morning. Crompton's is our A La Carte restaurant and there are two bars for you to choose from, Wave is only open during dinner, but the American Bar is open all day, 'till late." She cocked her head. "Will you be dining with us, Mr Cogan? Crompton's is always busy, and a reservation is recommended."

Des examined his key and gave the girl a smile of his own.

"I dinnea think this Crompton's place is my kindae eatery, do you? I was hoping that ye might be able to recommend a good wee Indian. I do like a curry."

The girl raised her brows.

"Well, you're just a twenty minute stroll from the waterfront, Mr Cogan.

There are lots of places to choose from there, but I like UnI on Renshaw Street. It's really old fashioned with little booths that you can pull a curtain across for privacy if you choose, and the food is absolutely amazing. I love their Baltis."

"That sounds more like it, hen, thank you," he said, turning towards the lifts.

As he moved away, the receptionist appeared to remember something and called after him.

"Oh, Mr Cogan. Sorry, I almost forgot. There is a package for you. It was delivered earlier this morning. It's rather heavy. Shall I get it brought to your room?"

Cogan considered this information for a moment. Whoever had sent the package had obviously made the presumption that he would indeed travel to Liverpool. Probably the same someone who had arranged for young Warren Casey to visit him in Scotland and bait the hook. The very someone who knew that he would be unable to resist the temptation of working alongside Rick Fuller again. And that could only be one person, Damien Cartwright.

So, Cogan presumed, whatever was in the package, was both valuable and important.

He shook his head.

"No, I'll take it up myself hen," he said. "The exercise will do me good."

Minutes later, Cogan sat on the end of his bed with the mysterious package at his feet.

"Now then," he said to himself. "Let's see what the old bugger is sending to Desmond, special D."

He took his knife and slit open the cardboard box to find an aluminium flight case inside. He lifted it out, turned and dropped it onto the bed.

The lid was secured by a numerical combination lock. Attached to that, was a plastic fob with a white paper insert. On that was written. "Happy Birthday Desmond."

He scratched his head for a moment, then twisted the barrels on the combination to read his date of birth. Sure enough, the lock popped open.

"Well, that was easy," he muttered, lifting the lid.

Sitting in foam inserts at the top of the box were three mobile phones. Cogan didn't recognise the make or model, but they appeared substantially built with rugged cases, the kind you often saw builders carrying around.

He lifted the insert from the case and lay it next to the box leaving the three phones snugly in position. The removal of this layer revealed a second. This time three Sig Sauer P938's nestled there. He picked one out, removed the magazine and pulled back the slide to empty the breech. The weapon was exceptionally light. Cogan had fired one before. He'd been given the identical model by a US army officer as a gift when he'd served alongside him in Columbia. The P938 was unusual for a modern gun, being made from all metal, but Cogan knew just how accurate it was. It was immensely popular with combat shooters and private individuals alike. Unfortunately for the German/Swiss company, the weapon had been made famous in one of the many mass shootings on American soil. A guy called Adam Lanza had entered Sandy Hook Elementary School in Newtown, Connecticut, and shot to death six adults and twenty children using one.

Cogan re-loaded the pistol, sat it back in its place and lifted out the second layer of foam from the box. Beneath the Sigs, were another array of toys. Boxes of ammunition, covert comms sets, miniature binos, lock picking kits, wire, detonators, and what looked suspiciously like a block of C4 explosive.

"It's like opening a box of Milk Tray at Christmas," he said quietly.

He lifted the final foam insert to check that there were no further things to play with and discovered a brown envelope with the name 'Fuller,' written on the front. The script was handwritten by a man of senior years.

"A message from Cartwright himself then," he muttered.

Des squared everything away and tucked the box out of sight inside one of the large wardrobes in his hotel room.

He felt for his pipe again, noticed that Cartwright had chosen a non-smoking room for him, and decided that a smoke, a beer and a visit to UnI were in order.

Minutes later, his nicotine habit was satisfied, and he was sitting in the back of a cab pushing his way through Liverpool's evening traffic.

It was Des' first visit to the city and it instantly reminded him of home. Of Glasgow.

The borough of Liverpool was founded by royal charter in 1207 by King John. But it was the city's trade with Ireland that ensured its early growth. That, in turn, enticed wealthy men to the city who opened markets with Africa and the West Indies, notoriously including the slave trade. Liverpool's population grew rapidly, especially with Irish migrants, and by the mid 1800's one quarter of the city's inhabitants was Irish-born. Liverpool suffered shocking damage in the blitz and appalling unemployment and poverty with the decline of the docks, but the people had fought back, and Liverpool was once again on the rise. It was a rough old town with a heart of gold and Cogan felt instantly at home.

Fifteen minutes later, he found himself sitting in UnI.

The place had opened its doors in 1970 and it didn't appear anything had changed since that day. Cogan's first impressions were that it looked like a train carriage with compartments either side of a narrow walkway. That said, the smells emanating from the kitchen made his mouth water.

He was shown to a table, given a menu and offered a large bottle of Cobra. Des lay his 'burner' phone next to his napkin, checked he hadn't missed a call, and took a long, much needed drink.

The waiter was back in an instant, introduced himself in what Cogan considered to be the most comical Scouse/Indian accent, and took his order. Chicken Jalfrezi, mushroom rice and a garlic naan bread.

Despite his concerns for what he'd left behind, for Grace and the boy, Des couldn't prevent his stomach from tumbling with excitement as he considered what adventures may be to come. He'd lost count of how many times he'd taken 'one last job.' The truth was, there was nothing in the world that could match the feeling of a new mission. No food, no drink, nobody. He'd felt it as soon as he'd pulled that Sig from the case.

He was back, and the game was on.

NINE

Larkhill Lane, Formby, Liverpool

Organised crime in Russia had been around since the imperial period of the Tsars, but it was not until the Soviet era that the first real gangsters, the Vory v Zakone, or Thieves in Law, emerged. At this time, most of the Soviet population were peasants, therefore criminals who stole from government entities and divided the profits among the people earned Robin Hood like status, being viewed as protectors of the poor and becoming folk heroes. These early mobsters created, Vorovskoy Mir, roughly translated as, Thieves World. They had their own code of conduct that was based on strict loyalty with one another, as well as a fanatical opposition to governments of any persuasion.

By the end of World War II, more and more gangs emerged in the flourishing black market. Then, as the Soviet Union began its collapse, the now fully functioning Bratva, The Mafia, used bribery and violence to exploit the unstable governments of the former republics, becoming almost as powerful as the Kremlin itself.

By the time the USSR buckled, and the free market economy emerged, The Bratva had become so powerful that they began to take over large parts of Russia's economy. They recruited ex-KGB agents, former Spetsnaz operatives and veterans of the Afghan war as Bratok, or soldiers. Rather than fight each other, rival gangs held summit meetings so that top Vory v Zakone could agree on who would rule what and set plans on how to take over the post-Communist states.

Within a year of the collapse of the Union, The Bratva had built international operations that included, narcotics, money laundering, and prostitution. They'd made ties with the American Mafia and Colombian drug cartels and anyone who dared go against them were horribly murdered.

Semion Savalovsky began his criminal life as a Shestyorka to the Bratva. A Shestyorka, is no more than an errand boy and is the lowest rank in the Russian Mafia. They were sometimes assigned to an Avtoritet or Brigadier, providing intelligence for upcoming hits on certain targets, but were usually left out of the main action.

However, Semion had never been one to remain in the shadows when it came to violence, and after proving himself more than capable of taking a life, he had been accepted as a Vor, or Thief, a title denoting a made man. The honour of becoming a Vor is given only when the recruit shows considerable leadership skills, personal ability, intellect and charisma. Only a Pakhan, the Russian equivalent of a Godfather, or another high-ranking member of The Bratva could decide if the recruit would receive such a title. When you became a member of the Vor-world, you had to accept the code of the Vor v Zakone. Something Savalovsky did with open arms.

By the time Semion was twenty five, he had made Brigadier and ran his own crew as part of the Brothers Circle.

Born into a poor Russian Jewish family in Kiev's Podol neighbourhood, he used his newfound power to amass his first significant fortune. He did this by scamming fellow Russian Jews eager to emigrate from the Ukraine to the United States, UK and Israel. He made deals to buy their assets, sell them for fair market value, and forward the proceeds. Instead, once they were out of the country, he simply sold their houses and belongings and pocketed the lot.

Any remaining relatives who complained were found floating in the Dnieper River.

Semion later moved to the Middle East, to Dubai. Using a fake identity, he'd posed as a Russian property developer. However, his true role was as second in command to Pakhan and Godfather of all Godfathers,

Vladimir Asharvin. He quickly became head of the Obshchak, or Security Group, and held the responsibility of watching over the dozens of Brigadiers working the Middle East and Europe. It was Semion who ensured their compliance and loyalty to Asharvin. He ruled without mercy and was given the nickname Lezviye, meaning Blade, due to his love of a double sided knife he always carried.

After being bestowed with his own title as Pakhan, he moved to the UK, to Liverpool, once again using his bogus Russian credentials as a Bona Fide property developer, travelling under the name of Sergei Stefanovic. His task, to buy up the swathes of derelict property in and around Merseyside and turn them into fresh new industrial and retail developments for the benefit of the Brothers Circle.

Semion purchased the house he now sat in on Larkhill Lane, Formby for a cool two million pounds and spent another four hundred thousand on security. It was the closest thing to a nuclear bunker a private individual could own. Yet this was not razor wire and gun turret territory. Anything but. Savalovsky knew the value of discretion and the measures taken were inconspicuous, state of the art and went largely unseen by his equally security conscious neighbours.

Indeed, Semion was a pillar of the community. Heading charitable organisations, funding local sports teams and playing off a modest handicap at the local golf club.

He had a beautiful young wife, two equally attractive children, and appeared to all around him as the perfect doting father.

Semion valued his privacy and his public façade almost as much as he did his multimillion pound fortune. After all, they went hand in hand, did they not?

Nevertheless, as he sat in his study with his trusted Derzhatel Obschaka, or Bookkeeper, John Hodiak at his side, all was not well.

Standing nervously in front of the all-powerful pair was Erich Honecker, Brigadier for Frankfurt and Mannheim, and the man who had been responsible for the security of Russian Ambassador Alexander Solonik. That, and the now missing contents of his diplomatic bag.

"So, tell me again, Erich," said Semion quietly. "How could such a thing happen?"

"Solonik is a drunk and a womaniser, Pakhan," offered Honecker. "An irresponsible man with no morals, who chooses his bodyguards by his own standards."

Savalovsky rubbed his square chin thoughtfully. He was not a rash man and did not believe in apportioning blame recklessly or indeed any subsequent punishments, especially to one as loyal as Erich Honecker.

"This, I understand, Erich. But we were aware of Solonik's shortcomings before he was given the task of transportation, were we not? Hence the presence of your men. Your best men."

"We were, Papa, but his behaviour was worse than we expected. He knew we were providing extra security. He knew of the threat, yet he deliberately deceived the soldiers who were tasked with his safety so that he may meet with the whore."

Semion nodded slowly.

"And this whore, as you call her. Tell me more of her. Tell me of her escape with *my* goods."

Erich swallowed hard. He knew there was no way to dress up what had happened. After all, they had underestimated the woman. Indeed, to even call her a woman was exaggerating the fact. She'd been no more than a slip of a girl.

"She was in the company of two accomplices, Papa. Two men who fought and died well."

"Professionals then?"

"I would say so, yes."

"Working for?"

Erich shook his head.

"We cannot say for sure, they carried no identification, but they were British, and I would suggest that they had once been military men."

Semion pinched the bridge of his nose, closed his eyes for a moment.

"So they work for a rival then?"

"Possibly, Pakhan."

Savalovsky looked up, eyes sharp, stony.

"Or, given the content of the program, the British Secret Service?"

Erich felt his blood run cold.

"I could not rule that possibility out, Papa, as the girl was also British and well educated, but I would say that she was too young for such a role, too…"

Semion held up a hand.

"Too what? Too frail, too tender of years to be a threat? Did we not lose thousands of teenage men and women in the Great Wars? Were they too young to fight? To Die? And as this… mere child, managed to evade one of your best men, to snap his neck like a rotten branch, wouldn't you suggest that there is the possibility that she may have been a little more than a teenage temptress?"

"Yes Papa. I would, but…"

There was an edge to Semion's tone now, and it sharpened with each sentence.

"Then let us not dress this up. Let us call it what it is. A fucking disaster."

"Yes Papa."

John Hodiak leaned over and whispered in Savalovsky's ear. Hodiak was a man of immense importance to Semion. As his bookkeeper it was his responsibility to collect money from the Brigadiers' criminal enterprises. Their narcotics deals, prostitution, money laundering, and use it to bribe government officials. This was money allocated for use solely in the interests of the whole group, the Brothers Circle, and was sacrosanct. This responsibility, together with his ability to discover and play upon the weaknesses of corrupt politicians, police officers and other powerful public figures, made Hodiak almost as influential as Savalovsky himself.

Erich couldn't hear what Hodiak had said to his Papa, but he knew it wouldn't have been complimentary.

Semion nodded his agreement at whatever he had just been told. He sniffed.

"So, this girl, this youngster, escapes your clutches and runs. Yet, she doesn't run home to England.

Instead of turning the nine hundred kilometres home she flees nine thousand to Bangkok."

"Yes Papa," offered Honecker nervously. "We quickly used our contacts at the airlines to identify her movements and alert our men in Thailand."

"And?"

"We eventually traced her to Jomtien, Papa."

Semion sat back in his chair and made a pyramid with his fingers.

"And this is where the story gets really interesting, does it not? This is where, this slip of a girl, this harmless child meets up with another innocuous soul. A drunk. A middle aged alcoholic who spends his every waking moment in a whorehouse drinking cheap whiskey. And yet, this lush, this inebriated sex tourist, walks out of a beachside café, unarmed, in broad daylight, and slays three of our finest Bratok before disappearing into thin air with our target." Savalovsky slammed a huge fist into the table. "...And my fucking goods."

Erich couldn't bring himself to speak. He just nodded as his legs began to shake.

"And where are they now," hissed Semion. "This... this harmless pair?"

"We... we aren't quite sure, Papa."

Savalovsky was a big man. Naturally powerful, with huge forearms, thick wrists and massive hands. Erich noted that they were shaking in anger. Not a good Sign.

"Not sure?" said the Godfather, holding his temper in check by the finest of threads. "What about these wonderful contacts you have at the airports?"

"It would appear that they left the country before our men could..." Erich swallowed bile. "Re-group, Papa."

Hodiak, the bookkeeper, leaned in again. There was another whispered message. A longer one this time. Erich thought he may vomit.

Semion again nodded his assent, turned down his mouth. "Do you believe in coincidences, Erich?" he asked, his temper seemingly edging away.

"Sometimes, Papa. But not often."

"No," said Semion. "And neither do I. You see, it would appear that one of my Brigadiers has taken it upon himself to go swimming in the river Mersey. Brigadier Julian, to be precise. Now, stop me if you consider me mistaken, but I would suggest that this is not the kind of weather for a man to go bathing. Indeed, I would propose that the act would be inherently dangerous."

"Indeed, Papa," said Erich, grateful that the subject appeared to have changed from the Frankfurt debacle.

"Indeed," pointed Semion. "And this has certainly proved to be the case, as poor Julian is now lying in the morgue, drowned."

Erich didn't quite know what to say.

"My condolences," he managed.

"Quite," smiled Semion. "However, all is not as it seems. Yes, the police have discovered poor Julian's shoes, wallet and other trinkets on the riverbank, suggesting his entry to the water had been of his own volition, yet, after discussions with Julian's soldiers, nothing is cut and dried. Our Brigadier had recently organised to meet a youth, curiously... coincidentally, another slip of a child outside Altcourse prison. A boy by the name of Shenton. Now, whatever their business had been, Julian had chosen not to share it with his men, so, as of this moment, we are none the wiser. That said, it would appear that this industrious teen has somehow turned the tables on Julian and his Bratok and left the scene holding our Brigadier at gunpoint. Now, hours later, Mr Nix, is drowned."

"I'm sorry, I don't see the connection, Papa," muttered Erich.

"Don't you?"

"No, Papa."

"Well, the connection is this. Julian Nix was the keeper of the only computer that is capable of reading the lost program." Semion pointed again. "The very program you were responsible for. And now, that machine has disappeared along with this boy, Shenton."

Semion stood, slowly trod the thick carpet of his study and looked out of his window into the night.

"I want them back, Erich. The machine and the program. They are of the utmost importance.

That software contains pure political dynamite. Intimate details, secrets, photographs, of one of the most powerful politicians in this country. That program will not only destroy a Minister of the Crown, but her husband and her lover. This will bring down the government, Erich. The scandal will lose them the next election and we will have our very own friendly faces back at the top. I want that program, Erich, and the computer that unlocks it. And I want this slip of a girl, this boy and that drunkard… dead." He turned, face pale, eyes narrowed. "Am I clear?"

TEN

UnI Indian Restaurant, Liverpool

Cogan shovelled the last of his rice into his mouth then began the glorious task of wiping around his plate with the remnants of his Naan bread.

As he chewed gratefully, he gestured to the waiter for another Cobra. Moments later, it arrived exactly as he liked it. Ice cold, no glass.

He drank greedily from the neck, lay the bottle down and sat back in his chair pleasantly full.

Things didn't seem too bad after all.

That said, those things, like the weather, can change very quickly.

His 'burner' phone began to vibrate, spinning itself around on the polished surface of the table. Des clocked the screen which announced, 'private number.'

He answered.

"Cogan."

"Of course it is," said a rather croaky Cartwright. "How was your curry?"

Des instinctively looked around him for any sign of a tail, saw none, looked quizzically at the phone and put it back to his ear.

"Don't panic," said Cartwright, a mere hint of mirth in that ageing voice. "You have always been a creature of habit, Mr Cogan. I can't recall a single time you have visited a new city in the United

Kingdom when you have not sought out cuisine from the Indian continent. Personally, I find the whole concept rather dreadful, but each to his own as they say."

"Your idea of a wee joke eh, Cartwright?"

"I do try," he said.

"Aye, well, as it happens, the answer to your question is, yes, it was excellent. Now, may I ask how you are yersel, Sir? I understand from young Warren that ye have been poorly."

"The reports of my demise have been somewhat exaggerated, Mr Cogan. My surgeon has done a masterful job and informs me that there is quite a bit of life in the old dog yet. However, those that would see me in my grave have ensured that my role at the Firm has been downgraded. I'm currently on gardening leave."

"Well you send out very interesting gifts fer a man on his holidays."

"Ah, yes. So you got the package. Excellent. I have an inkling that you may need pretty much all of the contents of that particular box in the coming days."

"Expecting trouble then. These boys, Russians I believe, have it in for yer wee niece?"

"In my experience, Cogan, the Russians have always been a cause of great anxiety. And this particular shower are no exception." Cartwright cleared his throat. Des thought he heard him take a drink. "Now, as you are aware, I have an inherent distrust of mobile telephones, indeed telephones of all types, so I'll keep this brief. As I understand you travelled south by train, by the time you return to your hotel, there will be a hire car waiting for you. Tomorrow afternoon, I need you to collect Mr Fuller and my niece, Harriet from the airport. They are on the Emirates flight from Bangkok, via Dubai. Give Fuller that note I left him. It may help.

However, things are moving along a pace and I require you to begin your enquiries tonight, before Fuller and Casey arrive."

Des reluctantly put down his Cobra.

"Go on," he said.

"There's a boy," said Cartwright. "A young man by the name of Shenton, Jack Shenton. He was released from HMP Altcourse earlier today and was involved in an altercation with a man called Julian Nix, a particularly unsavoury character with connections to the very men that would do Harriet harm. However, I'm reliably informed that Mr Nix was later found floating in the Mersey minus his shoes, and that young Shenton has disappeared."

"Sounds like this wee lad is a handful," said Des, eyeing his near full bottle of beer with some regret.

"A solid character, I'm led to believe, who found himself in an unassailable position. That said, the boy's actions towards Nix are of little consequence. What is of more pressing concern, is the suggestion in criminal circles that Shenton may now be in possession of a valuable item that is essential to the positive outcome of your mission."

"I thought my mission was to protect your niece?"

"It is, at any cost, Cogan. However, there is another element to this assignment that is best not discussed on these dreadful devices. All I can say right now is that this item, a computer of some sort, must not fall back into the hands of the Russians. Find Mr Shenton, Cogan, tonight if you can, and lay hands on that computer."

Des blew out his cheeks.

"That's a tall order, Sir."

Cartwright coughed again.

"The boy has a mother, Sadie. She resides in an area called Croxteth. Apparently, she is well known in the neighbourhood for her particular brand of adult services. I'll send the address to your mobile phone presently. Memorise it then destroy the handset immediately. Good luck, Cogan."

And the line went dead.

Seconds later the address of Sadie Shenton popped onto the screen of his phone. Des took a long swig of his very palatable beer and reluctantly left the rest.

After paying his bill, he stepped out into the very nasty night, turned up the collar of his leather and found his pipe. Cogan huddled himself into a nearby shop doorway to shield himself from the wind, and driving rain, filled the bowl and lit up. Three drags later, the pipe was stowed. He pulled the 'burner' from his pocket, dropped it to the floor and stamped on the set, smashing it under the heel of his boot.

As he did so, a young girl walked by gripping a flimsy umbrella. She gave him a surprised look.

"Didnea like the ringtone," he said.

* * *

Jack dipped another handful of fries into his ketchup before pushing them into his mouth. He'd eaten two Big Mac meals already and was halfway through his third.

The guy serving him had given him the strangest look on his last visit to the counter, but he didn't care. The food at HMP Altcourse had been truly awful, and Maccy D's had been high on his list of post-prison treats for months. That said, he did feel somewhat uncomfortable each time the restaurant's automatic doors opened, expecting the appearance of overly muscled Slavic types brandishing automatic weapons with every swish.

And it wasn't just the fact that he'd just drowned one of the most feared criminals in Liverpool either. As Jack chewed on his burger, the clock ticked silently past the cut off time for his arrival at his hostel. He was now officially AWOL and any contact with the law, would ensure a swift return to jail, dead gangsters or not.

As he turned his attention to his large Coke, Jack did his best to formulate a plan to keep himself alive and out of custody. He'd never been on the run before and very quickly realised that despite the wads of money in the case at his feet, he had nowhere to go. No passport or other ID meant foreign travel was out of the question. He didn't dare visit any of his mates, for fear of implicating them, and he certainly couldn't go to the cops. So, Jack figured that eating three burgers in one sitting, was the least of his worries.

He finally finished his food, wiped his mouth with a napkin and carried his newly acquired case full of money to the Gents.

Once safely in the cubical, he opened it, removed a couple of hundred in cash, which he considered would be enough to get him a place to stay for the night, and stuffed the bundle in his still damp jeans. Jack was streetwise enough to realise that it wouldn't just be the cash that was important to the Russians. He knew that the notebook sized computer nestling between those bundles would be just as valuable in its own way. Maybe it was full of names and addresses of drug dealers or rival gangsters? Jack didn't know or indeed care, but he did consider that he needed a safe place to stash the case for a day or two, and the only place he could think of didn't fill him with confidence... his mother's flat.

It had been just shy of two years since he had last spoken to Sadie. His errant mother hadn't visited him in prison, not once. Neither had she replied to any of his letters. This, in itself, was not a surprise to the young Shenton. Even before his incarceration, on the few occasions he had stopped by her flat, she had always been out... 'working.'

Their relationship had broken down long before Jack was imprisoned, indeed, Shenton had been forced to fend for himself before he'd even made high school. Social services, care professionals, youth workers, even doctors and the police had spent hundreds of fruitless hours trying to create a parent-child relationship between them.

But Sadie was just not that kind of girl.

Jack had slept in hostels, care homes, even doorways. You name it, he'd been there. He'd been cold, scared and hungry more times than he could remember. Growing up with no father and a prostitute for a mother had ensured his education came more from the street than a classroom. Even the truant officer had given up on Jack Shenton. He and his other street urchin mates had got into all manner of scrapes, stealing cars for fun, stealing cash to eat. Jack was no angel, he'd never been able to afford that luxury. Throughout those times, his only saving grace had been his courage, and his ability to fight with his fists, yet now, it seemed even his beloved sport had turned against him. After all, if he hadn't been such a devastating puncher, both inside and outside of the ring, he wouldn't be sitting in McDonald's with a price on his head, would he?

He knew his mother would still have all her problems. She'd had them all his life. Drink, drugs, money and men had all conspired together to make her life difficult. That and Jack himself of course. Sadie had never wanted a child and had always seen her son as a burden, a chain to drag her down, hold her back. Yet despite all Sadie's shortcomings, she was still his mother, and you only got one of those. In fact Jack had always clung onto those rare memories when his mother had been both sober and loving. An occasional day out to Southport, an ice cream on the beach, a visit to the pictures.

And there was little doubt that he needed her now. Well, maybe not Sadie herself, but her flat, his old room and those loose floorboards where he'd always managed to hide anything of value away from prying eyes, including his mother's.

Stepping out into the rain, Jack raised his face to the inky sky. He felt totally alone, and if he was honest, for the first time since those awful childhood days, truly scared.

He hailed a black cab. On hearing his destination, the driver demanded his fare up front. Not unusual for anyone driving into 'Crocky'.

Jack was dropped at The Fir Trees pub, the infamous criminal haunt being just five minutes' walk from Sadie's flat. The bar and the surrounding area were notorious, particularly since Rhys Jones, an innocent eleven year old lad was shot dead on the car park.

That had been back in 2007 when Jack was still at school, but he'd grown up knowing all about the killers and the gang they were part of, The Croxteth Crew. This gang, and their great rivals, The Strand Crew, from nearby Norris Green, had been at war for years and gave Croxteth its shocking reputation for violence.

Shenton kept his head down and strode quickly away from the empty pub car park and its bright security lighting. Within minutes he was climbing the stairs of his mother's block of flats. His trainers squelched and rainwater dripped from his nose as he trod the concrete steps. They stank of stale urine and the walls either side of him were covered in graffiti. Somewhere above him, he could hear the sounds of a drunken argument and breaking crockery.

Another day in paradise.

Sadie lived at number 44. The fourth floor of a twelve storey block that had been due for demolition the last three years. Half of the flats were officially empty, the tenants already re-housed in readiness for the regeneration project. Nevertheless, empty dwellings in an area such as Croxteth, no matter how dilapidated, were gold dust for dealers, pimps and worse. This meant that no one really knew who lived in the block. It was as anonymous as it was decrepit.

Jack knocked.

"Mam," he shouted. "It's me. Let us in eh?"

There was no reply.

He had another go. "Mam, come on, I'm piss wet through here."

From somewhere down the corridor he heard a male voice shout, "Shut the fuck up, soft lad," but that was the sum total of the response.

Jack sauntered towards the end of the walkway where a thick red fire hose was housed in a broken glass case. He pushed two fingers inside the end of the hose and removed a door key. He knew it would be there. It had been hidden in that very spot for as long as he had been tall enough to reach it.

The argument above him seemed to be raging on and he heard more bumps, bangs and crashes mixed with screamed insults. He shook his head ruefully and pushed the key into the lock.

The flat was unusually in darkness. Sadie had never been one for switching stuff off. In fact, the TV had never gone quiet in his living memory. Not so today.

Jack found the light switch and the hallway was instantly bathed in a soft orange glow. No doubt Sadie's idea of what a working girl's flat should look like.

"Mam?" he called, pushing open the door to the lounge. "Mam, you there?"

Yes. Sadie was indeed there.

She lay on her back, her left leg tucked awkwardly underneath her. Her bleached blonde hair soaked with blood. Her tired but still pretty face, battered and bruised, lips grotesquely swollen, eyes wide open, unseeing.

Jack dropped his case.

"Oh no, Mam," he said quietly.

He stepped forwards and knelt at the side of his mother's body, feeling his tears fall, but making no sound. Sadie Shenton had never been a good mother. She had never showed her son love or affection. There had been no Christmas or birthday gifts, no parent's night visits, no praise for his achievements. But, despite it all, Jack had loved her.

"Oh, my God, Mam. What have I done?" he said, his voice breaking. "This is all my fault."

He looked about him, and for the first time, noticed the devastation to the flat. The place had been burgled many times before and he'd seen the wreckage thieves left behind, but this was on a scale he'd never witnessed. Whoever had done this, killed his mother, ripped the flat apart, had been looking for something valuable, something special.

He tore his eyes from Sadie's corpse and shot a look at the case he'd dropped on the carpet.

"All my fault," he muttered again.

Jack could feel himself losing control of his emotions. He fought back more tears, sucked in a deep breath and took hold of his mother's hand.

It was cool, but not cold.

That stopped him in his tracks.

Not cold? How long does a body stay warm? Jack didn't know. But he knew enough to realise that the killer, or killers were not far away. Were they watching the flat? Had they seen him climb the stairs? Were they…?

As if to answer his question, there was a scratching sound at the front door. Jack thought his heart would burst. The adrenaline coursing through his veins hit him like a hammer. His pulse raced. Pulling himself to his feet, Jack trod quietly back into the hallway and switched off the light.

He stood in near pitch darkness, listening to the scratching noises and his own blood pound through his veins. He felt sweat trickle down his spine as whoever was doing the scratching, sniffed and shuffled their feet.

He had never felt so afraid in all his young life.

Forcing himself to control his breathing, he stood with his back to the wall just feet from the door. The scraping noises continued for a few seconds more. Jack thought it sounded like a drunk trying to get a key into the lock.

His mind raced for a solution to his problem, then Shenton remembered the Colt, the gun he had taken from Julian Nix. Yes, it was in the case. He moved as quickly as he dare, back into the lounge, quietly opened the metal box, and there it was, glistening in the half light.

Shenton picked it up. It felt slippery in his wet palms. He swallowed hard. Would it fire? Could he fire it? He unconsciously shook his head, raised himself up and trod quietly back into the hall. This time, he faced the door, feet slightly apart, both arms outstretched pointing the Colt forwards, just as he'd seen all those actors do on the TV.

There was click from the lock. It was a quiet sound, but to Jack it may well have been a thunderclap. He felt his skin prickle and his legs begin to shake.

The door swung open and a man stepped quickly inside.

Jack aimed at the figure. To his surprise, the man instantly charged at him. Shenton went to fire, felt the pressure on the trigger and waited for the inevitable explosion, but it didn't come. Before he could complete the action, with one swift movement, the man had slapped the gun away with the back of his left hand, grabbed the muzzle with his right and twisted the weapon from Jack's grasp. It had obviously been an undertaking the intruder had practiced hundreds of times, just as Jack had rehearsed what he tried to do next. Punch his way out of trouble.

Shenton went for the man's body, head down, full power, but he easily tied him up with his own defences. He was like iron. Not a big guy, similar height and build to himself, but immensely strong, determined and experienced.

Jack had just pulled back his right in an attempt to land a decent shot, when he heard the unmistakable sound of a weapon being readied and felt the cold steel of a muzzle under his chin.

"Now, wee man," said his opponent. "Calm the fuck down eh? Is this the way ye welcome all yer house guests?"

"Most visitors knock, mate," said Jack, pressed against the wall, the Colt pushed into his skin.

"Aye," said Cogan. "I reckon they do. But I'm not in the business of announcing myself."

Des found the light switch with his spare hand and got a better look at the kid.

"There, that's better eh? Now, my name's Cogan. Des Cogan. I work for the government, son. I'm here to get ye out of this mess."

"You don't look like a Bizzy."

Des screwed up his face. "A what?"

"A Bizzy. A Copper."

Cogan shot a glance into the lounge. He saw the case still open on the floor, the cash, the laptop. Then he saw the pitiful sight of Sadie Shenton.

"Is that yer Mam, son?"

Jack swallowed, nodded slowly.

Des pulled the gun from under the kid's chin and pushed it into his belt. Jack thought him the scariest man he'd ever seen.

Cogan couldn't help but feel for the boy, but there was no time for sentiment.

"We need to get ye out of here the now," he said. "I'm sorry son, but there's nothing we can do fer yer mother. But I promise ye this, I'll do everything I can to keep you alive. Now, grab that case eh?"

Jack did as he was asked. After all, what choice did he have? This Scot who had expertly picked the front door lock, disarmed him in a split second then batted away his best punches without a second thought, looked like he was made of wire and leather. Yet he had a kindness about him. It was the look in his eyes. And Jack had seen that look before, seen it in the face of his old boxing trainer, a genuinely hard man with a heart of gold.

"Where we goin'," he asked.

"No far," said Des. He gestured towards the case. "Is that what ye took fe the Russian boys?"

"Well, he wasn't Russian," said Jack. "But he worked for them, I reckon. He was going to kill me. He…"

Des held up a hand.

"Just tell me. Is that a computer in there?"

Jack nodded.

"Okay, well ye can tell me all about it when we're away fe here, son."

Cogan knelt at the body of Sadie Shenton and gently pushed a finger into her mouth to part her swollen lips. As he suspected, several of her teeth were missing. If the Scot were a betting man, he'd wager that they were scattered around the grubby flat somewhere.

Sadie had been tortured before her body had given up the ghost.

"Yer Mam know where to find ye, did she?"

Jack shook his head.

"Not seen her since before I was locked up. Almost two years, I reckon."

Des turned down his mouth.

"And she knew nothing of the case, the money, the computer?"

Jack bit his bottom lip, the guilt flooding back into him, tearing at his young heart.

"She knew nothin'. I was just gonna hide it here for a bit. Y'know, till I figured out what to do, like."

Des raised himself.

Whatever was on that computer was of no consequence to him, but Cogan knew one thing, the Russians would stop at nothing to get it back. Both he and the boy were in terrible danger and would continue to be so until the machine was out of their hands. Of course, luck could shine down upon them both, they could go back to the Adelphi, sleep soundly, collect Rick and the girl from the airport and all would be well.

Job done.

Yeah right.

"Come on, son," said Cogan pulling the Colt from his belt. "Do you know how to use this?"

Jack shook his head.

"No mate. I wouldn't have a clue. I only pointed it at yer cos I was scared, like."

The Scot nodded ruefully.

"Well maybe that's my first job. You tired?"

Jack sniffed.

"A bit."

The Scot handed him the Colt.

"You can sleep when you're dead, son."

* * *

Cogan had parked two streets away from the block and used all his anti-surveillance knowledge to approach the flats undetected. He had seen Jack enter. The boy had been lucky. A black Merc carrying five men had only pulled away moments before he had crossed the street to his mother's. Cogan too had noticed that Sadie hadn't been dead for long, and that could easily mean that the Merc was connected to her murder.

Tenuous, but possible.

The unlikely pair made the bottom of the stairwell and Des held up a hand to stop Jack in his tracks. He scanned the street for any signs of danger, another car with misted windows, a shadowy figure in a doorway, but saw nothing.

"I'm going to get the motor, son," he whispered. "You stay put."

Jack watched as Cogan strode away, carrying the case with him. The guy may have promised to keep him alive, but whatever was in that metal box, was obviously worth more than an eighteen year old convict. That or he didn't trust Jack to be there when he got back.

Shenton shivered as he tucked himself out of sight behind a pair of large metal waste bins. The rain had finally stopped, but his clothes were still wet, and the cold February night began to eat into his bones. As the minutes passed, he began to worry that Cogan had left him behind. After all, he'd got what he came for, and whoever he was, whoever he worked for, he had no real reason to help Jack out.

The lad began to think of his mother, about how she had died so horribly. In less than twelve hours, his life had been turned upside down and instead of starting a new episode with a clean slate, his mother had been murdered and he was now on the run from both the authorities and a set of fearsome criminals.

After what seemed like an age, he saw a white car slowly approaching, headlights off. Cogan pulled up, opened the passenger door and Jack gratefully slipped inside.

The Scot gingerly edged the car away. After several minutes of painfully slow, deliberately quiet progress, Des exited the estate, put on more power, turned on the headlights and they were away.

Jack felt much better.

"Do you know any big open spaces where we can make some noise, son?" asked the Scot.

Jack thought for a moment.

"There's loads of disused warehouses and stuff on the old docks. We used to rob cars an' take 'em down there for the crack like."

Des shot the kid a look. He didn't look old enough to drive, never mind steal a car.

"Sounds like a plan," he said.

Twenty minutes later, they stood inside a cavernous old building that had been laid empty since the demise of the Liverpool docklands. Containerisation had been the Liverpool dockers' downfall. The left wing trade unions, fearing job losses as a result of the 'new' way of working had refused to change their methods and business had steadily moved away to other yards, notably their neighbours in Manchester. Thousands of jobs were lost, and Liverpool was once again hit by recession and the docks fell into dereliction.

Des found two old planks of wood and stood them on end, leaning them against a bare brick wall some six feet apart. With only a smattering of distant yellow sodium lights shining through the broken windows, there was barely enough light to see, but time was of the essence and Cogan knew that the next forty eight hours were going to be the roughest of rides for the young lad. If he were to have any chance at all, he needed to know how to use that Colt he'd acquired.

Des had clocked the boy a few times on the drive over. He'd looked pale and ever so immature. He reminded Cogan of himself in some ways. A young man that took matters to heart, yet incapable of showing his emotions.

He had to remember that the lad had been forced into killing a man, and that would weigh heavy.

Des had been even younger than Jack when he'd been posted to Northern Ireland. He too was still in his teens when he'd first taken a life. Different times, of course. Different circumstances, definitely. But it was the same mental and physical outcome, you never forgot it, no matter what the reason.

Neither would Shenton, and to top it all, the kid had lost his mother in the most horrendous of circumstances. Des couldn't even begin to get a handle on that one. How the lad would react was anyone's guess, but as the streetlights had flickered across Jack's face on the drive over, Des considered he saw a deep rage in there.

His hatred towards his mother's killers would churn in his gut, but who could blame the boy?

"Okay, kid," said Des. "Take that Colt from your belt and hand it to me." Jack did as he was asked.

"So," said the Scot, holding up the gun. "There is no safety catch on this baby, ye see this wee lever here? This wee latch that fits snug into your palm when you hold the gun? Well that is the safety, it pushes in as you squeeze the grip, so no need to fumble for a lever. Now, that doesn't mean you can walk around with your finger on the trigger. I see you doing that, I'll snap it off for ye… understand? Unless ye are about to shoot some fucker, ye keep yer finger outside the guard, pointed forwards, like this…okay?"

Jack nodded and looked ever so slightly worried.

"Now," said Des. "This is a .45, a big old round for such a small weapon. It will kick in your hand, but don't worry too much, by the time you feel the recoil, the round has gone, and if you've done the job right, your target is down. So," Cogan gripped Jack by the shoulders. "Stand here the now, set yersel. Just like ye did when ye pointed the gun at me in the flat."

"That didn't go too well," said Jack quietly.

Cogan looked in the kid's eyes.

"Aye, and ye know why I'm still here, son? Ye know how I managed to strip this wee gun fe yer hand? Because ye hesitated. Now, ye box d'ya not?"

"Yeah."

"D'ya wait te see what yer man does before ye throw yer own punches?"

Jack wrinkled his nose. "I understand what yer saying, Mr Cogan."

"Ye cannea hesitate, son. Now, like I said, set yersel, feet apart, cup yer left hand and support yer right with it. You willnea be doing any one handed John Wayne shite, I promise ye. Right… good, so this is all about triangles, about stability and dinnea worry if ye don't hit anything at first… okay?"

Jack nodded.

Des pointed.

"With this weapon ye have an eight round magazine. I want ye to fire two shots at each plank in turn. Nice and easy, bang, bang, bang, bang. And fer fuck's sake relax. Ye should know ye cannea punch while yer uptight. Ye shoulders are up around yer ears, man. Take a breath son… Ready?"

"Suppose."

"Off ye go then… both eyes open. Ye no a fuckin' sniper."

Jack did as he was told. When the gun fired the first time, he thought he may drop it. The noise was atrocious, the shockwave of sound inside the warehouse rattled his teeth and his ears rang instantly. Of course, Cogan knew this would happen and he stood off to one side with his fingers firmly protecting his own drums. The kid had to learn, and learn quickly. Gunfights are noisy and lethal.

Jack fired again, changed stance slightly and fired another two, changed again, bang, bang, again, bang, bang.

Pigeons fluttered in the rafters, an owl hooted somewhere, and the unmistakable smell of gunfire filled the air.

Cogan wandered over to the two planks. Each had four holes in them around chest height. He shook his head and smiled to himself.

"Fuck me, I'm good," he said.

ELEVEN

The Fir Trees Pub, Croxteth

Erich Honecker threw the shot of vodka down his throat, head back, and slammed the glass down on the bar.

"Another," he barked.

The young woman serving him gave him a sharp look. She dealt with hard men every day. Criminals of all shapes and sizes, from mountainous steroid filled bouncers, to skinny kids in black tracksuits. Marie Rose Gerrard certainly wasn't scared of this middle aged, broken nosed Russian.

"You break that glass, and you pay for it," she said flatly.

Honecker sneered at the young brunette. She was attractive in a whore-ish way. Too much makeup, too few clothes.

"I could buy this whole pub sweetheart," he spat and pointed at the glass. "Another."

Marie turned to the optics and poured a double.

"Two ninety," she said, petulantly, hand out.

Honecker slapped a ten pound note into her palm.

"Keep it," he said.

The girl shrugged, still unimpressed but happy for the extra cash.

"You know a boy called Shenton?" asked Honecker, loudly enough for the whole room to hear.

Marie shook her head. She was a Croxteth girl born and bred. You never knew anyone… ever.

"Never heard of him."

Honecker smiled, nodded.

"Of course you haven't. You must be a similar age, what are you eighteen, nineteen? Maybe you went to the same school?"

"I went to Broughton Hall, mate," said Marie. "Catholic. All girls. Like I said. I don't know him. I just serve drinks. I'm not a fuckin' information service."

Honecker wanted to slap the girl. Well, actually, he wanted to do more than that to her. Maybe he should remove some of her teeth with the same pair of pliers he'd pulled Sadie's molars out with? Maybe that would change her tone?

"Whatever," he snapped and turned to find himself a seat.

Sadie had been co-operative, even before he'd began his dental work. She'd given him two addresses that Jack had been using. He'd instantly dispatched his men there, an old boxing gym and what turned out to be nothing more than a flop house. Neither bore fruit, hence the need to play dentist. That work had resulted in two more addresses and the surprising death of his subject. Weak heart maybe? Even so, they too turned out to be little more than squats, so Erich had returned and called into the Fir Trees pub, to stir up the locals.

Prior to their arrival in Croxteth, the crew had paid a visit to Julian Nix's men, the four sorry characters who'd managed to let an eighteen year old kid kidnap and murder their boss, stealing the most valuable piece of equipment Papa Simeon Savalovsky owned in the process.

The terrified men had pointed out that Nix had been the engineer of his own downfall, underestimating the boy and allowing his blood feud to get the better of his common sense.

That said, mistakes of that magnitude could not be seen to go unpunished, and three of the Bratok, one Liverpudlian, one Estonian and one Ukrainian had been summarily executed, leaving the last man, a Russian by the name of Jacob, to do Honecker's bidding and, of course, live to tell the tale of just how ruthless the Brothers Circle was.

Erich himself had been a loyal servant to the Brothers, yet he was well aware that had it not been for the good grace of the Papa, his own errors in Germany may well have resulted in the same punishment as Nix's unfortunate soldiers.

This mission, the return of Savalovsky's goods and the execution of the people responsible for the theft, was one that simply could not fail. It was literally a matter of life and death.

His.

Honecker could feel the animosity towards him in the room. Dozens of pairs of criminal eyes watching his every move. Of course, that had been his plan. Jack Shenton had been born in that flea ridden flat not five minutes from where he sat, played on those mean streets outside. He may not have been the doting son, but he still visited his mother. He'd written to her from his prison cell. Honecker had seen the unopened letters. His DNA was here, and someone, someone sipping warm beer from a dirty glass in this shit hole that passed for a pub, knew him. And knew where to find him.

Honecker could feel it in his water.

He waited for the inevitable, and he didn't need to wait long.

One lanky youth with a ridiculously long gold chain around his neck dropped himself onto the stool opposite, He had a zero crew and eyes that had, 'I just did a line' written all over them.

"You Five-oh or what?" he said, giving Erich the evils.

"Just looking for Jack Shenton," said Honecker flatly. "It's a family matter."

The guy wiped his nose with his palm, curled his lip.

"Well you ain't family are yer, soft lad? Jacko weren't a Russian that's fer sure." The guy turned to his watching pals hoping to milk his audience. Three shaven headed teens grinned, nodded. One pointed his finger, pistol-like, winked.

Erich was unimpressed.

Now, it wasn't the fact that Honecker didn't realise what a perilous position he was in. Indeed, he knew these boys were perfectly capable of slotting him and dropping him in the nearest wheelie bin. However, he didn't think even they were stupid enough to make their move inside the bar, and he did have four heavily armed ex Spetsnaz soldiers sitting in a car on the car park awaiting his every command.

He raised his voice so, once again, the whole bar could hear.

"I am not a Russian, my friend, I am German, of Ukrainian heritage."

He smiled to reveal thousands of pounds of recent cosmetic dentistry.

"I am also a lawyer and I seek Mr Shenton on a legal matter regarding the last will and testament of his Great Uncle William. All I desire is to complete my business with the boy. I shall pay a fair price to the man that can lead me to him."

Long chain snorted.

"Yeah right. Ye still sound like a Ruski to me. And I reckon you should do one, pal."

Erich held up a conciliatory hand.

"I know where I'm not welcome," he said, then raised his considerable frame from his stool and made for the door.

He stood on the steps of the pub a moment. His men were where he'd left them, one outside the car, ready to move into the venue if needed.

Erich lit his cigarette and waited. He was rarely wrong on these matters. Someone in that bar would be unable to resist the temptation.

Moments later he was proved correct.

The door swung open and a kid dressed in an unseasonal t-shirt and shorts stepped out toking on a fat joint.

"How much?" he said, getting straight to the point.

"How good is your information?" asked Erich blowing smoke into the kid's face.

"Well, from what I'm hearin', Jacko won't be around too long either way. Apparently, he pushed Jules Nix in the fuckin' Mersey this aft and nicked a big bag of cash from him." The guy took another toke. "I saw him an hour ago if that's worth a few quid to yer."

"Five hundred."

"Let's see it."

Honecker produced a wad.

The guy nodded, seemingly impressed.

"He got in a car outside his Mam's block, grey haired bloke drivin'. A white Sorrento, new shape, ten plate."

"Anything else?"

"Yeah, the guy drivin'. Not the biggest of blokes, but looked a right handful."

Erich counted out the cash.

"How did you know about Nix?" he asked.

The kid snorted and shook his head. He pushed the five in his shorts.

"This is Crocky, mate," he said.

* * *

Erich strode to his car, pulling his mobile from his overcoat as he did so.

"It's Honecker," he barked. "I need you to find me a man who can view the council CCTV from the Croxteth estate… I don't care about the fuckin' time… a white Kia Sorrento 2010 plate… two men, one middle aged, one teenager. And get on to your police contacts. As soon as you have the plate, I want ANPR checked. This city is full of cameras, these thieves cannot hide from me for long. You have an hour, or I call the Papa and tell him of your incompetence."

Erich closed the call and dropped wearily into the front passenger seat of the Merc. He opened his iPhone again, Googled 'Kia hire, Liverpool,' and came up with two results. Enterprise and Avis. He checked the addresses and noted that both sites were close to John Lennon and both were open until midnight. He pointed the screen towards his massive driver and bodyguard, Anatoly Ivanov.

"Take me here," he said. "And make it quick."

Ivanov nodded, put the car into drive and pulled away.

Honecker rubbed his tired eyes and addressed his trusted servant.

"Whoever planned the theft in Frankfurt, put that team together, did not intend her to escape to Thailand, Anatoly. Those agents were working black. She must have had help from elsewhere. So I ask, why did she run all the way to the Far East? And who is this mystery drunk she ran to? Who is this long haired, middle aged man? A man that can take down three of our best Bratok?"

Erich pointed.

"And… what if this grey haired soul that just collected Shenton from his mother's is connected to the man in Pattaya? Because, if that is so, then that would mean whoever controls these two men, now holds both sides of the puzzle. The program and the machine, and that spells danger, not just for my own wellbeing, but for the whole of the Circle."

The huge driver nodded but stayed silent.

Erich began to search his phone again.

"If I am correct, then the two must meet, and soon. Yes, here… 1235hrs tomorrow, Emirates, flight number EK17 Bangkok via Dubai into Manchester. That would fit the timeframe perfectly, would it not?"

Erich pushed his phone into his pocket. He had a good feeling about this. They were close and he knew it. The Papa would love him again and all would be well.

"Quickly now, Anatoly," he barked at the driver. "Like your life depends on it."

TWELVE

Dubai International Airport DBX

Fuller ordered another Scotch.

The thought of meeting Des again was playing havoc with his head. Part of him, a fucking big part, wanted, no needed, to see him again, to hear what the cantankerous old bastard had been up to, that and check on Grace and the kid.

Yet another darker, more broken part of him, did not.

He looked at the amber fluid spiralling in his glass and wondered if he could do that. Could he go back? Manchester? The place where it all happened?

Harriet watched him drink.

"We'll be boarding in four hours," she said.

He barely nodded, took the thick glass tumbler in his hand and necked the final dregs.

Casey scowled.

"Maybe you didn't need that, Fuller."

He raised his brows, waved at the barman.

"Maybe I don't need the advice."

She looked him up and down. There was an impish air about her.

"Y'know, that picture of you, the one I had on my phone, the one taken back in 2006, you were hot back then, Fuller. Quite the man about town."

He turned and glared.

"You suggesting that I need a haircut? A shave? You think that will change things?"

"I'm suggesting that the man in that picture looked a whole lot different to the man killing another few brain cells right now."

"And your problem is?"

She shook her head, managed a smile, sipped her Coke and played her ace.

"What will Cogan think of you?" she asked.

"Of my hairstyle?"

"Of the scarecrow that walks out of the airport. Of the broken man that once stood tall."

Fuller felt his dander rise.

"You don't know me well enough to take the piss, Casey, and you certainly don't know Des Cogan. He shaves when the mood takes him, shops at Marks and Spencer's, cuts his own hair and drinks Guinness like his life depends on it. And if folks don't like him, he'll tell them he hasn't got a fuck left to give. The only thing he has is…"

"Is what, Fuller?"

He found the words difficult.

"Is me," he said slowly.

"And the feeling is mutual?"

The barman delivered another Scotch.

"We're all that's left, Casey. Him and me. The last ones standing."

Harriet ran her hand through her hair. Her eyes sparkled as she spoke.

"Women have come and gone then?"

Fuller sipped his drink, scowled.

"They do, don't they?"

"Some."

"Let's not go there, Casey. I'm here to get you back to Blighty and to find this computer or whatever Cartwright is looking for. I'm good at that kind of thing, so is Des. It's a simple job, let's not complicate matters by getting personal."

She looked into his eyes and gave him a smile.

"Why don't you get that haircut?" she said. "Show your friend you've not lost your touch."

Fuller looked down at his shoes. They were cheap and worn, just like the rest of his clothes. His head spun. Losing Lauren had changed him hadn't it? Something like that must alter a man, should alter a man. His old obsessions with clothes, the good things in life, had deserted him the moment he'd held her lifeless body in his arms. He shook his head.

"I'm not sure it will help."

Casey gave him a nudge in the ribs.

"There are seventy one spas and salons in this airport, Fuller, and I feel the need for a facial. Come on, what d'ya say?"

He shrugged.

"Is Cartwright paying?"

She held up a MasterCard.

"All the fucking way."

"Then why stop at a haircut?" he said.

Fuller began with a Desert Aroma Massage. His Indian masseur using aromatic oils which claimed to improve blood circulation, maybe it did, either way, he smelled nice and it was a snip at £145 for the 50 minute session. Next came a haircut, beard trim and shave priced at £90, including a hot compress treatment with a cleansing cream and balm.

Then a wonderful visit to Salvatore Ferragamo, where Fuller chose two pairs of Oxford brogues, one black one oxblood for a mere £1,400. After all, he had never liked to scrimp on shoes.

He was delighted to find that Thomas Pink had recently opened on the mall and chose two tailored fit Royal Oxford double cuff shirts, one in pale blue, the other in classic white, together with a selection of silk ties, swiping Cartwright's card for a further £290.

Adding a Hugo Boss navy two piece, two pairs of casual Ralph Lauren chinos, four polo's, underwear, socks and a very serviceable Samsonite case to put it all in hurt the old spy's credit card for an eyewatering £2480.

With just forty minutes left before the flight was due to leave, he strode towards the gate, his new boarding pass in hand.

Casey barely recognised him.

"My word, Fuller, you scrub up well."

He shrugged and gestured towards a carrier between her feet.

"What did you buy?"

"Just some aftershaves for my brother, Warren," she said, now rather disappointed with her purchases.

He nodded.

"I'd better get to the gate."

Casey looked confused.

"We haven't been called yet. First only, so far."

"I am in first."

"We came economy, Fuller."

"That was the Thai Fuller. This is the Manchester model. I never fly in an orange aircraft, or one that plays a fucking bugle when you land, and whenever the option presents itself, I always travel in first."

She examined her boarding pass before looking into his face.

"So I get to travel in cattle, is that it?"

He managed a thin smile.

"Best we don't sit together. I mean, the Russians will probably have accessed the manifest by the time we land, so…"

"But you're using the name, Colletti. I don't see…"

"It's an old ID. One I've used before, so, better safe than sorry… enjoy your flight, Casey."

As he turned, she called after him.

"Don't take too much advantage of the complimentary bar."

Fuller turned, straightened his tie and adjusted the cuff of his shirt.

"I'm on the wagon," he said.

THIRTEEN

Avis Car Rental, Speke, Liverpool

Erich Honecker peered over the counter at the young man's body.

Jacob, Nix's soldier, the man he'd recently spared, had been somewhat overzealous in extracting the information they'd required about the Kia car. He was probably trying to impress. Possibly Jacob's way of showing his gratitude for the fact that he was still breathing.

Either way, he'd beaten the man so badly that he now lay dead in a pool of his own blood.

Honecker shrugged off this minor issue and began to read the hire agreement for a white Kia Sorrento, delivered this very night to the Adelphi Hotel in the city.

The car had been hired by a company called Bright Trading, giving a London address and telephone number. Honecker suspected that the details would almost definitely be those of a bogus holding company. However, the car itself had been delivered for the use of one, Desmond Cogan who was currently residing in room 422 of the hotel.

Of course, until they could confirm the registration number by the local CCTV, this information, this vehicle, could be nothing more than a wild goose chase. Maybe another Kia Sorrento picked up young Shenton?

No.

Honecker felt good about this one.

Since the Papa had explained about the politically volatile information contained in the missing program, he was in no doubt that Whitehall would have been desperate to prevent the memory stick reaching its intended destination.

And it was true that MI6, like any branch of the Security Services you cared to mention, used deniable operatives from time to time. So maybe, just maybe, the three players in Frankfurt had indeed been dispatched from Vauxhall Cross.

It was a conundrum.

Yet Erich was convinced that whoever aided the girl's escape to the Far East did not now tread those hallowed corridors of power, certainly they were not party to the original plan.

No, more likely a rival gang, some other group who also knew the true value of the secrets contained on that device. Maybe they had got to the girl. Probably offered her great rewards. A band of criminals who needed to influence British politics for their own reasons.

No, MI6 was not behind the Thai killings. Criminals were. Criminals just like him.

And now, due to a bizarre chain of events, a young boy, straight out of a prison, a boy with no connections to the Brothers or the Secret Service, ends up in possession of the computer needed to open the stolen program.

As the Papa had pointed out, the strangest of coincidences.

Fluke, chance, quirk or not, whatever the mishap, these events had drawn out two men that were very skilled and dangerous. Two men that were inextricably linked. One had already slaughtered three excellent Bratok and this other grey haired mystery man who was one step ahead of Erich and his team, now possessed the boy and therefore the machine.

The question was, did Erich take the man currently sitting in room 422 tonight, or did he wait until he met with his partner in crime and the girl?

His phone rang in his pocket.

"Sir, we have the number of the car," said the voice. "RT10VCX. The plate is clear on the CCTV, no mistake."

Honecker scanned the hire document, even though he was sure the registration matched. He ran his finger under the number and smiled.

"Excellent work. Now, get your police contacts onto it. I want to know where it has been, every move it made and a picture of the driver. Make it quick."

He closed the call, pointed at the dead body behind the counter of Avis Car Rental and turned to Jacob.

"Clean this up. I'll wait in the car."

Just over an hour later, the Russian team had found the Kia parked two streets from the Adelphi Hotel.

"A bird in the hand," muttered Honecker.

He had decided that they would take Cogan and the boy, first. Once they were dispatched and the team had hands on the computer, he still had nine hours before the Emirates flight disembarked in Manchester. Nine hours to plan the demise of the mysterious long haired killer and the girl thief he was protecting.

Before the day was out, Erich was confident that he would have possession of the stolen items, and that his Papa's tormenters would all be dead.

Easy pickings.

As the team sat in their Mercedes, just yards from The Adelphi's entrance, Erich's contacts sent through a clear picture of Shenton and his mysterious middle aged companion. It had been taken by an ANPR camera at a road junction close to the Liverpool Docks. He now held the final piece in the jigsaw.

They knew the number of the hotel room the pair were in and they had the expertise and the firepower to dispatch them easily. For the first time in a week, Erich felt good.

"Okay, Jacob, Dimitri, Mikhail. You know what to do. Make it quick, clean and as quiet as you can. Bring the laptop back to me. And don't forget this is a fucking hotel, I don't want half of Merseyside Police chasing me for the rest of my days."

The three men nodded, checked over silenced weapons, then slipped out into the night.

Anatoly Ivanov, Erich's long trusted bodyguard and driver, sat back in his seat and watched the three men stroll confidently towards the front entrance of the hotel.

"You should have let me go with them," he growled.

Honecker turned.

"I need you here, Anatoly. And this is a straightforward job. Like shooting fish in a barrel."

"As you wish, Sir. But I don't like."

"Don't like what?" spat Honecker.

Ivanov reached across and tapped the screen on Erich's phone. It had Des Cogan's face enlarged on it.

"This man. I don't like the look of this man."

* * *

Cogan rummaged through the box of tricks that Cartwright had sent him. Jack sat on a narrow chair flicking through the hotel's pay per view channels.

"There were no need to change rooms on my account, Mr Cogan. I'd have slept on the floor," he said scrolling past some soft porn.

In Cartwright's box, Des had found three noise suppressors to fit the Sig Sauer pistols. He selected two and screwed them onto each barrel in turn, then he checked over the weapons one last time before dropping them both on the bed.

"That wee Colt ye practised with is no good to you now, son. Fer a start, we dinnea have any .45 ammunition until we get back to Manchester." He turned and gave the lad a withering look. "So how about you stop watching Brazzers, drop yer old gun in the box and help me stow the rest of this kit."

Jack jumped to his feet.

"Sorry, Mr Cogan."

"And will ye stop with the mister business. Does my head in. Just dinnea call me Jock, eh."

Jack removed the empty magazine from the Colt, opened the slide and lay both inside the box alongside the other ancillary kit.

"There, just like you showed me, Mr... I mean, Des."

Cogan shot the kid a look.

"Have ye wiped it down?"

Jack looked sheepish, lifted the Colt back out and gave it a good rub with his t shirt.

"That's better, son," said Des. "Now, I didnea swap rooms so ye could have a comfy night. I did it in case we had any unwelcome visitors."

He picked up one of the silenced Sig pistols and handed it to Jack.

"Hence the need for a wee bit of discretion."

Shenton examined the pistol and frowned.

"I take it this is the safety?"

"Aye, lad, it's called a thumb safety, ye push it upwards to fire. Dinnea fret yersel, you'll learn as ye go."

Jack looked worried, a hint of fear in his eyes.

"And you think they'll find us? The Russians? Come here? Tonight?"

Cogan took a moment.

From being a sixteen year old boy soldier, Des had put himself in harm's way. It had come naturally to him. He accepted the danger, revelled in it at times. Even now, as he neared his half-century, he couldn't hide his excitement at finding himself at the centre of a new mission. Ever since young Warren Casey had paid him a visit, he'd felt alive again. Sharp, focused, ready for the inevitable conflict. And if he were honest, once he'd learned that Rick was onboard, it was the best he'd felt in over a year.

Yet in his haste to prepare for the upcoming inescapable violent encounters, he'd forgotten that Jack Shenton was just a boy. A young man unused to guns, blood and death.

"Sit ye down, son," he said.

Jack did as he was asked, resting his pistol across his knees, pale faced and wide eyed.

"Look," began Cogan. "I cannea even start to understand how ye are feeling the now. I mean, ye get yersel in a wee bit of trouble with the Polis, ye keep yer head down, do yer time and that should have been the end of it eh? But it wasnea to be. Ye walk out to a nightmare. Before ye know it yer forced to kill another man in order to survive."

Des' eyes lost their focus a moment.

"I know how that feels Jack. I really do."

He rubbed his face with his palms, his calloused hands scratching his stubble. When he'd finished, his blue eyes had sharpened again.

"But I cannea lie to ye, son. These boys, these Russians or whoever they are, they're serious players, and they are vicious bastards. You've seen it first-hand lad."

Des saw Jack's eyes fill with tears. He rested his hand on the lad's shoulder.

"I'm sorry son. I didnea forget about ye Ma. It was shocking fer ye, I know."

Des added a little pressure, gave Jack a quick shake and moved the subject on.

"Look, son… what you did in that warehouse back on the docks, that shootin', not many folks could do with years of practice. Yer a natural, and that gives you… us, a fighting chance here. And what ye need to remember, is that we're the good guys."

Cogan held up a finger.

"Not that we can go to the polis eh? We never bother with those fuckers. But we're on the right side of the argument sure enough. And once we meet with my pal Rick Fuller in Manchester, hopefully this will all be over, and we can get you sorted out."

Jack wiped his eyes and did his best to swallow his heartache.

"It was my fault they killed me Mam," he whispered. "If I hadn't nicked that case, she'd still be alive. And now… now I've nowhere to go, Mr Cogan."

"Yes, ye have, son," said Des. "I'll see to it myself, so I will. And I'll see those bastards that did that to ye Ma, get what's coming to 'em n'all."

Jack nodded. He'd always been resilient, he'd had to be. And even though he'd just met Cogan, he believed him when he said he'd help. If they both lived long enough that was.

"So… we're going to Manchester?" he asked, clearing the tears from his throat.

"Aye. First to the airport to collect my old buddy, Rick and a wee lassie called Harriet Casey. Then I reckon we'll be off to a few old haunts until we know how the land lies."

"Never been," said Jack, examining his new gun. "Manchester, I mean, it's not far or nothin', I realise that, just never fancied it like. Me being a red and all that… Do you follow the footie, Des?"

Cogan sat on the end of one of the twin beds in his new room and smiled to himself.

"Aye, well I used to like. My old man took us to Celtic Park when I was a kid. I'll tell ye this too. Liverpool and United ain't got nothing on an Old Firm game. Jeezo, it's a war, kid."

Jack instantly came to life. It was as if he finally had a moment of normality. A brief portion of time where he could forget where he was. Why he was there. Cogan noticed it at once, the bright eyes, the buoyancy.

"Did you ever see King Kenny?" Shenton asked excitedly.

Des couldn't hide his smile.

"Aye, I did kid. 322 appearances, 168 goals. I had a wee greet when he signed fer your mob in '77. It was just before I joined the army."

The enthusiasm immediately left Jack's face. The mere mention of the military bringing his situation back with a bang.

"I figured you was in the army," he said quietly, looking at his feet. Then, looking up, "Did you like it? My boxing trainer, Danny was a soldier. All forces champ he was. Danny Blatchford, did you know him?"

"Doesn't ring a bell, but I've been retired a while now, son. He probably came after me. But I did like the job." Des stood and pushed his hands into his jeans. "I joined up to get away from Glasgow, from the poverty, the lack of jobs. My brothers all worked on the docks, but by the time King Kenny as ye call him was on his way here to Liverpool, I could see there was no future in shipbuilding on the Clyde. I wanted somethin' different and the army gave me that. I loved it fe day one."

Jack cocked his head, quizzically.

"So have you ever jumped out of a plane or anything?"

Des was about to answer when he heard hefty footsteps in the corridor outside. He'd chosen his new room 425, on the pretext that it had twin beds. However, his real reason, was that it was directly opposite his old one, 422. He held a finger to his lips. Jack nodded, gripped his Sig in his hand and stood, warily.

Cogan trod quietly towards the door, looked through the spyhole and gestured for the lad to join him.

Des could see three men, all heavy set, two fair, one dark, grouped around the door opposite. All three carried what looked like suppressed Russian military issue MP-443 Grach pistols.

He watched as one of the blonds produced what appeared to be a standard electronic card key, except his was attached to a small black control unit by a multi coloured wire. He pushed the card in the door lock and began pressing buttons on the unit.

Des looked over at Jack and noticed beads of sweat were forming on his forehead. The kid seemed paler than ever. He gave him a reassuring smile and a wink.

Cogan knew it would be easy to allow the three men to make their entry to the room, find it unoccupied and let them walk away, empty handed. But that was three more soldiers to deal with down the line. The way he saw it, better to dispose of your enemy in the here and now.

Timing was of the utmost importance. He wanted all the Bratok inside the room before he could open his own door and make his move.

Jack stood watching Cogan, he held his breath, biting his lip, not knowing what was happening on the other side of the door. He could hear whispered voices speaking in a language he couldn't understand and a bleeping noise that sounded like someone texting with an old Nokia.

Jack couldn't take his eyes from Cogan. He couldn't believe how calm he was. Not a hint of nerves. In fact, he seemed to be actually enjoying himself.

Shenton felt the sweat trickle down his back again, just as it had when he was waiting for the Scot to burst into his mother's flat. The gun he held in his hand felt slippery and his jaw ached from clenching his teeth.

Could he do this? Should he do this?

Des looked over to him and nodded. With his left hand, he grabbed at the door handle. In his right, he held his pistol skywards but with three fingers laid against the barrel. Then two. Then one, and then he tore at the door.

Des was out in an instant. Jack followed, heart racing.

Cogan stepped quickly across the corridor, pistol in the aim. It sounded to Jack like the men inside the room were tearing it apart, lifting up beds pulling open wardrobes, cursing to each other.

He watched as Des stepped into the open doorway, his left elbow brushing the jamb. As he did so, the darker haired man of the three twisted his head towards the noise.

Cogan fired twice in quick succession, a double tap to the man's chest. He fell against the bedroom wall and slithered down on his haunches.

Jack was at Cogan's right shoulder. He was amazed just how quiet the shots had been, the slide on the pistol making more noise than the round exiting the breech.

For a split second, the room appeared empty to him. Then, another huge blond guy popped up from behind the upturned double bed in the centre of the room, swinging his weapon towards Des.

Shenton could hear Cogan's words in his head.

No hesitation, son.

There was no time to pause. Just as when an opponent dropped his guard after a body shot. The window of opportunity would be brief.

Jack felt the pistol kick in his hand, even before he'd realised, he'd pulled the trigger. His first shot was a little low, hitting the bed itself, yet punching its way through the mattress into the guy's gut. His second was on the money though, smack in the centre of his chest. The blond monster toppled against the long drapes behind him, tearing them from the rail as he fell, Jack heard him exhale as he dropped, and just knew it would be his very last breath.

Shenton felt instantly sick to his stomach, but there was no time to wretch.

The third man was in the bathroom and by now, fully aware that he was under attack. Cogan gave Jack a look, pointed to his right and indicated for him to keep low.

Shenton crouched down and edged himself into position, his Sig pointed at the open bathroom door. But before he could set himself, the man popped out from behind the frame and fired once, twice, three times. Mercifully, the rounds flew by him and buried themselves into the wall behind his head. It was the most terrifying thing he'd ever experienced. He actually felt the bullets pass him, felt the air move, felt the heat on his face.

Cogan moved forwards, took a step right, and opened up towards the shooter, but his two rounds only splintered the doorframe where the Russian took refuge, missing their target.

The fair haired gangster wasn't done. He once again twisted his body, remaining half in cover, and fired again, this time towards Cogan.

Des threw himself left to avoid the white hot rounds before dropping into the kneel and letting go with his own Sig. This time it was a solitary shot, but again the round simply slammed into the wood and plaster the Russian hid behind.

In that very moment, Jack saw his chance. He vaulted over the upturned bed in the middle of the room, changing his angle of fire. He narrowed his eyes and let fly four times.

He hit the man in his forearm, shoulder, neck and cheek, the bullets tearing into his skin, sending claret spattering onto the white bathroom tiles behind him. The big Russian staggered forwards, out into the bedroom, gun hand useless, weapon dangling from his fingers.

Cogan lifted himself, casually placed his pistol to the man's temple and pulled the trigger.

The gangster's legs folded like card, and he dropped with a heavy thump to the carpet.

Jack stood panting like he'd just finished a hard ten rounds and stared at the carnage. Then he examined the smoking Sig in his hand, the slide sitting in the open position.

"Yer out of ammo, son," said Cogan, changing his own magazine. "Next time, keep count."

Jack was incredulous.

"Next time?"

Cogan ignored Jack's scepticism and began to rummage in the pockets of the man from the bathroom. He pulled out a wallet and looked up at the young Liverpudlian.

"If you think this is over, Jack my boy, you are very much mistaken. Now, don't just stand there gawping, check that guy's pockets. We'll have their weapons too. The ammo will come in handy."

* * *

Erich Honecker turned up the heater on the Merc, then looked to Anatoly Ivanov.

"The boys are taking their time," he said.

"Maybe the machine is well hidden," said the massive bodyguard.

Erich snorted his derision and pushed his tired bones down in his seat. He was getting too old for all this shit. Too old to be sitting in damp clothes in a cold car in the middle of the night. On the other hand, he considered that his options were limited, and being a trifle soggy was certainly preferable to having his body parts strewn across half of Merseyside.

He watched as the first police patrol arrived at the front of the Adelphi, blue lights flashing.

"I don't care for the look of this, Anatoly," he muttered.

"No, Sir."

Then a second patrol, this time an ARV crew slid to a halt and sprinted into the hotel, fully armed.

Erich rummaged in his overcoat, pulled out his phone and called Jacob. It was answered on the second ring.

"Jacob! What is happening, the police are here," he shouted.

"That will be because I called them, pal," said a calm Scottish voice. "And as you seem to be in the know, I take it you and the rest of yer pals are outside watching?"

"Who is this?" spat Honecker.

The man on the other end of the line sounded like he was smiling.

"This, my old china, is the boy who will be knocking on your door sometime soon and giving you the good news. Oh, and I wouldnea bother hanging about fer ye pals. They won't be playing out today."

There was a bleep, and the line went dead.

Ivanov looked across at his boss. Honecker was shaking.

"Whoever that was, whatever it takes, I want that bastard Scotsman's head on a plate," he seethed. "Now drive."

FOURTEEN

Terminal 1, Manchester Airport

Cogan had parked the Kia out by the Skypark. It gave him a great view of the runway and beyond. He had always enjoyed watching planes take off and land. And, right on time, the massive Emirates A380 that carried Rick Fuller and Harriet Casey came into view. It was on its final approach, the unmistakable red, green and black tail flash glinting in the very welcome February sunshine. He saw the pilot drop his landing gear, before steering the largest passenger aircraft in the world effortlessly down to the tarmac. As the twenty two wheels touched down and gave off a puff of tyre smoke, he pulled out his pipe, filled the bowl and stepped from the car to light up.

"Welcome home pal," he said to himself as he blew out a long plume.

Jack was asleep in the passenger seat. To be fair to the lad, it was probably the first zeds he'd had in twenty four hours, and what a day it had been for him.

Cogan tapped out his pipe, slid back into the Kia and gave him a shake.

"Come on son, let's go meet the rest of the team."

Jack rubbed his eyes, puffed out his cheeks.

"I could go a brew, Des," he said. "Me mouth's like the bottom of a budgie's cage."

Cogan looked over his shoulder at the huge eight hundred and fifty three seat plane as it began its taxi towards the terminal, then back at Jack.

"I reckon we've time fer a swift cuppa," he said.

Des moved the Kia to the short stay, and minutes later, the pair sat in Costa sipping most welcome hot Americano coffees.

"So, have you known this bloke Rick for a long time then, Des?" asked Jack, hugging his cup two handed.

"Longer than you've been alive, son," he said.

"And is he like you?"

Des had a think about that one.

"We were both in the same Regiment if that's what ye mean. He was kind of my boss I suppose… but we're different. He's a Cockney fer a start."

Jack took a sip.

"Bet he's a Gooner."

Des smiled.

"Rick's not a big football fan, son."

"What does he like then?"

Cogan sat back in his chair his mind a whirl of memories. Flashes of when he and Rick were young squaddies, his old Cortina car, the boozing, the fist fights, the girls. Then the dark days. How he'd changed after losing Cathy, the flash cars, the designer clothes, the obsessive behaviour. Then of course there was Lauren North.

He took a long breath.

"Rick's doesn't care for much, son."

Jack looked Des in the eye.

"Except fer you then?"

Des nodded slowly.

"Aye son, except fer me… Come on the now, let's go meet Rick Fuller."

The arrivals hall was full to bursting as eager relatives and friends mixed with businessmen, taxi drivers and travel reps. The Emirates flight had landed a few minutes early so its passengers were mixed with travellers returning from Rome, Zakynthos and Copenhagen.

Des leaned against a pillar, eager to see his friend once again, his stomach reminding him of just how they had parted in that cemetery just over a year ago.

What kind of shape would Rick be in? Physically? Mentally?

All would soon be revealed.

Cogan caught the first glimpse of him as he pushed a trolley between a group of tanned revellers. He looked remarkably well. The trademark suit, shirt and tie were immaculate. He walked with that Fuller confidence, eyes darting around the hall.

Was he looking for Des, or the enemy? Cogan considered it would be both.

Then Rick saw him.

Fuller didn't smile often, but when he did, he lit up a room with it. He shoved his trolley off to his left and gave the job of pushing it to a young woman that Des could only presume to be Harriet Casey. Leaving his baggage behind, he strode over and took Cogan in his arms.

Des hugged his friend back.

"Ye all right there, pal?" he said into Fuller's ear.

"Not as good as you," he said. "You ain't been sat next to some fat bloke from Bournemouth for the last nine hours."

They released each other.

Fuller scowled.

"He collected Toby Jugs… you know the type?"

Des grinned.

"Aye, an interesting kindae chap then. Well at least there was a free bar."

Rick turned down his mouth. Des thought he read something in his eyes but couldn't be sure.

"I've been off the booze for a while," he said, tapping his flat stomach. "Been getting some in."

Fuller turned and noticed Jack standing uncomfortably to Cogan's right. "And this is?"

Des put his hand on the kid's shoulder.

"This is wee Jack Shenton, pal. He saved me from being slotted by a big hairy Russian last night. He's a good boy."

Shenton held out a shaky hand. He didn't think anyone could look scarier than Des Cogan, especially dressed in a designer suit, but this bloke seemed to manage it.

"Pleased to meet you Mr Fuller," he said.

Rick was about to speak when Harriet Casey appeared, slightly red in the face pushing the pair's luggage. She instantly let go both barrels, her finest Queen's English on display for all to hear.

"When you've quite finished with the old boy's from the Regiment act, may I suggest we find a slightly less conspicuous place to make our acquaintances. That, and I need to phone Uncle Damien as a matter of urgency."

Fuller shrugged and gave Des a look.

Jack leaned over into Cogan's ear.

"Fuck me, she's fit," he said.

* * *

"So you already have the computer?" Casey asked, a mixture of incredulity and excitement in her cultured voice.

"Aye," said Des, finding his pipe as he stood at the driver's door of the Kia. "Young Jack managed to get his hands on it. Caused a right old stoater of a row it has. We were paid a visit by three shockingly angry Spetsnaz boys last night, who were rather disappointed not to leave with the goods, I'll tell ye."

"They aren't Spetsnaz," said Casey wearily.

"They aren't anything now," muttered Jack, sliding into the back seat, rather pleased to be sitting next to Harriet rather than the scary looking Fuller.

Harriet cocked her head quizzically.

"Meaning?"

"Meaning they're dead," said Jack, flatly.

Casey blew out her cheeks, shook her head and found her mobile.

"I really need to call Uncle Damien," she said, opening the screen.

"That secure?" asked Fuller, nodding towards the set.

Casey shrugged.

"Then close it," he snapped. "Cartwright hates mobile phones at the best of times, and if I were a betting man, he already knows the score."

"Aye," said Des, dropping into the driver's seat after finishing his smoke. "The gunfight at the Adelphi Hotel was all over the news this morning. He'll know the craic fer sure." Des pulled his personal Browning SLP from the glovebox. "But there's Sigs, mags and secure phones in the boot, if ye want to sort yersels before we set off. The old boy sent us a right box of tricks, but I took the liberty of sending it on. I'll collect the rest from the DHL depot in Trafford tomorrow."

"Probably wise," said Rick, loosening his tie. "Meantime, we need to get somewhere secure and work out the best way to get this stick and computer to Cartwright."

"True enough," nodded Des.

Rick turned to Jack. "Shenton... do the honours, son."

Jack gave Rick a confused look, finally got the message and slipped out of the car around to the boot. Moments later he was back with three Sigs complete with spare mags and three robust looking mobile phones.

"Told ye, he's a good lad," said Des firing up the Kia.

Rick pushed his newly acquired mobile into his jacket without switching it on, then checked over his SLP before turning his attention to the car.

"What the fuck is this, by the way?"

"Kia Sorrento," said Des, moving off from the multi-storey short stay park. "Nice wee motor. It has everything."

Rick rubbed the dash disdainfully.

"What it does have, is a badge that says it was put together by shoeless Chinese children."

"It's South Korean, Fuller," said Casey, pushing her own Sig into her jeans.

Rick twisted his head around from the front seat. He had that 'I will say this only once,' look about him.

"I like to ride in British or German cars, Casey. Prefer to walk in Italian shoes, fight in American boots, and won't be seen dead wearing anything that says, George, Florence or Fred on the label. The only people who drive cars like this are those unfortunate enough not to be able to afford a Range Rover." He shot Des a look. "We need to change this heap."

"Actually, we do," said Des. "The last set of Russian boys traced us because of it, so it's best we dump it in town, then pick up something from the lock-up eh?"

Fuller sniffed.

"Nothing there. I sold everything. The Aston, the Porsches, even the van. All that's left is a few bits of kit, some clothes, rations… cash, a few grand, walking around money."

Des gave his old friend a quick eyeball.

"You weren't intending a quick return then?"

Fuller didn't answer that one. Instead, he turned and looked out of the window, seemingly deep in thought.

They were heading along the airport spur. Then it would be the M56, which would turn into Princess Parkway. In minutes, they would cross the Mersey, pass West Didsbury, then Moss Side and Hulme, before peeling off at the Cambridge Street junction and hitting the usual traffic at the University District. At that point, they would be just minutes from the place where Fuller had kept some of his beloved cars, weapons and himself, on more occasions than he could recall. His trusty lock-up.

"Never thought I'd be back," he said to the window, still musing.

"Well, I'm glad ye are," said Des. "I got so bored I even bought a dog."

Fuller gave his friend a smile and a nod, before looking back out at the passing landscape.

Moments later, Rick frowned.

"You clocked the Chrysler 300? Silver one. Been with us since the spur?"

"Aye," said Des.

"Aren't those cars for people who can't afford a Bentley?" said Harriet, with a hint of mirth.

Fuller watched via the passenger side mirror as the front of the big saloon sat up, its driver hitting the pedal hard, laying down the power from the three litre V6.

"It might not have the drinks cabinet, sweetheart, but as the fucker weighs in at just under two thousand kilos. It's a cheap battering ram."

As he spoke, a second vehicle came into view on their outside. A black Grand Voyager. Four up as far as Fuller could see, and the people carrier wasn't hanging around either.

"Another Chrysler," he said, pulling his Sig from his jacket. "With all that disposable income, you'd think the Russians would have more taste."

Des checked his mirrors and put his foot down. The Kia picked its feet up but was unimpressive.

"Now we need that Range Rover," he said.

Jack looked over his shoulder, through the rear window. The silver C300 was closing fast and the Grand Voyager was almost upon them.

"Can we not just outrun 'em, Des?" he asked worriedly.

"Not a hope in this, son," said the Scot, foot flat to the floor, the Kia slowly climbing past a hundred miles an hour.

Rick was looking around him, eyes darting left and right.

"They're going to box us in," he said. "Push us off the road."

Des edged the Kia right, half into the outside lane, cutting off the progress of the Voyager.

"No if I can help it," he said.

"Did I mention, I'm not keen on hi speed pursuits," said Harriet, checking over her pistol. "I'm a slow and steady kind of girl if I'm not behind the wheel."

Before anyone could deride her comment, there was a massive jolt as the rear of the Kia was hit hard from behind. Seconds later, they were struck again, and the back window exploded, showering Harriet and Jack in dozens of pearls of laminated glass. The South Korean marque skittered left and right, the tyres screaming as Des fought to keep her steady.

The C300 had indeed rammed them.

Jack risked a peek over his shoulder.

"Looks like four up," he shouted over the wind noise.

"Next time he comes close, put a couple into the screen," shouted Rick.

"Give him something to think about."

Harriet turned to Jack.

"That's not protocol, Shenton. You should never fire at or from a moving vehicle. It's far too dangerous."

A split second later, the massive bulk of the Chrysler smashed into the rear of the Kia for a third time.

Des twisted the wheel of the car as it slewed to the right.

"Fuck the protocol, son," he shouted. "Lay down some rounds. Just like I showed you."

Shenton twisted awkwardly before settling himself, his knees on the back seat, forearms resting on the glass filled parcel shelf, both hands on his Sig.

Jack's presence was not wasted on the Chrysler's driver who stamped on the brakes so hard, tyre smoke billowed from the front wheels. Shenton exhaled slowly and squeezed the trigger firing twice at the fast retreating saloon. He saw his first round hit the screen, causing a web shaped crack. His second effort buried itself into the grill, sparking as it entered the engine compartment. Steam instantly poured from the gaps in the bonnet.

"I've done his radiator, I reckon," he shouted.

The youngster's elation was short lived. Whilst the team's attention had been centred on the C300, the Grand Voyager had made it alongside them, and one of its rear passengers, a huge shaven headed man, opened fire into the Kia with what looked like an M4 carbine.

Four rounds punched through the driver's window, slamming into the instrument panel just inches from Des' hands. A second controlled burst of 5.56 clattered into the rear passenger compartment, mercifully missing both Harriet and Jack, before burying themselves into the headlining just inches from their heads.

"We're sitting ducks here," shouted Des. "Hang on."

At that he too stamped on the brakes, the Kia's ABS kicking in, preventing the wheels from locking, but delivering machine gun like vibrations through the car. That put some much needed distance between them and the Voyager. But the chase was far from over.

Des flicked the car left, darting behind an articulated truck, stamped on the brakes, then pushed left again, onto the hard shoulder, before accelerating hard, undertaking the wagon and drawing a long blaring angry horn from the driver.

The Scot pushed the Kia to its limits, touching a hundred and twenty miles per hour as he re-joined the carriageway. But the C300 had followed his every move and was closing fast. Despite the steam pouring from its front end, the one hundred and fifty five mph top speed of the big saloon, gave it the ultimate advantage.

The team couldn't get away by speed alone.

Rick was making his own judgements.

"The traffic will start to build in the next few miles," he said. "As soon as we slow, these boys will just rake the car. They won't give a fuck about casualties. We've got to get off this motorway."

"The nearest exit is four miles away," said Des. He shot a look in his mirrors. Both enemy vehicles had closed in on the team and were manoeuvring to box them in again. "We're not going to make it, pal. We're going to have to fight our way out of this."

Rick sniffed, cricked his neck.

"Eight against four. Carbines against, SLPs. I always did like a challenge. Let's make the decision for them, pal."

Des shot Rick a look.

"Really?"

Fuller turned down his mouth. Nodded slowly.

"Really," he said.

Des shouted to his rear passengers.

"Okay folks, this is your captain speaking. We're going to leave the motorway. Seatbelts on, please. Secure your weapons. When I give the word, keep your heads down and prepare for a bumpy landing."

Harriet had worked out the plan, and she didn't like it one bit. Off to the left of the carriageway, was a steep grass bank. At the bottom of the slope was a barbed wire fence. Beyond that a wooded area with a narrow track leading to… well of that she wasn't sure.

"You can't be serious, Cogan," she said, checking about her, racking her brain for a safer option. "You'll kill us all if you put this car down that banking at this speed."

Cogan ignored Casey's plea.

"Hang on," he shouted, pulling the Kia sharply left, tyres screaming. "Head's down."

The manoeuvre took their pursuers by total surprise and they overshot their target.

As the Kia crossed the hard shoulder, Des stamped on the brakes as hard as he dare. He needed to slow the car enough so that it didn't roll the moment it began its descent down the bank. He felt the front wheels hit the grass and lifted off the pedal. The seemingly endless February rain had made the surface of the sharp gradient soft, and the car instantly began to slide. The all-wheel drive Kia was an able off roader, but it wasn't designed to travel sideways down a steep wet grassy slope at sixty miles an hour.

Cogan fought with the car, hoping to point the nose downwards and stabilise their descent, but the Kia's natural impetus only buried the front wheels into the turf and unbalanced it further. He felt the offside rear wheel lift and knew he'd lost the battle.

"We're going over. Hold on." he shouted, seconds before the Kia began to tumble.

The car slammed onto its passenger side. Rick and Jack crashing into their respective doors, gripping onto anything they could find. Harriet fell into Jack, grabbing at his jacket, screaming in his ear.

"These guys are fucking crazy."

Then the Kia began to roll.

Casey felt her seatbelt cut into her shoulder as the Kia turned onto its roof, it held her torso so tightly that it forced the wind from her, disorientating her further. As the car rolled onto its offside, the internal airbags began to go off like gunshots. One slammed into the right side of her face.

Although the devices were designed to save her life, the blow from the exploding equipment was like being punched by a heavyweight, knocking her senseless. Her limp body began flopping around, smashing into Jack, who'd taken the decision to assume the crash position and say what he could remember of the Lord's Prayer. As the Kia continued its acrobatics turning faster with each rotation, he reached out and grabbed at Harriet, wrapping his arm around her, pulling her in close.

Finally, the Kia rolled to the bottom of the slope, destroying the wire fence at the bottom, before coming to a halt on its nearside, just before the tree line.

A strong smell of petrol instantly filled the car as Jack began to fight with the multiple airbags that surrounded him. Harriet lay on his shoulder, moaning quietly. He lifted her off him, just as Des' head appeared between the front seats, eyes wild, knife in hand, slashing at the bags.

The Scot pushed his wiry frame forwards so he could cut both their seat belts. Once he was satisfied the pair were free, he had a quick look at Harriet, and gave her a shake.

"Come on Casey. The fun's over. Move yersel."

Her eyes flickered open and she exhaled down her nose.

"Bet I have a black eye," she said drowsily.

Des wriggled backwards and began his exit.

"Yer still a bonny wee thing, dinnea fret yersel, now, come on, we need to move, we have company."

Rick had clambered out of the Kia through the missing windscreen and was watching six of the eight men that had been pursuing them as they half slipped, half clambered down the sodden banking towards them.

The Russians had reversed their respective vehicles back down the hard shoulder to where the team had left the road, seemingly oblivious of the danger and blasting horns of Manchester's motorists. The men were all heavy set, typical Baltic gangster types, zero crews, black bombers, their recruiters obviously seeing brawn as a major plus in any conflict. Had they seen these guys attempting to negotiate such a simple obstacle as a wet slope, they may well have changed their mind.

He rested his Sig on the front wheel of the upturned car and let off a single round.

Fuller knew his enemy were too far away for the 9mm pistol to do any real damage, but it had the desired effect and sent the six brutes scurrying for the treeline, heads down.

"Shenton," he shouted. "Get the computer… and don't fuckin' let it out of your sight. Casey, you're on me, come on, shake a leg."

Harriet still looked dazed but was moving gingerly, her head clearing by the second.

Jack scurried around to the rear of the Kia. It took him three attempts to prise the tailgate open and pull out the suitcase containing the laptop and cash.

"What about your luggage?" he shouted.

"Are ye fuckin' serious, son?" said Des, dropping a lit box of matches into the car before sprinting towards the nearest mature tree. "Move yer arse."

Seconds later two of the Russians, who had jogged into the wooded area, opened up with their M4s.

"Holy shit," shouted Jack. "What the fuck was that?"

Des grabbed him by the collar and dragged him into cover.

"Get yer fuckin' head down, son," he snapped. "Stop askin' stupid questions and get switched on."

Jack thought his heart would leap from his chest. Being shot at by a man with a pistol was one thing. Being shot at by a team of gangsters with combat rifles, after rolling down a mountain in a Kia, was a whole new level of scariness. That said, Des Cogan appeared in no mood to make allowances for his lack of maturity or experience.

The Scot gave him a sharp clip behind his ear. "Are ye listening son?"

Cogan didn't wait for a reply. He returned fire with his Browning and instantly clipped one big youthful looking blond guy in his gut. Jack sat on the sodden ground, legs shaking, as he listened to the Russian screaming in agony. Cogan took careful aim a second time, and the guy went quiet.

"Fuck, fuck, fuck, fuck," muttered Jack, fighting to get his head together, case between his knees.

He twisted his body and punched out his own Sig, scanning the woods, his breathing reminding him of the last seconds of the final round of a tough fight.

"Calm the fuck down, Jacko," hissed Cogan. "Just do as I say and ye'll be fine. Move two trees to my left... there, yes, that one... and keep low." Des was wide eyed. "Do it now, ye tube," he barked.

Jack did as he was told and drew another burst of 5.56 from the Russians. As the rounds slammed into the ground around him, he hopped, somewhat comically, foot to foot, holding the case at head height.

"Fuckin' Russian bastards," he shouted as he dove for cover.

Cogan shook his head and shot him a look. Shenton couldn't decide if it was sympathy or distain.

"It's not fuckin' funny Mr Cogan," he offered, red faced.

Des pointed towards Jack's field of vision.

"Stop yer fuckin' greetin' and keep yer eyes peeled, lad. If they get around us, we'll really be in the shit. And no fucker will be laughin' then, I'll tell ye."

Rick was headed towards the enemy, jogging bent at the waist. A mixture of 5.56 and 9mm peppered the undergrowth around him as he zig zagged towards the Russians, a dangerous ploy, but a necessary one. He fired occasionally, drawing the crew ever closer to him. Des did his best to keep the enemy busy, firing single aimed shots as they scurried in and out of cover. The good news was, they were following Rick's path and falling into his trap. Finally, Fuller had the gang where he wanted them, deep in the wood, facing the open ground where the Kia had come to rest. He peeled off, taking up a position, off to Jack's left, Casey was knelt behind a discarded washing machine a thoughtful fly tipper had dumped just on the edge of the track. She was back in the game, Sig at the ready. The team were now all in cover in a rough arc, with their backs to open ground and the motorway. Fuller had drawn the Russians deeper into the woods than they needed to go, and they now had a big problem.

He knew the cops would already be aware of the incident, and as thick black smoke poured from the ruined Kia, sending a huge toxic plume into the clear sky, he was pretty certain they wouldn't be too long about it.

The only way the Russians could recover the case, or the program, was to attack Rick's team head on, and time was running out.

He leaned a shoulder into the trunk of his tree and scanned the woods ahead.

"Come on, boys," he muttered to himself. "Let's dance."

Rick didn't have long to wait.

There was movement to his right.

"Shenton," he hissed. "Come on, son. Wake up. He's your target."

Jack saw that a big bull of a man with a bald head and impressive full set, was edging ever closer to his position. The Russian's M41A carbine was tucked into his shoulder and he swung it, left and right as he moved, searching for his prey.

Jack steadied himself and did his best to control his racing heart. He slipped his finger through the trigger guard of the Sig and lifted the thumb safety upwards to the fire position, exhaling as he did so.

Then there was that moment, that split second where one shooter spies the other. Jack saw the man's body tense, his eyes widen. He watched as the massive Russian aimed his M4 and curled his mouth into a sneer. But Shenton had learned his lesson and was instinctively quicker than his opponent. He fired, hitting the guy in his midriff. Jack watched the man drop his weapon and stumble backwards, hands clutching his stomach. Shenton took another long slow breath before calmly putting a second into the Russian's chest.

The contact immediately drew an onslaught of fire from the remainder of the dead man's crew. Rounds clattered into the tree he was using as cover, sending wood splinters flying past his face. He ducked down, eyes narrowed, trying to see where the rounds were coming from, but all he could make out were muzzle flashes and shadows.

Casey had a far better view and cut down a third Russian with a burst of four shots. Her cavalier use of ammunition drawing an admonishing look from Fuller, who barked, "You've only four left," as the guy fell and lay motionless on the woodland floor.

Harriet pulled her spare mag from her jeans, waved it at him and shrugged.

Fuller turned away, clocked another target and dropped him with a single shot.

Then the sirens started.

Des knew the cops' first port of call would be the rolled Kia. He also knew that what was left of the Russian team would want to be on their toes. After all, jail wasn't high on anyone's list of priorities. He moved out of cover and edged closer to Jack.

"On me, son," he said, and gave him another friendly clip. "And well done eh?"

Shenton smiled briefly, before dropping in behind the Scot. The pair carefully edged their way through the undergrowth until they picked up Rick and Harriet. Finally, they all hunkered down in cover.

"Everyone okay?" asked Rick as the first police vehicle pulled up on the hard shoulder some two hundred metres away. He got nods all round. "Good," he said. "Casey, Shenton, check over your weapons, drop in a full mag. We still have two possible targets out there, so stay in sight of each other, but just in case they try any last heroics, don't bunch up." He waved an arm. "I think this place is Kenworthy Woods, which means if we keep the Parkway to our right, we should be able to cross the river via a footbridge which will take us towards the water park at Chorlton.

"And then what?" snapped Harriet.

"Then we call a cab, sweetheart," said Des rooting in his pocket for his pipe. "But in the meantime, do as Rick tells ye, keep yer eyes peeled and yer head down. It's no more than a couple of K's. Piece of piss."

* * *

A muddy but uneventful tab eventually brought the team to the grounds of Chorlton Golf Club. Rick, being the best dressed, went inside and told the extremely helpful Steward his tale of mechanical breakdown and mud filled trek across the park. The guy called him not one, but two cabs. Rick once again paired with Casey, Des with Shenton, and a twenty minute drive, followed by thirty minutes of on foot anti-surveillance moves around the city, saw the team sitting in Rick's lock up, drinking a much needed hot brew.

"What was all that about, Des?" asked Jack, removing his sopping trainers and rubbing some feeling into his feet. "All that running about town, in and out of the shops without buying nothin'?"

"This is our one clean, safe space," said Rick sharply. "And I intend to keep it that way."

Harriet wandered the lock up, taking in her surroundings and cradling her tea with both hands, "So this is your bat cave then, Fuller?" she said.

"It's where we plan, rest up, and hide if need be," offered Des. He pointed to the area where they always kept their vehicles. "This space here is usually filled with cars. There's a log burner over there to keep us toasty, shower's in the corner. There's enough cots fer us all, and some fighting and civvy clothes to change into."

Rick sat at his old table. The place where he'd spent hundreds of hours planning missions with some of the fiercest fighters known to man. He sipped his tea and allowed his mind to wander. Fuller had never been religious. neither did he believe in ghosts or the spirit world. But J.J. and Lauren had both sat around his gnarled wooden table, and as he absently ran a palm across the heavily worn timber top, he felt their presence.

"How much cash is in that case of yours, Shenton?" he asked quietly.

Jack shrugged.

"Not counted it, Mr Fuller… a lot, I'd say."

"Pop it on the table, son," said Des. "Let's have a look."

Jack did as he was asked, and Rick flipped open the lid.

Des let out a whistle. "There's a few bob there eh?"

Fuller lifted the precious notebook computer from the centre, stood and locked it away in the weapons safe.

He then turned to Casey.

"Maybe you should put the stick in here, too? Where is it?"

Harriet blushed slightly.

"I'll recover it when I get a shower, Fuller. If you don't mind."

He nodded knowingly and sauntered back to the table. Once seated, he lifted one bundle of notes from the case and did a quick count.

"Ten grand," he said. "Ten bundles of ten grand."

Jack rooted in his jeans, pulled out some crumpled notes and lay them on the table.

"I took this out of one bundle, last night. I was gonna use it to get a hotel like. You can have it. I never used it."

Harriet wandered back to the group and sat.

"You do realise that we need to hand this money in."

"Oh aye," said Des, rooting in his own pockets. "We're full of bright ideas like that, lassie." He found his pipe. "And just who do ye think we're going to give it back to? The Russians? MI6? Yer Great Uncle Damien? I mean, fe where I'm sitting, I'd be calling this our Brucie bonus, eh?"

"I agree," said Rick, picking up a ten thousand pound bundle and tossing it to Jack. "Wages, son," he said. "You did good back there."

Shenton went the colour of a ripened plum but held onto the bundle like his life depended on it. He looked to Des for his approval. The Scot smiled and nodded. Jack swallowed hard, "Thanks Mr Fuller."

Rick tossed a second to Des, then another to Casey who caught it, but frowned.

"I'm not a thief, Fuller. I may work dark, but I'm not a criminal."

Rick snorted.

"Don't come the holier than thou shit, Casey. I'll be calling Cartwright later and I'll tell him that this is in lieu of our fee. Besides, you can't walk around in those cheap shoes much longer."

Harriet inspected her feet for a moment, then pulled her face.

"I like Converse. And what do you mean, Our fee?"

"I mean, until this job is over, you work for me. Didn't you see that coming, Casey? Don't you understand your dear Uncle's reasoning? He wants the program, yes. He wanted you alive too. But he also wanted this." Rick pointed a finger around the table. "He wouldn't have banked on young Shenton here, but you, Des and me? The return of his old dark ops team? Even if it's just for this one job, I can hear the old bastard chuckling as we speak."

"How can you be so sure?" she asked.

Rick sat back in his seat.

"I've known Cartwright for years, Casey. He's known of me, since I was Jack's age, maybe even younger. Look, I'm sure you are very precious to him, but Cartwright is an old school, pragmatic, hard arsed spy. He'd have sacrificed you in an instant had the job required it, just as he would me or Des or anyone else. But if I'm correct, he has a major problem, and it's not just his bowels."

"And what major problem is that?" asked Casey, rolling the wad of cash around in her hand, blue eyes flashing.

Rick gripped the bridge of his nose, closed his eyes for a second.

"Look someone at The Firm wants him out of the loop, and I think it's because of what's on that stick. There's something on there that he'd got wind of. That's why he needs us. Now he has us on board, he has a few more cards he can play. He's back in the game."

"I never really thought of it that way," said Casey. "So what next?"

"Well, that is the million dollar question," said Rick. "I reckon we discuss our options over dinner… I'm starving."

"I need a smoke before we do anything," said Des.

"Can I get a shower?" asked Casey.

* * *

Des pushed open the door of the lock up and stood on the dank pavement. The weather had stayed dry but there was a real winter nip in the air and the ever darkening skies threatened another round of sharp showers, ready to drench Manchester's evening commuters.

He filled his pipe and watched the traffic pass the end of the street. The rush hour was just beginning, yet the cars were already bumper to bumper, full of people going home to… well to what? Marital bliss? Lonely bedsit?

It had been thirteen months since he'd left Manchester for a better, quieter life. He lit up, took in the smoke, shook his head.

Quieter? Well it had certainly been that.

Better?

As he topped up his bowl and pushed down the mixture with his thumb, he noticed his hands smelled of gunfire. He held his fist under his nose for a moment, closed his eyes and took in a satisfying, deep breath. It had been an aroma he'd lived with since he'd turned sixteen. The smell, and the excitement that went along with it. Could anything ever replace that elation, the euphoria that true fear brings?

Better?

No.

As Des pondered his lot, the door of the lock up opened, and Jack Shenton popped his head out.

"Mind if I join you, Des?"

"Knock yourself out, kid," he said, smiling. "Didn't know you indulged."

"I don't. Just wanted a word really."

"Well, before ye do. Let me tell ye, you did a fine job today, son, and I'm sorry fer clippin' ye like I did. Ye showed true courage."

Jack wrinkled his nose.

"Well I don't know about that, like. I was shittin' myself for most of it. And I reckon we all need a clip once in a while, Des."

"Aye, suppose so, son. Anyway, what was it ye wanted?"

Jack scratched his head nervously.

"Well, I was wondering, like. I mean, you know all about me, what I've done wrong, where I've come from. And you know I don't have any place to go or nothin.'"

"I do."

"And I know I'm young and all that, but I was thinking that maybe I could work for you and Mr Fuller, y'know, run a few errands, anythin' really. I'm a quick learner, Des, honest."

Cogan tapped out his pipe.

"Can I ask you a question, son?"

"Course."

Des looked into the kid's eyes.

"In the last day, you've slotted three men. Three living, breathing, human beings, and that will stay with you forever. Trust me, I know. Now, I realise that all three of those people would have murdered you had you not done what you did. But my worry is that those shootings will change you. Harm you in some way. You're a good kid, solid, tough, but those faces will come back and haunt you. Those dead men will come knocking again. I promise they will. And if you stay around Rick and me long enough, you won't be running errands… there'll be more. More faces in your dreams. Do you think ye can cope with that, son?"

Jack looked down at his worn, sodden trainers, the only pair of shoes he owned, his tattered jeans soaked to the knee. He sniffed, wiped his nose with his palm and looked into Cogan's face.

"I've seen stuff that a kid should never have seen, Des. Long before you and Mr Fuller came along. Seen horrible stuff, and I know what bad dreams are like, but they're just that… dreams. Believe me, where I lived, and in prison, the real stuff was always worse than the nightmares."

Des smiled again.

"Rick threw you that cash for a reason, son. It's early days, but if Rick is right, and Cartwright wants the team back together, then I reckon there might be a place for you in it… you can buy yourself some new runners too, eh?"

Jack beamed. It was an event in itself. His smooth youthful features creased, and his eyes became little more than slits.

"Oh that's boss that is, Des."

Jack's smile slowly faded as he pulled the wad of cash Rick had thrown him from his pocket.

"There's somthin' else, Des... I... I want to make sure me Mam has a good send off, and I wondered if you could help me get some of this cash over to the right people. Y'know, without anyone knowin' like?"

Des dropped an arm around the boy's shoulders.

"I reckon we can do that, son... now, why don't we have a wander up the street and find you some dry footwear?"

* * *

Casey examined the shower cubical. She'd not expected it to be quite so beautifully tiled and finished. Off to one side was a cosy changing area with a stool, a small chest of drawers and a full length mirror.

"You decent?" shouted Fuller holding a large towel through the gap in the door, keeping his distance.

She took it, and as she was still dressed, pulled the door open.

"Thanks, Fuller," she said, gesturing towards the facilities. "This is great, real home from home stuff."

He nodded.

"Careful," he said. "Water's hot. I'll light the fire. Shout when you're done. I'm next."

Casey followed him a beat.

"Erm, Rick?"

He spun on his heels.

"What?"

Harriet held her arms out at her sides.

"We left our cases in the Kia so I've nothing to change into. I've been in these same clothes since Dubai. I know it's a long shot, Fuller, but I don't suppose you..."

She watched as the man in front of her deflated. That scarred, yet handsome countenance, those dark chocolate eyes, lost all expression. The switch from brusque, organised, military man to broken, damaged, individual happened so fast, it took her breath away.

What had she said?

Fuller swallowed, and for a moment, was unsure what to say or do. His legs felt like lead, his stomach stirred and in that very instant, he yearned for a drink. Beer, whiskey, anything. The brand, the flavour didn't matter. What had he been thinking? Did he really believe that he could return to Manchester, to where she had lived, worked, laughed, fought... died? To this very hallowed place where she had slept, showered, eaten, argued... kissed?

He could see the confusion on Casey's face. She, of course, had no way of knowing what a tremendous task she was asking of him. For him to walk over to Lauren's locker and open it. To look inside, stare into the past, touch what should stay sacred.

He took in air through his nose, then exhaled slowly, eyes closed.

"You see the three lockers over there. The one on the left used to be Lauren's. There'll be clothes in there. You're about the same size. Take what you want."

"Lauren?" asked Casey.

Rick strode over to a small cupboard by the fireplace, found a bottle of Black Label and a glass, cracked it open and sat heavily at the table.

Harriet watched him pour, then drink and pour again. After the second glass, he turned his face to hers.

"Go on, Casey. I told you, get what you need."

She felt rooted to the spot.

"Was Lauren your wife?" she asked nervously.

He shook his head.

"Colleague."

"And she died?"

He poured again.

"Murdered. Now, like I said. Get something to wear. The sob stories can wait for another day."

She walked tentatively to the locker, opened it and quickly selected a pair of pants, jeans, and t shirt. As she turned back towards the shower room, she saw Fuller pouring again.

"It won't bring her back," she said quietly.

"Be quick in the shower," he snapped. "I'm next."

FIFTEEN

The Thirsty Scholar, Oxford Road, Manchester

The team stepped under the railway arch at Oxford Road station just as the rain began to fall again. Jack was looking much better for his shopping trip, sporting new trainers, jeans and a polo shirt. Des couldn't take his eyes off Casey. Not because of her obvious beauty, but because he recognised the t shirt she was wearing only too well. He also had one eye on his old pal who was looking just a little worse for wear.

The Scholar had long been a regular haunt for the team. Good beer, lively atmosphere and a friendly landlord, ensured a decent night. However, Des couldn't recall them ever eating there.

"Vegan?" said Casey with some degree of surprise as she examined the menu. "I had you guys down as steak and chips types."

Des scanned the list of plant based delicacies with some suspicion.

"Ye have me to a tee there, hen," he said taking the head off his Guinness. "I dinnea even understand this mysel. What is vegan anyway? Why can't we just have a curry?"

"Not everyone likes curry," said Rick, sipping a large bourbon. "And to answer your question, a Vegan rejects the commodity status of animals. Martin the Mod threw all his toys out of his pram when Egghead came in here eating a pork pie, I'll tell you."

"I'll get a kebab after," said Jack, dropping his laminated sheet to the table.

"You could have the Moving Mountains B12 burger, Jack," offered Harriet.

Shenton shook his head. "Nah, all this vegan stuff is a con. Makes you think you're eating all healthy like, but that burger has thirty grams of saturated fat in it. That's your total daily allowance. They fill their meat substitutes with plant fats to make it taste good. When you think that a Big Mac has nine grams, including the bun, makes you wonder. Not that I'm suggesting Mackie D's is healthy."

Rick raised his brows.

"Listen to the nutritionist here."

Jack went slightly pink.

"I know some stuff cos of my boxing like," he said slurping his Coke.

"Did they teach you about the six spoonfuls of sugar in that glass of pop you're drinking," sniped Harriet.

"Let's not fall out over the menu," said Rick finishing his Jack Daniels all too quickly. "I say we have another couple in here, then find somewhere else to eat."

Des gave him a look. He'd seen Rick drink on many occasions, but that was in his younger years. In recent times it had rarely been to excess, and he could already see his friend's eyes were glazed.

"Are we celebrating your return, pal?" he said.

Rick sniffed and stood.

"Somethin' like that. We've had a quick result today ain't we? Fire's lit, the cots are all made up. Why not have a few drinks to take the edge off?"

"Aye," said Des, playing the game. "Why no? And seeing that you're in the chair, I'll have a wee Jamesons chaser."

The moment Rick left the table, Des turned to Harriet.

"How many did he have whilst we were out shopping, hen?"

Harriet pursed her lips.

"Half a bottle of Black Label, give or take."

Des nodded.

"Wouldnea have anything to do with that t shirt yer wearing, would it?"

Casey darkened.

"Look, Cogan. All I know is, I asked if he had some clothes I could change into."

"So that is Lauren's shirt then?"

"That's what he called her."

"Who's this Lauren?" asked Jack.

Des look a long drink, licked his lips.

"Lauren North was a nurse who was recruited by Rick and me. She worked alongside us for almost four years. Lauren and Rick became… close, shall we say. She was murdered just over a year ago. He blames himself. It's a long story."

"Hence the drinking? The Thai hiding place?" asked Casey.

"I suppose, but he's in far better shape than I expected, hen. That boy has seen some bad luck when it comes to the fairer sex, I'll tell ye. And I'll say this too, there's no a man breathin' better at this job than Rick Fuller. Drunk or sober."

Harriet sipped her wine.

"Well, that remains to be seen, Cogan. If Uncle Damien expects me to stay up here in Manchester, Fuller needs to lay off the booze."

Des' eyes flashed; his lip curled.

"Listen sweetheart, I'd wager Rick Fuller got ye out of the brown stuff over in Thailand, eh? Am I right? Would it be fair to say he's the reason yer still breathin'? Now, I can see that yer a smart kid, but from what I've seen so far, ye have a long way to go before ye can call yersel a player. So take a wee bit of advice from someone who knows." He tapped his lips with his finger. "Use less of that, and try and learn from the master, eh?" He pointed to the roof of the pub. "That, or the trains are running right above ye head, all the way to London. I'll even buy ye a ticket."

Casey bit her lip, took another drink.

"I don't give up that easily, Cogan," she said.

Des gave her a thin smile.

"Is that right? Well then, hen. Drink ye wine and enjoy yer night. Ye never know when you'll get another chance eh?"

He sat back and gave Jack a dig in the ribs with his elbow.

"You takin' all this in, son?"

"Yes Mr Cogan."

"Ye hear that, Harriet," he said, head cocked. "That's called humility. Now, enough gossip, the big man's back."

* * *

It would be fair to say that drink was taken. The couple in the Scholar, turned to three, then it was to The Salisbury and then The Font, before Jack, as the lone sober reveller, offered to wander down towards Rusholme and buy kebabs all round.

Just before midnight, the team sat around Rick's sturdy old table once again, this time devouring delicious chicken tikka filled naan breads.

"Boss these," said Jack through a mouthful of food.

"Aye, tasty enough," agreed Des.

The team's antics had been plastered across every media outlet, and reports of dead Russians in woodland, together with shots of a rolled and burnt out Kia Sorrento were big news. Rick figured those storylines would give Cartwright a firm clue as to how the job was progressing, and in his current state of inebriation, concluded that this negated the need for a late night phone call to the old spy.

However, one thing wouldn't let Fuller rest.

He was particularly curious as to why the Firm hadn't simply instructed Casey to destroy the memory stick once she'd stolen it. If the job had been simply to keep it out of the hands of the Bratva, why not just stamp on the thing and fuck off home.

He put that very question to her.

Harriet had lost some of her tetchiness. That edge, that petulance, had mellowed somewhat. Be it the Chablis or the company she was keeping, it was an improvement. Not much, but enough to make her bearable.

"I told you, Richard," she said, chewing on her chicken. "Our orders were to deliver the stick back to our handler, not smash it."

"And your handler was?"

"Abrahams," she said. "Aaron Abrahams. He's a Vauxhall Cross hot shot. His brief is anti-corruption. He reports directly to the Home Sec."

"So he wanted to see the content?"

She shrugged.

"And Uncle Damien doesn't trust this Mr Abrahams?" asked Rick.

"Appears not," said Harriet, hiccupping slightly. "And before you ask me why, just think back to your dealings with the Firm. No one trusts anyone. Besides, Abrahams is a tosser."

"Fair enough," said Rick throwing the remnants of his kebab in the trash. "But what do you think this Mr Abrahams will do next? I mean, he'll know by now that he ain't getting his stick back, and you aren't going to follow your orders."

Casey turned down her mouth.

"You've mistaken me for someone who gives a shit, Fuller. He left me hanging out to dry. If it hadn't been for…"

Rick tapped the table.

"Wait a minute. So you called Abrahams to extract you after the rest of your team were slotted. Then what?"

Casey sat back in her seat. She ran her hands through her hair, her beautiful eyes never leaving his. The edge had returned to her voice.

"I'd just been in a fight to the death, Fuller. Broken a man's neck. Listened to him choke as he fought for his last breath. Other than pissing blood, I was in good shape, almost home and dry. I needed a safe house for a night, maybe two."

"But?"

She bit her lip.

"When I called him, Abrahams that is, I got the impression he was more interested in the safety of the stick than in mine. He gave me the location of a Dead Letter Box in Manheim. He insisted I drop the stick there and get a train to Calais next morning. Then, and only then, he said, would he help repatriate me. Look Fuller, the mission was planned by him, the players were recruited by him. There was just something about the way he spoke on the phone... something shady. I don't know. Anyway, I called Uncle Damien and here we are."

Rick scratched his newly trimmed beard. The alcohol was dulling his senses and he inwardly cursed himself for weakening so easily. He shot a look over to Lauren's old locker and steeled himself. He would empty it tomorrow.

But this was not a time for weakness. No, what was important right now was this memory stick and what it contained. Of course he knew what Casey had said about the election interference, but that in itself was nothing new. Yes technology improved by the hour, but surely this was a program that could be recreated time and time again, so why not simply pay for another? Let's face it, the Russians were not short of a Rouble or two.

"We need to go and see Egghead," he said. "There's more to this than meets the eye."

"Why don't we just call Uncle Damien?" asked Harriet, yawning.

Rick stretched.

"Because he may not want to tell me what I need to know. He's a fucking spy, Casey. And a damned good one. If we are going to move the goods again, I want to know exactly who I'm up against and why. How many fronts I'm fighting on? If anyone can open this program, it's Simon. He may even shed some light on who wrote it. Now, come on guys, bedtime."

Jack didn't need telling twice, he sauntered over to his cot, pulled off his new clothes, slipped into his bag and appeared to be asleep the instant his head hit the pillow. Harriet padded to the bathroom and closed the door behind her.

Des sat opposite Rick. He pulled out his pipe ready for one last smoke before bed.

"How long you been hitting the scotch?" he said.

Rick looked at him from under his brows.

"Since day one," he said. "I promised myself I'd knock it on the head when I got back here but... well, it won't happen again. Not on a school night anyway."

"Was it the clothes?"

"In a way… I see her everywhere, pal. Smell her, hear her. It's like she's sitting at this table."

"Aye," said Cogan. "I get the picture."

Slipping his hand into the inside pocket of his leather, he pulled out an envelope. "Cartwright left you this. It was in the box with the weapons and other kit he sent over. He said it would help."

Rick took it from the Scot. "I'll read it later," he said, laying it flat on the table. "You going to pick up the rest of that kit he sent tomorrow?"

"Aye, suppose. And now I've got some expenses in my pocket, I might treat mysel to a wee motor too." Des filled his pipe, stood and smiled. "I've no really had the chance to chat te ye but… it's grand to see ye, pal," he said. "And I know it's a cliché and all, but Lauren wouldnea want te see ye pished all day long eh?"

Fuller gave his friend a long look.

"Go have your smoke and get to bed," he said.

Fuller lay in his cot, listening to the other three breathe. Casey muttered to herself on occasions, Des snored quietly, Jack slept like the dead. He opened the envelope Cartwright had left for him and began to read.

Dear Richard,

As you are probably aware, I have been unwell. Shortly after you left for Thailand, a scan of my upper bowel revealed three tumours that subsequently proved to be malignant. As a man who has been blessed with good health all my days, this came as somewhat of a shock, and as you can imagine, it has taken me some time to come to terms with my own mortality.

You see, we are all vulnerable, Fuller. We are all weak.

When Harriet Casey called me in the middle of the night with fear in her voice, I didn't hesitate to send her to you. Harriet is somewhat feisty and opinionated, not unlike your good self. However, you will discover she is extremely loyal and despite her youth, a competent operator.

I took the liberty of keeping an eye on you and Cogan this past year. Retirement, for whatever reason, can be hard on a fighting man, and both of you have sought solace in your own way, either in the arms of a woman, or, in your case, the bottom of a bottle.

It would appear that neither option has been a success.

Richard, take some advice from a man who has been given a reprieve, an un-expected yet welcome extension to his existence. Live your life. Live it the only way you know. Take Mr Cogan along for the ride, because life is short, rarely sweet, and to have someone around you that would lay down their life for yours is something exceptional.

I told Desmond that I hoped this letter would help you, and I'm sure that you expected details of Russian oligarchs and hi-tech shenanigans in these pages, but that was not my intention. For that, we shall meet face to face. No, these words, clumsily written, are meant to impart something that you have been missing this last year, and that is your sense of belonging.

There are times when we all feel that life is not worth living, Richard. That is until you discover that something, or someone, is about to take that very life from you.

Do what you do best, Fuller. Lead your team. Get to the bottom of this puzzle. God's speed.

Cartwright.

P.S.
I do believe it is your turn to buy luncheon.

* * *

Des and Jack had been dispatched to buy supplies for the lock up. Food, drink, more clothes, wood for the fire.

Rick caught a cab to Evo car hire in the city and returned with an Aston Martin V12 Vantage in quantum silver.

Harriet, who had concluded some diplomatic clothes shopping of her own, seemed impressed.

"Well, I'll say this for you, Fuller, you don't do things by halves."

"Jump in, Casey," he said. "We're going for a ride in the country."

She slid into the car, dropped her bag containing the stick and computer into the rear seat and took in the opulence of the Aston.

"Nice… very nice," she said. "V12 too. You can tell straight off by the bonnet louvres."

Fuller glanced over as he pushed the Aston into gear.

"You know your cars then?"

"I love cars, Fuller. This is 5.9 litre, no turbo, naturally aspirated, six speed manual box, ceramic brakes, and it has the carbon pack too." She settled into her seat. "Bit big and beefy for me. More of an old man's car, but a nice vehicle. I have the Porsche 911 3.8 turbo with the PDK box."

"Old man's car?" said Fuller, frowning as he edged out onto Oxford Road. "I hope your 911 is guards red or you'll look like a hairdresser."

"Hairdresser? Five hundred brake horsepower in a car that weighs just 1785kg. And that's with a full tank. Hair curler more like. And for the record, she's black."

"My second choice," he said. "Still, I suppose you didn't get to choose the options if Daddy bought it for you."

Fuller eyed Harriet's new outfit. It was similar to everything else she seemed to wear. Strappy tight top, no bra, cut-off jeans, bare legs, and those awful Converse bumpers.

"Still," he said. "I suppose you save him money on your outfits."

Casey shook her head and chose not to retaliate. She was getting to grips with Fuller and his ways.

"So, how far is Rossendale?" she asked.

"Not far, Casey. It's a quaint little place… You do like cats I take it?"

Simon Small, or Egghead to his many customers, lived with his mother in a dilapidated farmhouse, just off the M66 motorway in the Rossendale Valley.

His father, Peter, had died young after contracting Q fever, a bacterial infection caught by inhaling dust particles in barns and other enclosures where infected animals had been present. Q fever usually results in little more than mild flu-like symptoms, but unfortunately, left untreated, it causes serious damage to the liver, lungs and heart. Peter Small had never been one to make a fuss, and it wasn't until he began to have breathing difficulties, that he sought treatment. After being diagnosed with heart and liver failure, and realising he was dying, Peter sold all the land around the farmhouse to ensure his wife and son could remain in their family home, mortgage free.

Once his father passed, Simon took it upon himself to find numerous ways of getting himself into teenage troubles. Running with Manchester drug gangs and stealing cars whilst under the influence of cocaine were just two of his favourite pastimes. Several serious accidents and many weeks in intensive care finally brought him to his senses and, after much deliberation, he turned his undoubtedly massive intellect to good use.

Hacking.

Fuller pulled the Aston up to the front of the dilapidated farmhouse. Even though it had been almost two years since his last visit, little had changed. The small plot around the building was still overgrown, the rusting chain link fence surrounding it leaned precariously in several places. A discarded washing machine and a set of bald tyres were piled at the side of the path that led to a front door that had needed painting since Preston last won the cup. Ominously, three mangy looking cats prowled the front step.

"I thought you said it was quaint?" said Harriet, easing her trim frame from her seat.

"They call it shabby chic, don't they?" said Fuller, hiding his mirth. "Wait until you get inside. You'll love what they've done with the place."

Rick had deliberately dressed in a pair of faded Levi's and an old polo he'd found in the lock up. Gone were the days when he risked Paul Smith suits or John Lobb brogues when visiting Simon.

Fuller stood on the front step and knocked loudly. As usual, there was no answer. The three scruffy looking moggies that had been waiting to gain entry, wrapped themselves around his legs, purring in anticipation.

"Damned things," he muttered doing his best to push them away with his Timberlands.

"Maybe no one is home," said Casey.

Rick gave the old door another bang with his fist, and finally the pair heard movement from inside.

Moments later the door swung open.

Simon's mother stood holding a knife in one hand, and a cat by the scruff of its neck, in the other. A cigarette dangled precariously from the corner of her mouth. The three waiting felines slipped inside without being asked and four more de bunked the place mewing as they went.

"Simon!" she bawled. "Folks here to see yer."

At that, she turned and shuffled her way back towards the kitchen, where the smell of boiling mince fought for priority over the stench of cat deposits.

Harriet looked horrified.

"You have to be joking, Fuller," she hissed. "If I have to go in there, I reckon I'll throw."

"Man up, Casey," he said. "Come on."

The pair tip toed up the staircase, avoiding the usual accretions as best they could until they were met on the landing by Simon himself.

"Mr Fuller, sir," he bellowed. "Damned fine to see you again."

Rick took Simon's outstretched hand and shook.

"And you, Simon. Are you well?"

Simon puffed out his red cheeks and rubbed his ever growing paunch.

"I'm fit as a butcher's dog, Mr Fuller. Never better. And as the old crone is cooking mince and tatties for lunch, thing are looking up."

Simon leaned slightly to his left so he could get a better look at Harriet.

"And who might this fine looking young lady be then?" he asked, giving Casey his best beaming smile.

She too held out a hand.

"I'm Harriet," she said. "Harriet Casey."

"By heck," said Simon. "I've an Aunty Harriet. Bit more meat on her than you though, love."

Casey was doing her best not to breathe through her nose. Desperate to move matters on, she tapped her bag that contained the laptop and stick.

"We were hoping you could help us with something, Simon," she said.

"Ha, yes," said Egghead, prying his gaze away from her tanned legs and turning his attention back to Rick. "Mr Fuller mentioned something about a dodgy program." He turned swinging an arm theatrically as he did so. "Prey enter my boudoir."

Harriet was delighted to see that Simon's work area was cat deposit free. She handed the bag over to him and sat next to Fuller, who was playing with his newly acquired, substantial looking phone.

"Do you wish to explain matters, Fuller, or have you more pressing matters," she snapped.

Rick shot her a look and pushed the set into his jeans pocket.

"Patience, Casey," he said. "Now, Simon. The program on that memory stick can only be opened by using that particular laptop, which I find unusual. I wondered if you could tell us anything about it. Maybe who wrote it, how effective it would be." He glared at Casey again. "And what it would be worth to someone."

Simon rubbed his palms together excitedly.

"Ooh sounds interesting."

He picked up the laptop but didn't open it.

"Okay, Mr Fuller. Now, when folks do this, marrying a program to a specific device, it's usually all about security, and ensuring payment for services rendered. So, you buy the first half of the puzzle, ergo the laptop, at a premium, and once the programmer has the cash for the machine, he completes the deal for the software side of things," he held up the memory stick. "Voila… So, contained on this very laptop, will be a line of code that tells this little program to fire up. However, these folks are very sneaky. If you were to try inserting this stick in your own home set up, the software would see that the marrying code wasn't present and delete itself." Simon beamed at Harriet. "Clever eh, Miss?"

"We'd already got to that, Simon," she said flatly.

"Really? Oh, well... moving on," he said, a hint of disappointment in his voice. "Let's have a look what these boys are up to then."

Egghead first plugged a cable into the laptop and began tapping keys on one of his own machines.

"Hmm," he said. "No booby traps. Looks straightforward enough. I'll just pop in the software... here."

He tapped some more. This time on the recovered laptop.

He blew air down his nose, sat back in his seat and turned to Fuller.

"Straightforward social media phishing program, Mr Fuller."

"Meaning?" said Rick.

Simon rooted in his desk drawer for a moment, then found what appeared to be half a sausage roll wrapped in a paper napkin. He stuffed the whole thing in his mouth.

"The old bird was at Bury market again this week," he said, spraying flaky pastry across the keys of the recovered machine. "World class sausages there, Mr Fuller. I can ask her to pick you a dozen up, if y'like."

Rick held up a palm.

"I'm fine, thanks, Simon."

Harriet shook her head.

"You were saying, Simon," she said. "Before your snack?"

Simon was wide eyed.

"Oh, yes, sorry my love. So, erm yeah. This is nothing new. Something I could knock up for you in a morning. Maybe some Ukrainian kid wrote this in his bedroom in between playing with his Xbox. These programs do get a bit more refined each time I see them, but the only difference between this and the older versions, is that you don't need a room full of Tweeters and Facebookers to physically type the disinformation in. It does it for you. It has a bank of false social media profiles already installed. You tell it which lie you want to spread and... bingo."

Fuller scratched his beard and made a mental note to shave it off.

"And how much would something like this cost. Simon?"

"I'd knock this out for a bag of sand, Mr Fuller. However, this one was written in the Ukraine. I know that because these boys use a certain type of Cyrillic script, similar to Polish, but no, this is definitely Ukrainian. And as they don't command my hourly rate, whoever bought this would have paid about half that, a monkey, I reckon."

Fuller was incredulous.

"Five hundred quid?"

Simon picked pastry from his teeth.

"I reckon."

Rick leaned forwards.

"Look, Egghead. You can't be serious here. People are dead because of this program. People in high places are desperate for it back. There has to be more to it than you're telling us."

Simon swung his chair around and peered at the screen again. He tapped some more.

"There are more files on here, but I reckon it's just the fake info that the hackers want spreading, so things like... oh, just a mo. This looks a bit dodge."

"What?" snapped Harriet impatiently.

"Keep yer hair on, Miss," said Simon tapping away. "Right, I have two encrypted files here, one labelled, Perelyubnyky, which roughly translates as 'the wrong doer,' and another 'Spetssluzhby,' which means..."

"Secret Service," finished Rick.

"In one," pointed Simon.

"And just who is this wrong doer?" asked Fuller. "Whose dirt are they digging?"

Simon turned down his mouth.

"Hard to say until I get these files open."

Harriet gave him a thin smile.

"And just when might that be?"

"Well Miss," said Simon, smiling back. "That depends if it's cash or card."

SIXTEEN

Prenton Golf Club, Wirral, Merseyside.

Semion Savalovsky watched his ball circle the hole before it dropped. John Hodiak, his bookkeeper shook his head.

"That's your third birdie, Pakhan," he said ruefully. "The Gods are with you today. Maybe I should concede before the rain comes."

"Nonsense John. You will catch me. You always do."

Hodiak frowned. Not only was he a distinguished forensic accountant, and wonderful golfer, but he was a reader of men. He sometimes considered he knew what a man was about to do, even before the man himself. And this day, despite Semion's form on the greens, he knew his lifelong associate was troubled. And a troubled Pakhan, meant only one thing.

Bloodshed.

"Positive thinking," he said, taking his own ten foot putt and watching the ball drop. "That's the thing."

The two men walked side by side, on the deserted course, pulling their trolleys towards the next tee. Savalovsky had deliberately booked several tee slots at once to ensure privacy.

"Honecker is on his way," said Savalovsky. "Ivanov brings him to me."

"And how is Erich?" asked Hodiak.

"Sore. I heard he took a bullet in the ass." Semion grimaced. "How does a fighting man take a bullet in the ass, John?"

"How do eight of our Bratok allow themselves to be outwitted and outgunned by two middle aged men and a pair of teenagers?"

Savalovsky shook his head.

"Who knows, John. This whole business has begun to wear me down. Maybe it is time to cut our losses, approach this whole sorry tale from a different angle. Do things the old way."

"Meaning?"

"Look, my friend, ever since our man in Kiev obtained those emails, photographs, and phone records, we seem to have been chasing shadows. Back in the day, we would have simply blackmailed the woman and her Zionist bedfellow, and if they still refused our offer, dropped them in the Mersey. All this political interference, this Facebook, this Twitter. I ask you, my friend, is it really worth it?"

Hodiak selected his driver and took a long look down the fairway.

"Pakhan," he began. "Rosemary Longthorn Grey is the Home Secretary. The most powerful woman in this country and Member of Parliament for Liverpool Walton. Her husband, Peter Grey, is the head of the Sustainable Development Commission who insists his team of environmentalists embrace a form of capitalism that moves away from large scale city developments and concentrates on a 'green space economy.' This woman and her husband are preventing us from realising our dreams. Our plans will never be passed whilst she is in power."

Savalovsky's patience was wearing thin.

"And the Jew?"

"We are all Jews, Papa. And Abrahams' plans will be scuppered at the first hurdle. Have no fear, Papa, he will die along with his treacherous comrades, all in good time. But now, our priority is the dock development."

"Yes, I realise all that, but what I'm saying is…"

"Papa," Hodiak soothed. "I understand your impatience, but if we can re-establish possession of the software, not only can we demonstrate Longthorn Grey's infidelity, but we could easily suggest that she used her position as Home Secretary, to deploy a Security Services team to Frankfurt in an attempt to spare her blushes. A mission that cost the lives of two British citizens. She will be finished both as a politician and a wife. And using that information in this new modern way, via social media, as political interference, will strike fear into the whole government. The days of pushing brown envelopes across a bar in a smoke filled room are long gone, Papa. Paper can be burned, photographs torn, but no one can stop Facebook. Once the evidence is out there, real or imagined, it spreads like a pandemic. That scares politicians." He smiled. "And is not fear of the Bratva our greatest weapon?" Hodiak addressed his ball, "The recovery of that program and computer is essential, Pakhan. Without them, our plans are nothing but a dream. Remember it was us that insisted on the terms with our man in Kiev. We would pay his price, but there were to be no copies. No chance of a rival using the same information. It was our decision, Papa."

He took a deep breath and began his swing. Both men watched his shot power straight and true down the fairway.

"A fine drive, John," said Semion, deep in thought.

"Thank you, Papa."

Hodiak slid his driver back into his bag. As he did so, he saw two men approaching. One was the unmistakable figure of Anatoly Ivanov. At six feet nine inches tall and weighing in at just under twenty two stones, it was hard to miss Erich Honecker's bodyguard. Erich himself cast a lonely figure, doing his best to keep up with his huge minder, limping badly.

"We have company," said Hodiak.

Savalovsky pulled out his driver, turned his back on the approaching men and took his shot a little too quickly. His ball skewed left towards the trees and disappeared.

"See, John. What did I tell you?"

"We have eight more holes, Pakhan," offered Hodiak.

The Godfather sniffed, and turned, leaning on his club as Honecker and Ivanov arrived.

"How's your ass, Erich," he said, head cocked.

"Damned sore, Papa," Honecker moaned. "I can't sit down, can't sleep. I can't even fuck. It's shocking."

"How did you manage to get shot in such a delicate place?" asked Hodiak.

Erich darkened.

"I don't know who told you that I was shot, I wasn't. It was a wood splinter. The bullet clipped a tree and the splinter hit me in the buttocks. Took that butcher of a Polish doctor forty minutes to dig the bastard out."

The bookkeeper barely managed to hide his smile.

"I see, well I wish you a speedy recovery, Erich."

Semion Savalovsky gave Anatoly Ivanov a look.

"Give us some privacy, Bratok," he said.

The huge Ukrainian nodded and stepped away out of earshot.

"Tell me, Honecker," began Savalovsky. "Just how did you allow this motley crew to evade you a second time?"

Erich went pale.

"Papa, they are devils." He pulled a crumpled sheet of paper from his overcoat. "But we are closer to them now. We have information. The two older men are accomplished professional mercenaries. The smaller one, Cogan, is retired Special Forces, 22 SAS. The other, who is using the name Stephen Colletti, has connections in Manchester. We believe he too is ex-military but turned against his Regiment and became a criminal. He was once associated with a drug trafficker by the name of Joel Davies. We understand, he was his enforcer."

"And the babes?" said Savalovsky, rubbing his chin.

"The boy Shenton, the one who drowned Brigadier Julian, is a Liverpudlian, an unemployed amateur boxer. I would suggest that he has simply been caught up in this mess. Wrong place, wrong time. However, the girl... Harriet Casey, she's more of a concern. She's twenty three and was a former GCHQ employee."

Semion rubbed his face with his palm, his temper rising.

"Jesus Christ. So who are they working for now? The Secret Service? Some Moss Side drug lord? Or are they all just caught up in this mess, as you call it, by accident, Erich?"

Honecker took a long slow breath.

"Our people in Vauxhall Cross suggest that there is no official connection between this group and the Security Services. They believe that Casey was, and still is, working under the instruction of a retired handler with an axe to grind, and that the remainder of the team, are simply mercenaries, working for the highest bidder."

"And whom might that be, Erich?"

Honecker felt in his coat for aspirin, found two and dropped them into his dry mouth.

"I…I don't know, Papa," he stammered.

"You don't know?"

"No, Papa. But I promise, I will find out. I…"

Savalovsky looked at his feet, wrinkled his nose, lifted his club above his head and smashed it into Honecker's skull. He used every sinew, every ounce of his strength, to bring the club down onto the head of the man that had failed him. A fountain of blood spurted from Honecker's cranium as the titanium head of the number one wood buried itself into his brain.

The German stood stock still for a moment, eyes wide, jaw slack, the 45.5 inch shaft of the club bizarrely pointing in which ever direction he chose to look.

John Hodiak noticed the massive bulk of Anatoly Ivanov begin to race towards his boss. He held up a hand and shook his head.

That was enough.

As Honecker's legs buckled and his lifeless body toppled, Ivanov stopped in his tracks and looked to his Pakhan. He knew his own life was in danger. After all, he had been present for both disastrous missions.

Savalovsky walked over to Honecker's body, stamped his foot in his lifeless face, rived his club from deep in the man's skull and casually wiped the head on the grass.

"Get rid of him, Anatoly," he growled. "Then come to my house. You work for me now."

SEVENTEEN

The Old Wellington, Cathedral Gates, Manchester

"Nice place," said Harriet as the team were ushered to a corner table.

"One of the oldest buildings in the city centre," said Rick. "Built in 1552."

"Aye, it's bonny right enough," offered Des.

An attractive young waitress dropped menus on the table.

"Can I get you some drinks before you order?" she asked. Then smiling at Jack, added. "I'll need some ID for you sir."

"I don't drink, love," he said, flushing slightly. "I'll just have a Coke, please."

"I reckon I'll risk a pint of that Beavertown Neck Oil," said Des.

Harriet checked the bottled beers.

"Peroni, please."

"Evian," said Rick.

The girl gave Jack another admiring glance before she turned back to the bar.

"What time is Simon getting here?" asked Harriet. "I can't wait to hear his news."

Rick checked his watch.

"Any minute. When he said he'd cracked those files, I suggested I might save him from his mother's cooking, at least for one afternoon."

Des pulled a face.

"I wouldnea be eating anythin' that came out of that kitchen, I'll tell ye."

"I think he's here," hissed Harriet looking out of the window. "Change the subject."

At that, Egghead barrelled into the bar, laptop bag under his arm, red in the face.

Rick waved him over.

"Come and sit down, Simon," he said. "You look stressed."

"Oh, I am, Mr Fuller," he replied, pulling out a chair opposite Harriet. "City life isn't for me. I'm getting worse as I get older. Too many folks about. Too much hustle and bustle. Give me the virtual world any day."

"What'll ye have, Simon," asked Des. "We've not ordered the grub yet."

Simon twisted so he could see the pumps.

"I'll have a pint of that Gamma Ray, as yer offering, Mr Cogan."

Once the drinks arrived, Rick turned the subject to business.

"So Simon, before we move on to your favourite subject of food, what can you tell us about those files?"

Egghead was studying the specials board.

"Well, I'll tell you now, Mr Fuller, I'll be having the Game Pie. I do like a bit of pheasant."

"The files, Simon," snapped Fuller.

"Oh," said Egghead, "Yes, Mr Fuller. Well," he handed over the laptop bag. "Let me give you the hardware back first. The memory stick is inside the front pocket."

"You didn't make a copy, did you Simon?" said Rick sternly.

Simon looked hurt.

"Would I do such a thing, Mr Fuller?"

Rick didn't seem convinced.

"Go on then, what's the story?"

Egghead looked about him, before leaning forwards conspiratorially.

"Well, it's pretty hot stuff, I'll tell you. No wonder folks are getting bumped off over it."

Rick snorted.

"Just the facts, Simon."

"Sorry… sorry," he said. "Right, well, you know I said there were two files, one labelled Spetssluzhby, or 'Secret Service,' and a second file labelled Perelyubnyky, which I said roughly translated to 'the wrong doer.'"

"Go on," said Harriet.

"Well," said Simon, "I was a bit out with my translation. You see, Ukrainian belongs to a group of East Slavic languages, all of which use different variants of Cyrillic notation. They evolved from Old Russian, or Kievan Rus. In turn, many regional variations muddy the waters…"

"Simon!" snapped Rick.

Egghead held up his hands.

"Sorry again, Mr Fuller. It's just that I get stressed when I have to travel and meet folks. That, and I haven't eaten see, so…"

Casey reached across the table and took Simon's hand.

"It's okay. Take your time. We can eat first if you wish."

"I am starved, Miss," he said.

The team ordered as Rick sat back in his seat and brooded.

Once the food was on its way, Cogan broke the ice again.

"Go on, Si," said Des eyeing his irritated friend. "Why don't ye crack on with yer tale, whilst we wait fer the grub coming eh?"

Simon nodded.

"Yes, right, well, like I said. Two files. So, the one labelled Perelyubnyky, actually translates as… adulterer."

"I'm all ears," said Harriet, waving her empty bottle of Peroni at the waitress.

"In that file," said Simon. "Were dozens of pictures of a couple." Simon wagged a finger at Harriet. "Not the kind you're thinking of, Miss, not taken in the bedroom or anything, but of a couple simply doing stuff. How shall I say, enjoying each other's company. Parks, beaches, restaurants, that kind of thing."

"Keep going," said Rick.

"So, as I'm not avidly into the news or anything, that file, on its own didn't ring any bells. It wasn't until I decrypted the second folder, that all became clear. That folder contained copies of emails, Mr Fuller, emails from two accounts, both of which were highly classified. Whoever hacked those records, knew what they were doing and why. Marry those, how shall I say, somewhat racy emails up with the photographs, and you have a political bombshell."

"Political?" asked Rick.

"The woman in the pictures is Rosemary Longthorn Grey, Mr Fuller. The Home Secretary."

"And the man?" asked Harriet.

"Arron Abrahams," said Simon. I believe he's head of…"

"Anti-corruption, MI6," finished Casey. "Jesus H Christ. No wonder he wanted that stick."

Simon raised his brows and smiled.

"I do like to please, Miss Harriet."

Moments later, the waitress appeared with a tray of food.

"Game pie?" she asked.

"That will be me, darlin'" said Simon, rubbing his stomach.

* * *

Everyone relished their food even if the mood was somewhat pensive.

Once the bill was settled, Rick insisted that the team split and leave on foot, carrying out several further anti-surveillance routines before heading back to the lock up. The revelation of exactly what the team possessed, had made him even more cautious than usual.

Once inside the relative security of Fuller's lock up, Rick locked the memory stick and laptop in his safe.

He rested a palm on the bag a moment.

I still say, why not destroy the damned thing.

As he spun the combination, he turned and noticed a second vehicle had been pulled inside the unit. Nestled next to his hired Aston was a Land Rover Discovery. He sauntered over and gave the car a closer look.

"What do ye think, pal?"

Des was standing behind him holding two mugs of tea.

Rick took one.

"Cheers," he said. "It looks tidy."

"It is," said the Scot running his hand over the front grill. "2.7 TD V6. Low miles, seven seats, go anywhere. I treated mysel."

"So you left your old car up north?"

"Aye, came on the train."

"Makes sense to have a motor here. If you're thinking of staying that is?"

Des gave his old friend a look that he knew only too well.

"Do you really think I'd miss all the fun. pal? This wee job is getting more interesting by the hour."

"Isn't it just."

"More to the point," said Des. "What are your plans for the future?"

"One day at a time, pal," said Rick, sipping his tea as he walked around the Discovery. "You think us two old timers can still make a living?"

"Dinnea see why not, pal. There's life in the old dogs yet. We've certainly given the Russian boys a bloody nose the last couple of days."

"True," said Rick. "But y'know what still bothers me about this job, Des?"

"Go on."

"Why did this Abrahams guy not order Casey to crush that stick under her heel? I mean, he's been caught having an affair with his boss, who just happens to be the fucking Home Sec."

"Brave," said Des.

"Or stupid… Why not destroy the evidence?"

Des shook his head.

"Maybe he, or she wanted to see exactly how much had leaked? Maybe examining the documents and pictures would help them find who'd hacked the system, who took the pictures. Perhaps someone on the inside accessed those email accounts. Possibly the Home Sec wants a witch hunt."

Rick turned down his mouth, unconvinced.

"Okay, so how do you reckon Abrahams got to know about the existence of the leak in the first place?"

"I suppose he was being blackmailed."

"What? The Russians began to blackmail him, before they actually had hold of the evidence? No, I reckon Abrahams knew some information was lost, or stolen, early doors. Maybe some security alert within the computer systems. Maybe he'd left a laptop in the back of a car, or a hotel room. It wouldn't be the first time a civil servant has lost top secret files. Either way, they knew they were in the shit early doors. Then somehow, they found out the stick was being moved."

Des pulled out his pipe.

"It's way too complicated for a simple guy like me, pal. So, what's next?"

"I agree, pal, so as young Shenton has provided us all with some wages, I say we take the stick and computer to Cartwright and call it job done. Let MI6 clear up its own mess."

"When?"

"Tonight. I call him and arrange it. We'll travel in two vehicles, split the cargo and the team."

"You think they'll try and hit us again?"

Rick finished his tea.

"I think we're in danger until we hand over the goods. So, I say, let's make it hard for anyone who's thinking about it."

Des lay his cup on the old table.

"I'll nip and pick up the package Cartwright sent to the Adelphi. Take me ten minutes fe here. It's got binos, comms kits, some C4, dets, bits and pieces."

"Good idea. With the remnants of kit I left here, we should be okay for a trip south."

"What about ammo?"

"It'll be tight."

Des nodded.

"I'll get off. Give my new toy a run out."

Rick watched Cogan drive away then pulled down the roller shutters. Once he was happy the lock up was secure, he sat in the Aston for privacy, pulled out the phone that Cartwright had provided for him and dialled.

"Cartwright," answered the old spy, second ring.

"It's me," said Fuller.

"I realise that, Richard. I organised your secure line."

"Well, if it's as secure as the Home Secretary's email account, we're in trouble."

"You've managed to open the package then?"

"The package is burning a hole in my pocket, Cartwright."

"I can imagine. Are you any closer to identifying who the intended recipient was?"

"I wasn't aware that was in my remit. At a guess, I'd say a big hairy Slavic type with very deep pockets and Liverpool connections."

"Quite," growled the spy. "I'm working on it as we speak, Fuller. Maybe I'll have a clearer picture for you later today."

"Come on Cartwright, I'm not telling you anything you don't already know. You're not interested in the Ukrainians or the Russians. You just want to hang Abrahams out to dry. I bet he's the one who wanted you retired from The Firm. Am I right?"

"As a matter of fact, the Russians interest me immensely, Richard. As for Abrahams, don't underestimate that man. I believe he has more to hide than an affair with our very capable Home Secretary. He's under the cosh, Richard, so remember, a drowning man is sometimes more dangerous than the sharks that surround him."

"Did he run the Frankfurt job or was it his girlfriend?"

"That's classified, Richard. Need to know."

"So it was her then. Am I missing something here, Cartwright? Is there something else on that stick? Something you wanted by any chance?"

"Don't get ahead of yourself, Fuller. Deliver the package to me at my home tonight and let me worry about conspiracy theories."

"Just tell me this, Cartwright, why didn't your niece just destroy the evidence the moment she got her hands on it?"

"She was following orders, Fuller."

"From Abrahams? Or from you?"

"It's complicated. Like I said. Let me worry about the conspirators.

"So that's it, job done?"

"Job done."

"And this was Pro Bono?"

"I believe there was some spare change left in a Russian case that you might call a tax free bonus."

"Drug money."

"Wouldn't be the first time narcotics indirectly bought you a good suit, Fuller."

"You're all heart, Cartwright. See you in a few hours."

Rick killed the call and stepped out of the car.

Jack was sitting next to the log burner, enjoying the fire, whilst Harriet removed tags from her newly acquired wardrobe. She dropped the labels in the bin, folding each item neatly, before laying them on the table.

Rick ambled over to her.

"You may as well pack those, Casey. We're going south tonight, taking the goods to Cartwright. This is over for you."

She lay a pair of jeans on the table and looked at him, eyes wide.

"Really, I thought you said that Uncle…"

"Was hoping for a new team to emerge from the ashes, yes. I believe that was in his mind, but…"

"But what, Fuller?"

He scratched his beard.

"Well, for a start, once we drop that stick into Cartwright's sweaty palms, he says we're unemployed. So maybe I was wrong. This was a one off."

She shrugged.

"I see, but I can't exactly go back to my old post now, can I? Abrahams and his cronies will have it in for me. Probably have me sent to the tower in shackles."

"I'm sure your Uncle will smooth things over for you. And I reckon Abrahams' days will be numbered, no matter what happens from here on in."

She lowered her voice.

"What about, Jack?"

"What about him?"

"He has nowhere to live, Fuller. No job, his mother will be buried next week, and he'll have what's left of the Russian crew on his back the second he steps foot in Liverpool. He's just eighteen for God's sake."

"Look, Casey, I admit the kid did well yesterday, but he's just that…a kid, and I'm not a social worker."

"No, but you're a heartless bastard, Fuller," she spat. "You do realise we're all still in the firing line on this trip south, and that includes Shenton?"

"Hadn't realised," he said, his tone dripping with sarcasm.

Casey sniffed.

"So what you are saying is, Jack and I are good enough to watch your back for now, but once this job is completed, we're both surplus to requirements, is that it?"

Casey looked over her shoulder to see the young Liverpudlian standing there, eavesdropping.

"I don't want no charity," said Shenton, cricking his neck.

Casey instantly noticed just how the young boxer's eyes had changed. That sparkle, that cheekiness of youth, replaced by a cold hard stare.

"I think I've held me own, Mr Fuller," he said quietly. "But, when all's said and done, this is your crew, and if there's nothin' down for me, just say. And I'll do one, now."

"Don't get ahead of yourself, Shenton," snapped Rick. "There's another sixty grand in that safe to share out. Let's get this job over and then we'll take stock."

"I just want to know where I stand," said Jack, anger seeping into his tone. "And I'm not bothered about the rest of the money. That cash, and that stupid computer, got me Ma killed. So if…"

"Fer fuck's sake, what's going on here?"

Des had slipped into the lock up, carrying Cartwright's box and instantly picked up on the strained atmosphere.

Rick didn't take his eyes from Shenton.

"I was just pointing out to young Jack here, that Cartwright isn't offering long term employment prospects."

Jack gave Fuller one last hard stare before turning to Des.

"Thought it was too good to be true, Mr Cogan."

"Oh come on Jacko," said Des.

Shenton slumped back into his chair in front of the fire and sulked.

Des gave Rick a look.

"I cannea leave you for two minutes, eh?" he said, dropping the box on the table in exasperation.

Rick shrugged.

"Someone has to tell the kid the truth."

Des shook his head ruefully.

"I say we all play nice and get our kit sorted. Take our mind off the long game."

Rick muttered a few choice expletives as he walked over to a set of three heavily re-enforced firearms lockers, he entered a six digit combination into each electronic door lock, before opening all three in turn.

He lifted a heavy holdall from the first cabinet and lay it carefully on the table.

"SIG 552 Commando," he said, unzipping the bag and removing the Swiss made weapon. "Shenton, get your backside over here."

Jack reluctantly raised his frame from his chair and sauntered sullenly across the room, hands in pockets.

He eyed the gun suspiciously.

"This is mad," he said eyeing the evil looking weapon. "Proper on top. I'd get ten years just for holding that."

Rick curled his lip.

"If you want to be a player, Shenton, you need to learn how to use the tools of the trade."

Fuller gripped the gun, barrel pointing to the roof, finger outside the tigger guard.

"Okay, this is a 5.56 fully automatic assault rifle with an extended 30 round magazine. As you can see… here, it has a trigger mechanism with an ambidextrous safety and fire selector switch. There are four settings. S, for safe 1, for single shot, 3, for a three round burst and 20… for all hell just broke loose. The stock folds… like so. You insert the mag like this. And make the weapon ready…so. Are you with me son?"

Jack swallowed.

"Yes, Mr Fuller."

Rick was warming to his task. He returned to the second locker, removed another bag and returned to the table.

"Remington 870 Tac-14 12 bore shotgun, 14 inch barrel. Takes four in the mag and one in the spout. Nice, short, manstopper."

"I like the raptor grip," said Des picking up the jet black shotgun.

"Me too," offered Rick. "It doesn't feel like it's going to break your wrist every time you fire it either."

"Ammo?" asked Des, head cocked. "You said we were short."

"We are. When it comes to hardware, we have enough of everything, rifles, shotguns, pistols, but only 40 rounds of 00 for the 870s and a 100 5.56 for the 552s. We're down to two boxes of nine mil for the pistols and, before you ask, there's no time to search out the Greek for more."

The Scot nodded, rubbed his chin.

"I've got my Browning and half a box of nine milli." He lifted a shotgun from the table. "I'll take a Remington. Give Jack a 552 to go with his SLP. I'll run him through some drills before we leave."

Casey had been sitting in silence, watching proceedings. Finally, she could hold her tongue no longer.

"What the hell is this?" she spat. "Are we going to war, Fuller?"

"It was you who pointed out that this could be a hairy trip," said Rick, pulling out the third and final bag. "This is just a bit of insurance."

He dropped three sets of covert body armour onto the table, checked the sizing and pushed them towards each of his team.

"What about yersel," asked Des. "Or are ye invincible these days."

Rick shot him a sideways glance.

"What do you want me to do, share with Casey?"

Cogan shrugged resignedly and began to familiarise himself with the Remington pump.

"There's other toys in that box I brought over," said the Scot. "Comms sets, binos, some meds, morphine, antibiotics, some C4 and dets."

"Explosives," barked Casey. "Why in God's name would we need C4?"

Des picked up the square block of mouldable putty and held it up for all to see.

"This is grand stuff. Quick and easy to use, with enough velocity of detonation for metal cutting work."

"He means blowing up cars," said Rick quietly.

"Aye," said Des. "As Rick says, insurance. Better safe than sorry, I say."

Casey just shook her head and made for the kettle.

"Is there time for tea before we die?" she said.

"If you make it quick," said Fuller, selecting a SIG 552, two mags and a comms kit.

"We move in fifteen. From here to De Freville Avenue, is just over 3 and a half hours. We'll change our routine on this one. Jack, you're in with me in the Aston. We'll carry the laptop. Des, you and Casey are in the Disco with the stick. We stay in visual contact at all times and only use the comms sets if absolutely necessary. In the event of a contact en route, we go in hard. It's essential we get the goods to Cartwright tonight. Non-negotiable. Are we clear?"

"Aye, clear enough," said Des pulling his t-shirt over his head and grabbing his armour. "Where abouts is De Freville Avenue, anyway?"

"Cambridge," offered Harriet, dropping tea bags into mugs. "Uncle Damien's house is a stone's throw from the boat club."

"Very nice," said Des. "Few quid there eh?"

Casey shrugged.

"I believe he bought it back in the day for a modest sum. It's quite a humble little house really. Probably worth one and a half mil today."

"And you think that's modest, hen?" asked Des, picking up a mug and blowing on the surface of his tea.

Harriet pushed out her bottom lip.

"It's all relative, Cogan. Compared to my family home, it would be considered humble." She raised those perfectly plucked brows. "We can't all have been dragged up in a slum to make us more interesting."

Des looked over to Rick. He was shaking his head and smiling cheerlessly as he loaded magazines.

"Ye hear that pal? If I'd been born and bred in Milngavie, I'd have been a right boring bastard."

"I wasn't implying…" offered Casey. "I mean… I get slated all the time for being posh. And it's rather tiresome."

"No as tiresome as you, darlin,'" said Des as he pulled his shirt back over his head. "And as you and I are going to be sitting in the same motor all the way to Cambridge, I suggest ye climb down off yer very high horse, or we'll fall out."

Harriet coloured.

"Sorry Des, I'm awfully empty-headed sometimes."

"Aye, well," said the Scot. "Mind ye think on eh?"

* * *

"You don't like me very much, do you Mr Fuller?"

Jack had been sitting in silence for sixty miles, somewhat overawed by the opulence of the Aston and his company.

"Did I say that?"

"Not exactly, but…"

"Well don't make assumptions, Shenton."

"Sorry, Mr Fuller."

Rick moved out into the centre lane of the M6 so he could get better eyes on Des and the Discovery. The traffic had been unusually quiet through Staffordshire, allowing the team a good all round view of who was on the road, and who may be a tail. So far, all had been quiet.

He gave Jack a sideways glance.

"What weight do you fight at, son? Welterweight?"

Jack nodded.

"I reckon that would be the case if I ever got back in the ring. Before I went in the nick, I was light welter."

"But you kept growing."

"Yeah, ten stone is too light for me now. I still train hard most days, I even sparred with a couple of lads on the inside, but it wasn't the same."

"And is that what you wanted to do? Before you went inside. Box professionally?"

Jack wrinkled his nose.

"It was a pipe dream, Mr Fuller. I see that now."

"Not good enough?"

Jack smiled at Rick's directness.

"You remind me of me Mam. You wouldn't win any contests for tact, would yer."

Rick shrugged, waited.

Jack released a long breath down his nose.

"Danny said I was good enough. He said I had the skill to go all the way."

"Danny?"

"Danny Blatchford, he was my trainer, like. I was nine and oh, before things turned to shite. There was proper talk of me turning pro back then. Danny's old management were interested. But he got killed in an accident, I was on me arse, crashing at mates, nowhere to go. Then I got locked up."

"Life is like that, son."

"Tell me about it… I miss Danny though. He looked after me like I was his own. Like he was me Dad, y'know what I mean, Mr Fuller? A lad like me needs that." He smiled again, eyes like slits. "I need a bit of sense knocking into me every now and then."

"Don't we all, son," agreed Rick. "My old man was killed in action, Aden, 1967. I lost my mother soon after, so I know what it's like to be passed around. It was the army that gave me a chance."

"And that's where you met Mr Cogan?"

"For my sins."

"He's a good bloke."

"The best, Shenton. None better."

Fuller felt his phone vibrate in his pocket.

"I need to take this, son," he said opening the call. "Simon, what a pleasant surprise."

"Ah, Mr Fuller, sorry to disturb you like, but I have some further information for you."

"I'm all ears."

"Well, what it is, you see. I've been playing around with those files again."

"The ones that you haven't made a copy of because it couldn't be done?"

"Ah, sort of caught me out there, Mr Fuller. Well, I didn't actually copy the entire stick like…"

"Get on with it, Simon."

"Oh, right, well yes. You see, you know about those pictures, the park, the beach, all that?"

"Yes."

"Well I would suggest that they were all taken using a mobile phone. Selfies most of 'em."

"And?"

"Well then there was the emails. Looking at them again, it was just one account that was accessed. The arronabrahams@sis.gov.uk one. Mrs Longthorn Grey's account was never hacked, it was simply her replies we saw."

"I'm listening, Simon."

"Well I reckon the reason that the SIS account had been so easily accessible, was because Mr Abrahams had his password stored… in his phone."

"Are you going to tell me something of value, Simon?"

"Well, yes. With that in mind, I would suggest that all this has come about because this mush left his phone lying around, but, and this is the reason for my call, whoever got hold of this telephone, appears to have copied the phone book and call list too."

"So he made phone calls to Longthorn Grey, what a revelation."

"Yes, he did, Mr Fuller. But he also made a great deal of calls to the US."

Fuller turned down his mouth. "Maybe he has relatives there."

"Well, that's as maybe, but I've done some digging and he's not been calling his old mum. He's been chatting with a senior member of the JDL… a lot."

The JDL, or Jewish Defence League, was founded in New York City in 1968. It's original purpose was to protect Jews from antisemitism. However, the body grew in size and its fierce criticism of the Soviet Union increased its popularity. By the mid-nineties it had moved on from basic thuggery and in 2001 was classified as a right wing terrorist group by the FBI. Shortly after that, the JDL took to bombing Arab and Soviet properties in the United States and targeting various alleged 'enemies of the Jewish people,' for assassination. The JDL were spreading their wings too, having set up small but effective groups in Paris and London.

"Now I really want to know why this guy just didn't destroy the program," mused Fuller.

"Well," offered Egghead. "Again, looking at the evidence, he'd have been in the brown stuff if he did. I would suggest that MI6 would have insisted on having the software back in full working order. Any tech head worth his salt would be able to identify the writer, maybe even the intended recipient."

Rick nodded.

"I reckon you're right there, Simon. I bet he was under strict orders to return that stick, no excuses."

"Yes, Mr Fuller. But this Abrahams mush would have needed to clean off those phone records before his chums at The Firm got the data back. I mean, sleeping with your boss is one thing, being in bed with a banned terror organisation is quite another eh?"

"Mmm," said Rick. "Any other revelations?"

"Well, Mr Fuller, looking again at all the data, I would suggest that the reason for all these shenanigans, is that our Mr Abrahams simply lost his phone."

"Or had it stolen."

"Bonne da douche," said Simon.

Fuller closed the call. Things were beginning to make sense. The next question was, had Cartwright got wind Mr Abrahams' terrorist leanings? Was that the real reason he was still out in the cold, and was that the rationale behind why the old spy wanted his niece back in one piece, with the stick intact?

In the Land Rover, Des and Harriet were not quite so talkative. Cogan had finally got to grips with the stereo in the Discovery and had tuned it in to Radio 2.

Casey had tolerated Bob Harris' country hour for almost forty minutes before she made to change stations.

Cogan's reactions were like lightning and he slapped her hand the second she neared the set.

"Ye dinnea have much in the way of manners for a posh bird," he said.

Harriet rubbed the back of her hand and glowered.

"I was simply…"

"You were simply wanting yer own way, as usual. And bollocks to anyone else. It seems to be a recurring theme."

Harriet pulled down the passenger visor, opened the vanity mirror and checked her hair.

"Have you and Fuller always been so difficult?" she said, teasing a wayward curl.

"By difficult, you mean, playing by the rules, following orders and instructions, respecting people… yeah, pretty much, with the odd exception."

She turned to him, eyes burning.

"But you don't follow the rules, do you Cogan? And neither you nor your pal, Fuller, follow orders."

Des turned briefly, the light from the instrument display illuminating his weathered face.

"We, hen, are a team. My loyalty is to that team, to Rick Fuller. And you, as a member of it, should do the same. Follow his orders and respect the other members. Just because you were brought up with the silver spoon, doesn't give you the right to behave the way you do. Before you showed up, this unit was like a family. Rick, me, Lauren…"

"But she's dead, Cogan. She's gone and Fuller needs to get over it."

"See, there ye go again, shooting off yer mouth before ye engage that brain of yours. Not thinking that what ye say may hurt someone's feelings. Yer no big or clever enough to wipe Lauren North's boots, darlin'. And as fe Rick no being capable. It's no twenty four hours since I reminded ye he saved your pretty arse in Thailand, and if he hadn't led that Russian crew through the woods the way he did yesterday, we may all be goners. Ye have a long way to go and a lot te prove, lassie."

Casey turned her face to the window and fell into a sullen silence.

Des took a deep breath.

"Harriet," he said. "Look hen, take it from this old soldier. It's easy to get off on the wrong foot with folks, but the more you do it, the harder the bridges are to build."

She shook her head, then pushed some raven locks behind her ears.

"I'm a nightmare, I'm sorry, Des. I've always been a tad sharp, especially when the pressure is on."

"I can see that. I just reckon you need to wind that neck of yours in, and show some loyalty to the folks close to you. Prove yourself… then ye can take the piss as much as ye like."

"I'll try, Des."

"Aye," he said. "I'm sure."

EIGHTEEN

De Freville Avenue, Cambridge

Des pulled the Discovery into Cartwright's road. It was a long treelined avenue with cars parked in bays either side. The majority of the properties were Edwardian, with beautifully tended front gardens, many with electric security gates.

Cartwright's house was number 66.

Cogan let the Discovery trundle slowly along the road as they looked for it.

"There," said Casey. "That's Uncle Damien's."

Des depressed his comms pressel.

"Double fronted white painted detached, off to my left now. Gates open, no car on the drive, downstairs lights on, curtains closed. All looks peaceful."

"Roger that," said Rick. "Spin around and park as close as you can and wait for my order. Tell Casey to kit up and get ready for the approach. Tell her to meet me at the gate, thirty seconds."

Rick walked purposefully along the wide footpath, leaving Jack in the Aston to guard the precious laptop. Casey waited at the gate as asked.

Fuller pulled his secure phone from his pocket and dialled. Suspiciously, there was no answer from the old spy.

"Everything okay?" asked Casey as Rick joined her at the bottom of the driveway.

"He didn't pick up," he said.

"Well I can hear his TV from here," she offered. "Maybe the old goat didn't even hear the phone."

Rick examined the frontage of Cartwright's beautiful home. All seemed well.

"Mmm," he mused. "Let's go and knock."

"Let's," smiled Casey. "I can't wait to see him."

Harriet walked on ahead. Rick noted, that for once she'd opted for more substantial clothes, full length jeans, boots and a zip up black hoodie to hide her armour. Fuller trod cautiously behind, his trademark Timberlands crunching on the gravel drive.

Harriet rang the bell.

The pair waited, listening to the TV blasting away.

Casey rang again.

No answer.

Rick gave the substantial front door a push, and to his surprise, it swung open.

Instantly he opened his comms.

"Property is insecure. We have no contact with the subject. Des, you and Shenton make your way around the back."

"Roger that," said Des. "Jack, wait with the Aston, I'll come to you, we'll approach together."

Rick stepped quietly into the hall, the oppressive warmth from Cartwright's overworked central heating system instantly flushing his skin.

He pulled his SIG from his belt and held up his left hand, signalling Casey to stay behind him. She too drew her weapon, holding her position as instructed.

The blaring TV emanated from a room off to the left of the hallway. Rick edged his way forwards, ever closer to the half open door. As he reached the jamb, he motioned for Casey to join him. Once she was at his shoulder, he indicated exactly the area he wanted her to cover on entry. Low and to his right. She nodded calmly, her eyes never leaving his.

Fuller's comms crackled into life. Des and Jack were in position at the rear and the house appeared secure.

Seconds later, Rick gave the signal to move and the pair entered the room weapons in the aim.

Cartwright was sitting in what Fuller guessed was his favourite chair by the fire. The logs were nothing more than embers, in need of replenishing and a brandy balloon sat on the hearth, which still boasted a fair measure of his favoured Hennessy XO. One of his slippers was kicked off just feet from where he sat, and a small occasional table had been clumsily knocked over and not righted.

Cartwright's eyes were open, his jaw slack, skin pallid.

Rick shot Harriet a glance. She was motionless, gun still raised, her pure white teeth biting into her bottom lip.

Fuller stowed his weapon and pulled on latex gloves. He gently lifted the old spy's wrist to feel for a pulse.

Rick again turned to Casey. As he shook his head to confirm what both already suspected, he saw tears forming in those beautiful blue eyes.

He lay Cartwright's hand flat on the arm of his chair and grabbed Harriet firmly by the elbow.

"Hey," he whispered. "Stay switched on. Glove up and go and let the boys in through the back door... start a search."

She gazed at her Great Uncle for a moment longer, took a deep breath, nodded and strode out of the room.

Rick began a closer inspection of Cartwright's corpse.

First, he lifted each of his sleeves to examine his forearms, then his trouser legs to inspect his ankles and calves. Next, he worked carefully around the collar of his shirt and into Cartwright's hairline.

Finally, he found what he was looking for. At the base of the old spy's skull was a tiny puncture wound.

Fuller had seen two just like it before.

It had been in the mid-nineties. Rick and Des had been part of a four man unit covertly inserted into Bosnia, masquerading as United Kingdom Liaison Officers, working for the UN. They'd even worn the UN blue beret and carried standard weapons and ammunition to blend in with the rest of the force. However their real job was to gather intelligence on the various fighting factions in the area. It was during that torrid tour, that they met an Israeli mercenary who they suspected was part of Mossad. He carried the narrowest stiletto knife Rick had ever seen and used it to great effect. The blade left virtually no trace of a stab wound, enabling the guy to take out two Bosnian Mujahideen fighters as they'd eaten their dinner, silently and with hardly a drop of blood spilled.

Rick studied the room. The slipper and the table were the only things out of place, probably as a result of Cartwright kicking out in his final throes. The TV would easily have been loud enough to cover an accomplished assassin's entry. It would have been a straightforward kill. After all, his victim was elderly and recovering from major surgery. Hardly a challenge.

Des pushed open the door to the lounge.

"No sign of any forced entry or search, pal... Oh jeezo," he said eyeing Cartwright with a pained expression.

Rick gestured Des over and showed the Scot the old spy's tiny wound.

Des rubbed his chin.

"That's just like the one in..."

"In Bosnia, yeah. The Mossad guy," agreed Rick. "Just check the front door lock for me, pal. Give it a proper once over."

Des nodded and turned. As he opened the door of the lounge Harriet and Jack quietly stepped past him.

Casey walked straight over to Cartwright's body and stroked his hair with a gloved hand.

"Uncle Damien was a lovely man," she said. "He was the one who encouraged me into the life."

"And he always made that life interesting, I'll give him that," said Des walking back into the room.

"The lock?" asked Rick.

"Been picked," confirmed Des. "Nice clean, pro job."

Rick nodded then knelt at Cartwright's lifeless body. They'd jousted over many things the last four years. The MI6 man had revealed many secrets to him, some regarding Fuller's own past that he'd rather have stayed hidden, yet he had respected him, actually cared for him. He was one of the good guys, one of the unsung heroes. Rick patted the old spy's knee.

"Let's move," he said.

* * *

Jack had been deep in thought all the way along the A14.

Finally, he turned to Fuller.

"Who do you think killed that man then?"

"Cartwright," corrected Fuller. "That was his name, Cartwright... I'm not sure, son."

"You said it was the same type of knife that the Israeli's use."

"I said it was the same type of knife *one* Israeli used."

"But..."

"But what, Shenton?"

"Well, if he... Cartwright, I mean, was killed because someone thought he had that memory stick, why didn't they search for it?"

"Good question."

"Maybe they knew he didn't have it yet. Maybe they just didn't want him to have it?"

"Maybe."

"But that would mean, they killed him because..."

A light came on in Fuller's head.

"Because Cartwright already knew what was on there. He must have suspected Arron Abrahams was a double agent. That he was associated with a terror organisation. It had nothing to do with his affair with the Home Secretary. It was all about the JDL. Abrahams knew that once Cartwright obtained the stick, he could use it for his own devices and out him for what he was."

"Which means this Abrahams fella knew that we were on our way," said Jack.

Rick didn't answer, he was too busy looking in his driver's door mirror.

"What's up?" asked Jack.

"Cops," said Fuller. "Lots of blues and twos coming up behind."

Rick's comms burst into life.

"You clocked the Polis?" asked Des, two hundred metres ahead in the Land Rover.

"Yeah, they aren't hanging around either," said Fuller, easing off the gas and moving into the nearside lane. "Let's just give them a free run at who-ever they're after."

Des followed suit and dropped the speed of the Discovery. In his rear view he could see the convoy of vehicles approaching at speed. He count-ed nine sets of blue flashing lights, illuminating the night sky, reflecting off the crash barriers and wet road beneath them.

"Maybe there's an accident up ahead," offered Casey.

The Scot turned down his mouth. He could see that each police vehicle was less than a car's length apart, all travelling at high speed. That could only mean one thing. Each driver in the convoy must have been specially trained in defensive driving techniques. These guys were not your ordinary run of the mill traffic cops.

Less than a minute later the convoy were alongside, and Des got a far better look. Interspersed between the liveried police vehicles were four un-marked Land Cruisers. Inside each of those were four officers clad in wolf grey tactical uniforms.

Rick was straight on his comms.

"The only cops that wear those colours are CTSFO," he barked. "I think we have company."

No sooner had Rick announced the presence of the Counter Terrorist Specialist Firearms Officers, than the crack unit began to manoeuvre their vehicles in preparation for a hard stop on the carriageway.

Fuller was back on the airwaves.

"If this goes the way I think, I want everyone compliant and silent until I say otherwise, are we clear."

"Roger that," said Des.

Jack turned to Fuller, eyes wide.

"Am I going back to jail?" he said.

"Not if I can help it, son," said Rick, pulling onto the hard shoulder and slowing the Aston to a crawl. "Just remember, don't say anything, not even your name, until I say so... okay? Now, push your gun under the seat and make sure these fuckers can see your hands at all times."

Fuller knew all about the CTSFO, a heavily armed unit, a spinoff of SCO19, the Met's tactical firearms squad. They used live ammunition during CQC training and worked alongside UK Special Forces. This team were no mugs, and he knew it.

No sooner had the Aston come to a halt, than bright spotlights were shone into the windscreen blinding Rick and Jack.

They could hear the team bellowing commands as they dragged Des and Harriet from the Discovery, forcing them to the floor, then seconds later, Rick and Jack were given the same treatment.

Fuller found himself lying face down on the tarmac, cuffed, with two cops pointing SIG 516's at his head. He couldn't see Des or the others, but from his uncomfortable position he did see one cop pull a SIG 552 assault rifle from the boot of the Aston and drop it in a plastic evidence bag.

"Looks like you're fucked, mate," said one of the team standing over him.

Fuller snorted.

"Could have kissed me first."

Rick was finally lifted to his feet and searched for more weapons.

"Where are we going?" he asked.

"Disneyland," said the burly cop.

"Everyone's a fucking comic," he muttered.

Disneyland turned out to be an hour and forty minutes' drive away, in the form of Paddington Green Police Station.

For almost 50 years, the agepractiseding detention centre had been at the centre of the UK's anti-terror policing operations. During its bleak history, the Green has held IRA terrorists, Islamist would-be suicide bombers and prisoners returned from Guantanamo Bay.

Rick was marched into the custody suite where a surly Inspector asked for his details. After the third time of asking, and receiving nothing in return, the officer gave up and Fuller was taken to the forensic tent.

"This is new," he said.

"Been here before then?" said one of the cops tasked with Fuller's medical swabs.

Rick managed a thin smile but stayed silent.

"All samples are taken in here," said the cop. "We'd hate it if your brief were to suggest that you'd picked up traces of something nasty in one of our cells. After all, we do get to enjoy the company of lots of bad guys."

"Is that what you think we are?"

The cop shrugged.

"Possession of automatic weapons, C4, detonators, call me old fashioned, but it kind of looks that way eh?" He shook open a plastic evidence bag. "Boots first," he said, nodding appreciatively. "Nice Timberlands, I've got those myself in black."

Forty minutes later, Fuller was led to holding cell D wearing nothing but a paper evidence suit and shoes. The cell was cold and airless and remined him of a Victorian lavatory.

"Brew would be good," he said to yet another new cop.

"Too late, buddy. Next refreshments are breakfast, 0700hrs."

"Okay, how about my phone call? I want my brief."

The guy looked uneasy.

"We're a little busy right now dealing with your colleagues."

Fuller curled his lip. He knew that the guy was just toeing the line, following whatever protocols the bosses had laid down, but time was of the essence.

"Well, listen to me sonny," he spat. "You go and tell your superiors that if I don't get to call Martin Simpkins QC in the next fifteen minutes, he will have all your guts for garters, and any case you think you have against me or my… colleagues, will be as much use as a one legged man in an arse kicking contest."

Fuller looked up at the CCTV camera buried into the roof of his cell and waved.

"Did everyone get that? My brief and a fuckin' brew."

The cop scuttled off, leaving Fuller angrily pacing his cell to keep warm.

Rick didn't have long to wait. Just nine minutes later, his cell door creaked open and a middle aged suit stood in the opening.

"Mr Fuller," he said. "And before you make any further denials, we are fully aware of your identity. This childish behaviour from yourself, Cogan, Casey and Shenton is rather pathetic, don't you think?"

Rick stood, cricked his neck and balled his fists.

"I'll tell you what's pathetic, sunshine. What is particularly childish is I haven't been told why I've been arrested. I haven't been cautioned. I haven't been offered legal advice and I haven't been offered a cup of fucking tea."

The suit gave him a thin smile.

"All those things will come in good time, Fuller."

Rick took an aggressive step forward. The suit stood his ground.

"Adding a physical assault to your list of charges probably won't increase your sentence, but it won't win you any favours either, Fuller."

Rick took a breath.

"And you are?"

"I, Fuller, am of no consequence. However, it is my job to introduce you to someone who is."

"Really?"

"Yes, really, Fuller."

"Does it involve tea?"

The suit raised his brows.

"And biscuits, I believe."

Rick shrugged.

"Then lead on, McDuff."

ROBERT WHITE

Rick was ushered back along the cell block to the custody desk. There, two men were waiting for him. They were casually dressed, Levis, boots, sweatshirts. They had the look he knew only too well.

"Sterling Lines?" he asked them.

One quickly cuffed his hands, whilst the other removed a hood from his back pocket.

"Sorry chief," he said, pulling it over Fuller's head. "You know the script."

Rick was led away. He felt cold air on his face and intuitively knew he was outside. Moments later he was in a vehicle, a fast moving saloon car. The ride was short, twelve, fifteen minutes. Then he was out in the fresh air again, his two quiet minders keeping him moving, speaking only to warn him of steps, kerbs, doors. Then there was a lift, an old clanky affair. They were going down, a long way down.

Finally there was another lengthy silent shuffle along what sounded like a tiled corridor before he was led through a creaky door and made to sit on a hard chair. The room was again cold, and any small noise reverberated off the hard surfaces that surrounded him. He felt like he'd come full circle and was back in his cell in Paddington.

However, he was not.

His hood and cuffs were removed, and his two quietly efficient minders left him in a room that wouldn't have been out of place in a World War II movie.

Fuller had been positioned a discreet distance from an ornate oak desk with a single chair behind. On that, sat one of the most beautiful women he'd ever seen.

Rosemary Longthorn Grey was thirty six, making her the youngest Home Secretary in history. Tall and willowy with a shock of red curls that framed her near alabaster complexion, she boasted large, striking green eyes, and a full mouth. She bore no signs of makeup, the merest hint of freckles on her cheeks giving her a youthfulness of a woman ten years her junior.

The Minister wore a black two piece, buttoned at the midriff with a delicate plain white blouse underneath, open just a little too much for Fuller's comfort, the suggestion of a curve of cleavage enough to draw the eye.

A thick brown file sat on the desk in front of her. Stamped on the front in large red letters were the words, 'Top Secret. Eyes only.'

She tapped it with a French manicured nail.

"You have lived a most fascinating life, Fuller," she said, huskily. "Cartwright made a good decision."

"His choice of male friends appears sounder than your own, Ma'am," said Fuller, taking in the woman's obvious assets.

"Quite," she offered, showing no emotion, opening the file and pushing gold rimmed glasses onto her face. "Nevertheless, you appear to have served Damien well, and he you."

Fuller considered the addition of spectacles only made the woman more attractive.

"It's called respect," he said. "Comes with trust, honesty. Almost like a marriage."

She ran a finger under a line of text.

"Yes, I see you were married once. Catherine wasn't it? A sorry business."

"It was a long time ago."

"Yes, true and time heals, as they say."

"Do they?" said Fuller losing what was left of his patience. "Is there a point to all of this, Ma'am?"

Longthorn Grey cocked her head.

"Of course there's a point, Fuller. Indeed, I would suggest there are several points to discuss here."

Rick blew air down his nose, closed his eyes for second, then leaned forwards in his chair.

"What? Like how you and your lover sent government employees to their death to try and save your marriage and your reputation?"

The Secretary grimaced.

"Touché, Mr Fuller. You and your little team have already accessed the contents of the files, then?"

"Another fascinating part of my life, Ma'am. I like to get the job done."

"Then that makes this conversation somewhat easier. I never was one for beating around the bush."

"I'm shocked. A politician who answers questions."

Longthorn Grey sat back in her chair.

"Look, I don't want, or need you to like me, Fuller. And I certainly don't require a lecture on fidelity. I could spend the next hour listing the problems with my marriage, Peter's sweet young ecology students, the many days and nights alone, but what's the point? I could cry into my soup about how I have always been attracted to the wrong kind of men. Confident, bullish, self-possessed, handsome creatures that always turn out to be lacking in decency."

"My heart is bleeding, Ma'am."

"I'm sure it is, Fuller. However, this verbal jousting isn't getting us anywhere. So let's begin with Mr Arron Abrahams, shall we? A man totally unsuited to his role."

"He reported directly to you, Ma'am."

"True, but I inherited him. He was in post before he was… in me, so to speak."

Even Fuller smiled at that one.

"Cartwright didn't trust him."

"Of course he didn't, but I had to consider that there was bad blood there. Arron was instrumental in having Damien removed once his illness became public knowledge."

"Nice guy."

"He was actually. He was fun to be around. Handsome, charming. He came from a rich Jewish family with good city connections. All in all, a good egg, just…"

"Just?"

"Just damned unreliable. So it came as no surprise to me when he announced that he'd lost his mobile, his personal set, rather than his secure phone, whilst out and about in a Soho nightclub." She snorted.

"Lost my arse. He'd been in the company of some Polish ballet dancer. He'd always had an eye for Eastern European types. She saw her chance, before you could say Nureyev, she'd sold it on to the Kiev hackers who embedded the 'evidence' of our relationship into a social media phishing program before moving it on for an exorbitant fee to the Brothers Circle."

"And you, of course, got wind of this?"

"Yes, the chosen mule, Alexander Solonik was a whoremonger, a drunk and a notorious loudmouth. His diplomatic bag had proved a handy tool for the Brothers in the past, but he couldn't keep his mouth shut or his pants on."

"A man after your own heart, Ma'am."

"Very droll, Fuller. But let me be quite blunt here. At this juncture I was perfectly happy for matters to take their course. The tabloids would have had their five minutes of fame. Arron would have been moved sideways, and I would have been forced to accept some dreadfully dull advisory role in the city."

"And your husband?"

"Peter? He wouldn't have lost a wink. Anyway, as I was saying it's one thing making a political point, removing a high profile MP from her post, but quite another to attempt to bring down the whole government. These bally Russians just go too far."

"They do Ma'am."

She pushed herself back from her desk, unbuttoned her jacket, crossed wonderful legs.

"So Abrahams and I sent in the cavalry."

"Your plan?"

"I agreed to it."

"But I'd wager it was Abrahams idea, and he would have wanted the program and his stolen phone destroyed… correct?"

"I don't see what you are driving at here, Fuller."

"Two men were killed, Ma'am."

"Sadly, yes. But doing nothing is never an option. I demanded that stick be returned so our boffins could examine it and hopefully trace these gang-sters who would do our country harm."

"But, as I said, Mr Abrahams wanted it destroyed. Am I right?"

She leaned forwards and that blouse opened just an inch further.

"What makes you say that Richard?"

Fuller rubbed his annoying beard, did his best not to stare and moved the conversation sideways.

"More to the point, how did you trace us tonight?"

"Easy. When Casey called Cartwright from Frankfurt, he called me. I agreed with his little plan to clear up the mess, providing we could keep an eye on you."

"An eye?"

"Yes, those three phones you have... they contain trackers."

"So you knew we were going to visit Cartwright and hand over the goods tonight."

"We guessed as much."

"And your boyfriend? Did he know too?"

She pouted.

"Possible. Unlikely, but possible."

Fuller nodded slowly.

"And you know how Cartwright was killed?"

"I believe he was stabbed. Terrible business."

"Yes, it was, but his assassin was very particular and used a technique I've only ever seen once before. Cartwright was murdered using an extremely narrow stiletto blade inserted at the base of the cranium, the exact point where the cerebellar tonsils sit in the opening of the skull base. It's called the foramen magnum. This is the precise spot where the spinal cord attach-es to the brain. Death is instantaneous, but a sloppy or tired on call doc-tor could easily miss the wound. Add in Cartwright's recent medical prob-lems, and whoever did the dirty deed could easily have walked away scot free. Probably the killer's thinking."

Longthorn Grey swallowed.

"Sounds shocking."

"It is. Curiously, the technique is favoured by the Israelis, Ma'am. Mossad teach it."

Fuller examined the Home Secretary. There was something working extremely hard behind those beautiful features. He sniffed.

"Look, Ma'am, I don't know how much work your people have done on the stick yet, but my guy found that the men in Kiev had not just hacked Abrahams' email and pictures, but his phone records too."

Longthorn Grey shrugged indifferently.

"Arron called me most days. Hardly relevant in the circumstances."

"He called the head of the JDL most days as well."

"JDL?"

"The Jewish Defence League, Ma'am. A banned terror organisation based in the US. Anti-Russian. Anti-Arab. And there are other offshoots forming. One in Paris and now, oddly enough, here in London. Both linked to the Zionist leader Ze'ev Belinsky, a man, your lover seemed to have on speed dial. These groups, these offshoots, are predominantly formed from young middle-class men from the suburbs. However, they are trained and led by Mossad. Many of them schooled in krav maga, a hand-to-hand martial art used by the Israeli military, including the use of a stiletto blade. Do you consider that a coincidence Ma'am?"

The Minister went pale.

"Are you suggesting that Abrahams is Mossad... a murderer? A traitor to his country?"

"I'm suggesting that Cartwright already had wind of his connection to the JDL and that Abrahams wanted that memory stick badly enough to kill for it. He couldn't destroy it, that would have raised everyone's suspicions, including yours. So he had to get hold of the stick and wipe the phone records from the file before The Firm got their sweaty mitts on it and revealed him for what he is... A double agent."

Longthorn Grey stood and buttoned her jacket.

"Give me a moment, please," she said sharply as she opened the door.

A moment turned into forty minutes. Fuller had spent the last twenty of them pacing the chilly room.

Finally Longthorn Grey returned holding another file. This time a thin buff coloured affair.

"Sorry to keep you waiting, Fuller," she said.

"Dotting the i's, were we?" he said rubbing his hands together.

"Something like that. I've just spoken to the PM, and we've organised for your colleagues to be released. The chaps you met earlier from 22 have taken them to a safe house."

"A safe house?" snapped Fuller. "What the fuck is going on here?"

"Don't panic, it's just comfier than a cell, Fuller. And away from prying eyes for a few hours."

She held out the file.

"Home address and regular haunts of Arron Abrahams. And a bonus. A late present from our departed friend, Cartwright. The address of Semion Savalovsky, UK head of The Brothers Circle and intended recipient of the program." She placed the file in his hand. "To the best of my knowledge, you, I and the Prime Minister are the only people privy to this intelligence. I think you know what to do, Fuller."

Rick took it and quickly thumbed the pages.

"He knew it all, the old bugger," he muttered. Rick looked up from the file. "How long before I get my team back?"

"Richard. Contrary to popular belief, once someone is arrested in possession of automatic weapons and explosives in this country, it takes a few phone calls to secure their freedom. I realise The Firm can be a bit doddery in its ways of working, but once we arrive at the correct decision, things tend to move apace. Now, 22 Air Troop have the Kiev gig, with the brief to destroy the errant telephone and deal with the hackers. That will end any chance of the Brothers achieving their goals or making copies of the intel. However, as a result of 22's actions, I would suggest recriminations will follow. These Baltic types are a vengeful lot and before they get up a head of steam, they need to be dealt with. Therefore, your task is to eliminate the treacherous Mr Abrahams and our resident Russian gangster, Savalovsky before things get out of hand. I've briefed the PM, well… with as much as he needs to know, and he agrees that you are the man for the job. I've explained that you have a talent for making these unfortunate matters appear to be no more suspicious than an untimely accident. He, and I for that matter, expect that this is the way this game will play out."

Fuller dropped the file on the desk and got in close to the Home Secretary.

"So you hand me the address of your boyfriend and walk away clean, is that it? Come on, Minister, The Firm leaks like a sieve. Abrahams will know you have the program by now. He'll be on his toes to Tel Aviv before you can say Shalom."

She managed a brief smile.

"Oh dear, Fuller. How little you know him. Arron is a poor little rich boy with friends in high places. He won't even contemplate running. Not yet at least. He won't see the need. He'll believe he can worm his way out of trouble, the way he has all his life. Daddy will be on the blower to the PM before breakfast, explaining how these ghastly Ukrainians have planted this so called evidence of connections with the JDL and how it is nothing more than a racist plot against his family. This PM is more likely to swallow the tale, too. He's so frightened of being labelled anti-Semitic, he'd brush the whole thing under the rug in a heartbeat. Hence the need for discretion. The kind only a man like your good self can provide."

Fuller took a moment. Nodded.

"That may be possible with Abrahams, but Savalovsky will be a different ballgame. He'll have soldiers around him, he'll be well protected. That one could get messy. I can deal with our traitor quietly enough, but when it comes to the Brothers, I'll need my crew."

"And you will have them soon enough. I'm sure you and your rowdy little team will do a sterling job, Fuller," she said with a half-smile.

He turned down his mouth.

"Mmm…Okay, two things. First, feed the press a natural causes story on

Cartwright. Abrahams will be jumpy enough and I'd rather our boy be feeling he's home and dry on that count."

"And the second?"

"How much?" he said.

"I beg your pardon?"

"The fee. The spondoulies. In case you hadn't realised, I'm currently unemployed, and I have mouths to feed."

"I understood that Cartwright had…"

"Cartwright was as tight as cramp, Minister. The money young Jack recovered from Savalovsky's man in Liverpool will just about cover my winter wardrobe and a deposit on a new Vantage. You see Ma'am, you are right about one thing, accidents do happen, but they come expensive. Especially when the guys having the unfortunate mishaps are spooks with Mossad connections and Russian oligarchs with an army of ex Spetsnaz behind them."

"Hmm, I see. When you put it that way…"

"Let's call it a quarter of a mil. A nice round number."

"That's an awful lot of money, Fuller."

He shrugged.

"You slot 'em then."

"I'll need to clear it… with the powers that be."

Rick felt suddenly warm.

"Clear it with who you like, Ma'am." He scratched his beard. "But whilst The Firm are robbing their piggy bank, I could do with a good razor. I'll need some clothes too. Underwear, socks, shirts, shoes, and a couple of suits. Paul Smith preferably. You can't slot an Israeli spy wearing a cheap suit, now, can you?"

Longthorn Grey gave him a worried look, shook her head, turned and was gone.

Another tedious half hour passed before Fuller was joined by a grey haired gent of diminutive stature. As he led Fuller from the room, he made notes on a small pad.

"Now... Shoes sir? Type, make, size?"

"Oliver Sweeney brogues, size ten," said Rick. "Dark tan or black."

"As you wish Sir... any other footwear?"

"Boots, Timberland. The Radford six inch boot in sand... no, make that black. In fact I'll take two pairs, one of each."

"Of course, Sir. Shirts? Undergarments?"

"Alfred Dunhill, fitted, plain white and powder blue, seventeen collar. I'm not in the mood for a tie. As for skids, Tom Ford, long boxers, white, and a box of socks. Anything from the London Sock Company will do, but no bright colours, black or navy. And I'll need casuals. Levi 501s two pairs, thirty two long, and a selection of polos. Ralph Lauren, size XL, purple label, mind."

"Sir, and the razor?"

"What's your name, pal?"

"Henderson, Sir."

"Well, Henderson, what have you forgotten?"

"Ah, there could be a problem with the suits, Sir. The hour and..."

"I want the Paul Smith, tailored fit, all wool, two piece, in black, forty six long. And the same in deep indigo. No suits, no dead people."

"Yes, of course, Sir," said the guy, an anxious expression on his face.

"Thank you, Henderson."

"You're welcome, Sir."

He pushed open a heavy door which led to a courtyard. "The Ministerial car will be along shortly, Sir. The Home Secretary has requested you be taken to her flat in Kensington."

"Has she now," he said.

* * *

Arron Abrahams paced his open plan living room, reading the newsflashes on his phone as they popped up on his feed.

The Cartwright story had just broken in the local Cambridge Gazette.

It seemed genuine enough. That would buy him some time if nothing else.

The cantankerous old spy had been a thorn in his side ever since Arron's appointment to the SIS. Damien had always had his beady eye on him. Bugging his calls, having him followed. It had got so bad that Abrahams even considered his position untenable. Then, joy of joys, the old fart got cancer.

Of course, that good news was short lived. No sooner was Cartwright off his back than he'd stupidly 'lost' his phone.

The Frankfurt job had been a disaster. Casey had turned out to be less pliable than he'd thought, Rosemary had been insistent that the stick be returned and examined, and then the Russians began flexing their muscles at every opportunity.

Silencing Cartwright had been essential. God knows how, but the senile old goat had uncovered Arron's double life, and with his health improving, his return to The Firm would have caused all manner of problems that couldn't have been explained away. He'd even made a secret alliance with Rosemary and Casey, and somehow, the memory stick was now in the hands of the police.

Once the tech guys at Vauxhall Cross decrypted those phone records, Arron knew it would only be a matter of time before his connection to the JDL became common knowledge.

Okay, his father, a secret yet fervent supporter of The League would smooth things over politically, but Arron knew how these things worked.

He had time, but not much.

His current role gave him access to top secret intelligence regarding Russian political interference and their corrupt business dealings, and his department held thousands of pieces of delicate information regarding the Saudi's, the UAE and wider Arab world. In one fell swoop he had the ability to irretrievably damage all the enemies of Israel, and that had made him an extremely valuable commodity. However, once removed from such a position, he was vulnerable from all sides. The Russians, the Arabs and the backstabbers at The Firm.

Then, of course, there was the leader of the League, Ze'ev Belinsky himself.

A former Israeli soldier who had studied Jewish law, Belinsky had notoriously helped perpetrate a shocking massacre on the West Bank, in which thirty Muslim worshippers were murdered whilst at prayer. Prior to his leadership of the JDL, he'd been a key member of The New Kach movement, a group which advocated the expulsion of Arabs from Israel and the Palestinian Territories. Belinsky had promoted the use of terror all his adult life and was as vicious and coldblooded an individual as Abrahams had ever met.

Arron knew that it was his usefulness to Belinsky that had made him his true fortune the last five years. Numbered offshore accounts bursting with cash awaited him. His ability to obtain precious intelligence, to put names to faces, had been his financial lifeblood.

Nevertheless, Abrahams knew that his future now lay back in his homeland, and that the only way he could return and live there anonymously, in peace and prosperity, was to prove his worth to the JDL's near psychotic leader one last time.

On his personal laptop, he had amassed information priceless to the League. The addresses and hangouts of the enemies of Israel. Their wives' car registration numbers, the schools their children attended, their places of worship. The file was as precious as it was dangerous. Abrahams had always considered it to be his insurance policy, but now, the time was fast approaching to use it to secure his future, to open the floodgates, and let Belinsky wage the campaign of terror he'd always craved.

He knew he would have to ride out the current storm, answer some difficult questions, but that was of little consequence, a week, maybe two, was a long time in politics and people had short memories. A slap on the wrist, some bitter remarks from Rosemary, maybe even a change of department. Then one call, one last big deal and he was home and dry. With what Abrahams had to offer, Belinsky and the JDL would ensure the streets of London ran red with Arab and Russian blood, and what fair minded true supporter of Israel didn't want that?

* * *

Fuller stepped out of the black Jaguar still wearing his white paper evidence suit. The heavy rain had returned, and he was instantly soaked, the flimsy garment sticking to his skin as he stood shivering on the steps of Longthorn Grey's London flat.

The raised entrance to the Edwardian maisonette was directly opposite the Natural History Museum on the tree lined, Queen's Gate, just a stone's throw from Earls Court.

"Oh my," said the Minister, as she opened the heavy front door. "Come inside, Richard, you must be frozen."

Fuller shuffled his soaked feet inside.

"I'll get you a towel," she offered turning swiftly down the long corridor. "The lounge is on the right, fire's lit."

Moments later, she returned to find him warming his bones in front of the hearth.

"Very nice," he offered.

"It's Daddy's, not mine," she said, handing him a sumptuous Versace baroque embossed towel.

Fuller went about drying his hair as he took in the opulence.

"And what does 'Daddy' do?" he asked.

Longthorn Grey had changed her clothes. The two piece power suit had been replaced by a black and gold floral silk wrap. Fuller wasn't quite sure of the designer, or what if anything, was underneath.

She sat on the large corner sofa and crossed those legs again.

"He was in property renovation," she said. "This little place included. I do love it here. Close to everything, the West End, Oxford Street."

"The Houses of Parliament? Downing Street? Vauxhall Cross?" said Fuller.

Longthorn Grey shook her head and smiled, her luscious red curls falling around her face.

"Are you always thinking about business, Richard? Don't you ever relax?

Have fun?"

"Isn't business the reason I'm here, Ma'am?" said Fuller unable to take his eyes from the woman.

"Rosemary," she said, standing. "Don't be so formal, Richard. It's the middle of the night and we're not at work now. Call me Rosemary... please."

He walked to her, close enough to feel her breath on his face, smell her perfume, she rested her palm on his chest. Stopping him in his tracks.

"You need to get out of those wet clothes," she purred.

"And into what?" he said drinking in her beauty.

Rosemary grabbed at the neck of his paper suit. Instantly the saturated fragile fabric began to tear in her grasp. She pulled, gently at first, her eyes never leaving his, her lips parted. Fuller stood firm, arms at his side, watching her, listening as her breathing deepened. She stroked his cheek with her free hand. It was a soft, delicate touch, her fingers caressing the star shaped scar he bore. Then he saw her eyes widen, her face etch with determination. She took a firmer grip on his suit and began to tear in earnest, pulling at the seam, franticly ripping at the fabric.

Fuller in turn grabbed a handful of russet curls, pushing his free hand inside her robe, cupping her soft smooth curves, feeling her shiver as he kissed the corner of her mouth.

Rosemary was breathless, flushed with excitement.

"Take me to bed," she whispered. "For God's sake, take me to bed."

Fuller lay on his back bathed in sweat. Rosemary Longthorn Grey's head resting on his chest.

"You like to take chances, don't you?" he said.

"Do I? And what risk have I taken tonight, Richard? My reputation is already in tatters in certain circles."

"You don't feel guilty?"

"Do you?"

He stayed silent a moment. Strangely, he didn't... then.

"I'm not married," he said. "Or about to have my ex-lover slotted."

She twisted her naked body, rested both elbows on his chest and widened her eyes mischievously.

"Am I such a bad person?"

"We all make mistakes I suppose."

"Like now? Have you made a mistake, Richard?"

Again, he didn't quite know what to say, so stayed quiet.

She ran her hand through his hair, cocked her head.

"Tell me about Lauren. She was the reason you fled to Thailand, wasn't she?"

Fuller's eyes flashed.

"You read my file," he said flatly.

Rosemary pursed her lips.

"Don't get all defensive on me now. Cartwright was very diplomatic. Most of what he knew about people was in his head. That's what made him so dangerous. But I know she was killed. By a policeman wasn't it? Were you lovers for a long time?"

Fuller thought about that one. He shook his head.

"We'd made plans, but… I never took my chances."

Rosemary sat up.

"Oh my. I understood you were, well, you know."

He shook his head.

"Things always seemed to get in the way."

She smiled kindly.

"I see. That's sad."

There was a buzzing noise. Rosemary reached for her phone, pressed a single key and a live image of her front door appeared on the screen.

"Looks like your clothes are here," she said.

"Good job," said Fuller. "My others got ripped."

NINETEEN

Troeshchyna, Kiev, Ukraine.

Tango Echo Seven had dropped into Kiev under the cover of darkness and tabbed as far as the Almazne Lake. The four man patrol then RV'd with their contact on the south bank, who supplied them with a small boat in order to cross and land within a hundred metres of their target premises, a small garage that sat on the north bank on Pukhiska Street.

The road was made up of a mix of small industrial premises, car sales pitches and an enormously long grey block of flats that had more of a look of a Gulag than a welcoming home.

Joseph Lukashenko and John Sediuk rented the floor above CTJ Motorsport. They came and went about their business quietly. To all intents and purposes, the men ran a mobile phone repair shop. Indeed, to the outside world, even to those working just one storey below, there was nothing to point to the fact that the pair had carved out a concern that made them hundreds of thousands of Ukrainian Hryvnia per month.

It had been a busy time for the two hackers. Seemingly, every government in the world was beginning to see the benefit of using cybercrime to inflict damage on their enemies.

So busy were the pair, that they had taken to sleeping on the premises.

It was a bitterly cold night and Joseph was tending to the small gas burner that was the pair's sole source of heat.

"God damned thing," he said, changing the canister for the second time that night. "I have enough money to buy this whole block. Yet here I am with my nuts frozen in their sack."

John Sediuk was lying on his cot shrouded in blankets.

"Appearing poor, is what keeps us alive, Joseph," he said. "Another year, one more winter, and we can leave this hole, forever, rich men."

Lukashenko finally connected the gas bottle and lit the burner.

"There," he said, standing and pulling his own heavy blanket around his narrow shoulders. "That will keep the frost away until morning."

Joseph heard a click. It was a metallic sound, and he didn't care for it. As he turned towards the noise, the door to the room burst open. Three men rushed inside. They were cloaked in black, their faces covered with balaclavas.

The young man raised a hand in protest, just as the first round hit him square in the chest. The silenced weapons made little sound. Lukashenko fell atop of his heater. There was a hissing noise as his flesh burned, but he felt no pain. A second bullet had already entered his brain through the back of his skull.

John Sediuk was dead before he could slide one foot from his covers.

The three intruders quickly collected their empty casings, whilst a fourth set a crude incendiary device that could be purchased anywhere in the world.

On seeing the basic fuse light and begin to burn, the four turned and were gone into the night as quietly as they came.

As the troopers floated gently back across the lake, the premises of LS Mobile burned, lighting the night sky.

"Good job, lads," said one.

"Aye," said a second, "And back home for breakfast."

* * *

Fuller pulled one of his new polo shirts over his head and looked at himself in the mirror. He was clean shaven for the first time since the funeral, and somewhat miraculously, he'd woken without his hands shaking or his guts churning.

Rosemary pushed open the bathroom door and slid both arms around his waist. She peered over his shoulder at his reflection.

"Better without the beard," she offered.

"I'm glad it pleases you," he said, twisting from her grasp and making for the kitchen.

She called after him.

"My CP team will be here at eight. Probably best they don't see you."

He nodded.

"I'm the epitome of discretion, Ma'am. But I do need a place to work, and a laptop."

"The spare bedroom has a desktop," she purred. "The fridge is full. I have meetings until two, but I'll be back just after."

He picked up the coffee pot and poured.

"I was thinking it best you distance yourself from me... for the time being."

Her green eyes narrowed.

"Is this what you people call... the elbow?"

Fuller stepped closer and pulled her to him.

"You asked me about Lauren earlier," he said. "About us being lovers."

"And you said..."

"I said, I didn't take my chances."

"Yes."

"Well I don't intend to do that again. But like I said, I do need a place to work, and I need my guys with me asap." He sipped good coffee. "Look, Rosemary, things are about to come on top and you can't be seen to be involved in any way. With Cartwright gone, I have no one I can trust at the Firm, and my contacts for all things useful are all up north." He eyed her. "So I need you to do me a favour."

"Anything," she said.

He smiled at that. She thought it a wonderful sight, even if it was short lived.

"I need all the kit back that was confiscated by the cops last night," he said. "The cars, the weapons and…"

"And what?"

"And if you are serious about us taking Savalovsky out, then, some more ammunition too."

Longthorn Grey swallowed hard. The grim realisation of the task she had asked of him hitting home.

"I want you to come back to me, Richard," she whispered.

"Just get me a place… and that ammo," he said.

He packed his new clothes into a holdall he'd found in the spare room. Just for a moment, he wondered if it had been her husband's, or maybe Arron Abrahams'.

Fuller mentally shrugged to himself. What did it matter?

By the sound of it, Peter Grey had his own life and his marriage to Rosemary appeared to be nothing but a façade. As for Abrahams, he wouldn't be breathing long enough to be a problem.

Stepping into the blustery morning, he drank in the cold fresh air. It had been so long since he'd appreciated the basic things in life, he'd almost forgotten what it was like to feel alive.

Rick hailed a cab that would take him across the city, over the river to Battersea, where Rosemary, or whoever she had called, had found him a place to work from.

That place turned out to be a flat on Reform Street, just a short hop from Battersea Park. The Edwardian two bed flat was on a very pleasant estate that had been granted conservation status back in 1974. The area bustled with pubs and restaurants and even boasted its own theatre.

Rick, being a born and bred Londoner, felt instantly at home.

He dropped his bag in the pleasant open plan lounge-diner and slipped off his jacket, a three quarter Barbour that Henderson had kindly added to his list of desired clothing, and noticed the heating had been left on.

A quick check of the flat told him that the place had been hurriedly prepared for him. The fridge and freezer were stocked, bed made, everything was clean and ship shape.

Opening the door to the second bedroom, he discovered a small desk, laptop, printer and another rather robust looking mobile phone.

Fuller dropped that into a wicker wastepaper basket and made a note to himself to buy a cheap disposable burner at his earliest opportunity. Having an affair with the most powerful female politician in the country was one thing, having her know your exact whereabouts so soon into that relationship was another matter.

He opened the laptop, pulled the thin buff file Longthorn Grey had given him from his bag and began the delicate task of planning cold blooded murder.

* * *

Anatoly Ivanov was eating.

He'd completed his morning tasks. The children were safely in school and Ms Angelique had been dropped at her beauty salon. The Pakhan's Bentley had been delivered at the dealership for service and his spare car readied in case the garage were late returning his much preferred, bullet-proof marque.

Eating was something Ivanov found necessary every four hours or so. His sheer size, and the fact that he trained his body so hard each day, meant that the massive Russian bodyguard was permanently hungry.

As he shovelled what remained of six poached eggs and a full pack of salted bacon into his mouth, he considered himself fortunate to be able to eat at all. In his delicate position, as the former minder to the failure that was Erich Honecker, he could easily have found himself shipped to some hell hole Siberian prison, or worse still, the Papa, Semion Savalovsky, could have ordered his execution.

Ivanov wasn't scared of dying. Nevertheless, he wasn't keen on being made an example of either. People who let down the Papa were usually killed in ways that were intended to dissuade others from making similar mistakes, and having his kneecaps and elbows drilled before his body parts were scattered around Merseyside, was not the way he'd ever envisaged the end would come.

As he picked up his plate and walked to the sink, John Hodiak pushed his head around the corner of the kitchen door.

"Anatoly," he snapped. "Quickly, the Papa needs you."

He lay his plate on the worktop, wiped his hands on a towel and followed Savalovsky's trusted right hand to the Papa's study.

Hodiak stopped outside and knocked on the heavy, highly polished door.

"Enter," Savalovsky barked, and the pair strode inside.

As he approached, Ivanov thought his Godfather looked pale, his usually sharp eyes appearing somewhat listless, yet they still followed Anatoly's every movement, the way a feral cat would stalk an injured bird.

Finally the huge Russian stood to attention in front of his Papa, eyes front.

"Sit, Anatoly," said Savalovsky wearily.

Ivanov did as he was instructed. John Hodiak edged his way around the desk to stand at the right of his Godfather.

"We have the most serious of situations my Bratok," began Savalovsky. "As you are well aware, something extremely valuable to The Circle was stolen from us, and despite our best efforts, we have been unable to recover it. Our endeavours to catch the thieves have taken the lives of several good men, and your previous charge, the man given the task of recovery, has paid the ultimate price for his failure. Now, as of this morning, we have further bad news. Firstly, that the Police have arrested the people responsible for the Frankfurt theft, and taken possession of the said goods. They, in turn have handed the program over to MI6, who it would seem, have acted swiftly to protect their own. Our contacts in Kiev inform me, that the men who provided us with the software have been murdered, their business set ablaze, and the telephone that contained the precious information we required, is destroyed. Our people tell us that this was the work of professionals, possibly even British Special Forces. If this is the truth, Anatoly, it would appear that this whore of a Home Secretary has decided to fight back."

Savalovsky sat back in his chair.

"You know that I was born a Jew?"

"I do Papa."

He waved a dismissive hand.

"A mere label, my Bratok. A man does not choose his birthplace or his religion. I have always been a proud Ukrainian and supporter of the mother Russia. Yet Judaism is of no interest to me. The Circle is my religion, my faith, my creed. Do you understand that Anatoly?"

"Perfectly."

"Good, because your first task is to locate the Jew, Arron Abrahams. He is an enemy of Russia and therefore an enemy of The Brothers Circle. He is not only a philanderer and a traitor to his own country, but he is allied to The Jewish Defence League, an organisation who would see all Russian Jews expelled from Israel, a band of terrorists who would do our countrymen harm no matter their faith or location."

"Yes Papa."

"You were Spetsgruppa A, were you not? A soldier of the FSB, the most elite of our Special Forces?"

"I had that honour, Papa."

"A true patriot then. Excellent. I want you to take three good men of your choosing with you. My helicopter is fuelled and ready to take you to the capital. Make this Jew's death swift, my Bratok. Swift, but bloody and public. Make a bold statement that shows these Jew traitors just who is in control here."

"And the whore, Papa?"

Semion Savalovsky leaned forwards, both elbows on his desk. The tired, dull eyes suddenly alive, flashing with hatred.

"You bring her to me, Anatoly. We will show these people that no one is safe. No matter their protection, or their security." He turned and gestured to Hodiak who produced a thin brown envelope and pushed it across the desk.

"Rosemary Longthorn Grey's appointments for the next three days, and her London address," said the Bookkeeper. "She has a two man CP team, plus a driver. Kill them all if you need to, but bring her here, unharmed."

Ivanov took the envelope and stood.

"Thank you, Papa. I will not fail you."

Savalovsky smiled.

"Failure is not an option, Anatoly. Now go, pick your men and do as I ask."

TWENTY

MI6 Safe House, Northamptonshire.

Harriet Casey was bored. She flicked through the daytime TV channels, stopped at the BBC World News, turned down the volume and blew out her cheeks.

"Des," she called. "Are you making tea?"

Cogan popped his head around the door of the small lounge.

"Jack is in the kitchen, hen," he said. "I'm just nipping out to have a blether with our friends parked in the car outside. See if there's any update on Rick."

"Okay," she sighed. "But can you ask them if that update involves my bloody clothes, please. A girl can't live in a paper suit all her life."

"I'm sure they'll sort us out hen," said Des, closing the door.

Casey shuffled to the small kitchen where Jack was making tea and toast.

"Can you do me some?" she asked.

"No worries," said Shenton. "White or brown, they have everything here, y'know, it's great."

"Brown please… Better than that awful police station, that's for sure."

"Should try being locked up twenty three hours a day with some hairy arsed Scouser for company," said Jack, finding the butter.

"No thank you. I don't think I've ever been so relieved when they brought us here. I just wish we knew what was going on."

At that Cogan appeared.

"Our kit's here," he said, smiling.

"My clothes?" asked Casey, a hint of excitement in her voice.

"Clothes, cars, weapons… everything. The job's back on." He snatched a slice of toast from Jack's hand and took a large bite. "Come on my beauties don't slouch. Looks like the Firm cannea do without us. We meet Rick in two hours."

Traffic was light on the M1 and North Circular and the team pulled up on Reform Street right on time.

Casey had sulked when Des insisted on driving the Aston, however Jack had been more than happy to share the Discovery with her. She spoke out of the corner of her mouth as she and the Scot walked down the short path to Rick's newfound flat.

"He chatted me up the whole way," she hissed.

"Ye cannea blame the boy," smiled Des. "If I were his age, I'd be doing the same."

Casey shook her head.

"No help," she said. "You're all as bad as one another."

At that the door opened. Fuller stood in the opening and gave Casey and Cogan the once over. He then turned his attention to Jack who was struggling through the gate with a very heavy bag of what he presumed to be weaponry.

"You lot took your time," he snapped.

"Good to see you too," said Des, ignoring Fuller's tetchiness, whilst pushing his way into the flat. "Hey, very nice. I take it this is for all of us. What is it two bed?"

"Good area," offered Casey.

Rick shook his head.

"It wouldn't matter if it were Buckingham Palace. You won't be here long enough to worry about it." Rick gestured out towards the front door. "So why don't you two give the Homes Under the Hammer sketch a rest and help the kid with the rest of the kit?" He didn't wait for reply, just turned and added. "Put it in the lounge and meet me in the back bedroom when you're done."

Casey gave Des a look.

"See Mr Happy hasn't changed overnight."

Minutes later the team were all gathered around Rick's computer.

"Okay," he began. "We have two vastly different tasks ahead of us. First-ly, Arron Abrahams…"

"Sleazeball," muttered Casey.

"He's more than that," offered Rick "With all the excitement, I haven't had the opportunity to brief you, so I'll bring you all up to date on our Home Secretary's ex-boyfriend."

"Ex?" said Des.

"Very much so," said Rick. "Now, listen in."

Twenty minutes later, the crew were updated.

"So we're going back to Liverpool?" asked Jack.

Rick nodded.

"Yes, son. But before we can even look at the Russian crew, we have this guy Abrahams to deal with."

"You think he slotted Cartwright?" asked Des.

Rick shrugged.

"We'll probably never know, but the result will be the same. He's a double agent, a spy, and no matter who his father is, or what connections he may have, espionage only carries one penalty. However, this is a delicate matter, and it has to look like an accident."

Des nodded ruefully.

"Still, a quarter of a mil, eh? And you were summoned by the Home Sec herself."

"I was."

"Does that money include me then?" asked Jack.

"Sixty two and a half grand each, son," said Rick, opening a file on his lap-top. "Plus expenses of course… Now," he turned to Casey. "You've played Mata Hari before, haven't you?"

Harriet looked confused.

"What? Who?"

"Mata Hari," explained Des. "She was a Dutch exotic dancer and courtesan who was convicted of being a spy for Germany during World War I. She was executed by the French. Blew a kiss at the firing squad if you believe the tale."

"Oh, hang on," she snapped. "Abrahams has already tried to kill me once."

"He hung you out to dry," said Rick. "That's different. Plus, he can't keep his dick in his pants, which is the reason he lost his phone in the first place. Just flutter those lashes or whatever you did over in Frankfurt, and you'll be fine."

Casey pouted and went quiet.

"Talking about lost phones," said Des. "It sounds like the boys fe 22 did a number on the Kiev crew."

"Very neat and tidy," said Rick, "Just like old times."

He pointed.

"And whilst we are on the subject of mobiles, you need to bin those sets that Cartwright sent us. They have tracking devices fitted. That's how we got lifted. But, onwards and upwards… Let's talk about Arron Abrahams."

Rick hit some keys on his laptop and a picture of a beautiful modern detached house filled the screen.

"Our target is very much a creature of habit, and lives here, in this rather nice three bedroom number on Harleyford Road, just by The Oval. He bought it last year for a cool one point three mil."

"Jeezo," said Des. "Does nobody at Vauxhall Cross vet any bugger these days?"

Rick shrugged.

"Like I said, he comes from real money. Daddy owns half of Highgate. Anyway… moving on. Our Mr Abrahams works out, here, Sleven Fitness on Randall Road before walking to the SIS building each morning. But it's his after work antics we're interested in, where he goes for dinner most nights and where Casey will work her magic."

Harriet pulled her face.

"But he'll smell a rat instantly. He knows I'm Damien Cartwright's niece and I have an axe to grind. If I just rock up at his favourite eatery, he'll run a mile."

"No he won't," said Fuller.

"How can ye be so sure," asked Des.

"Because I've had a long chat with Longthorn Grey. She obviously knows him intimately."

"Obviously," muttered Des.

"And," glared Rick. "She believes he won't run because he considers his family connections will protect him. She thinks he'll try and ride out the political storm. Plus, he's close to Ze'ev Belinsky, head of the JDL, and that makes him a real player, he'll have influence in high places for sure. He'll disappear if he needs to, but he'll let the dust settle first. Daddy won't want his nearest and dearest leaving under a cloud, tainting the family name now, will he?"

Casey shook her head.

"So what do you want me to do, ask him to fucking dinner?"

"No," said Fuller. "You're just going to be there... here, by accident."

Harriet took a closer look at the screen.

"Massimo?"

"Very fucking posh," said Des. "Whatever happened to a fish supper?"

Rick smiled.

"Whatever, indeed. So, Abrahams uses this particular eatery because they not only know him well, but they know of his condition. He has a severe nut allergy and goes into anaphylactic shock if he as much as looks at a sesame bun, or particularly... this."

Rick held up small bottle containing a clear liquid.

"Sesame oil. It poses an even greater risk to Abrahams than the nut itself and will give us the result we're after. The allergy provoking proteins present in this, will have him choking like a dog in seconds. All we have to do, is get it into his tempura prawn salad, and bingo."

"He'll carry an EpiPen." said Jack.

Harriet gave the young Liverpudlian a sideways glance.

"The kid's right," said Rick.

"I'll see to that," offered Shenton casually. "I'll take it off him on his way in."

"You'll see to it?" said Casey, raising those perfectly plucked brows.

Jack shrugged.

"Well it's not somethin' you hide now is it? It'll be in his jacket pocket most likely. Honest, he'll never know it's gone."

Fuller looked at Des, head cocked.

"He's from Croxteth," explained the Scot. "Wayne and Colleen country."

"Okay, sounds like a plan," said Rick rubbing his palms together. "Jack rolls him on the way in, Harriet smiles sweetly and drops some oil in his Chilli Calamari, and Robert is your father's brother."

"And what will you two be doing whilst the junior members are earning their sixty grand?" asked Casey.

"The Fentiman's Arms is directly across the road," said Rick. "You'll have covert comms, we'll hear every word."

"Cracking boozer, that," said Des. "The Cumberland ring is for winners."

Casey shook her head.

"I should have stayed at GCHQ," she said.

* * *

Jack had changed into the smartest clothes he possessed. Fuller looked him up and down.

"That's what you bought back in Manchester? You look like a football hooligan."

"It's boss this Mr Fuller. Stone Island this hoodie, cost me a bomb."

Rick shook his head.

"You are not picking the pocket of a drunken tourist here, Shenton. This guy is a spy. Not only is he a paid up member of the British Security Services, but he's a double agent trained in the art of hand to hand combat. He may even be carrying that stiletto knife he used on Cartwright. The moment he sees you rushing towards him, he'll be on his guard. A teenage skinhead in a black hoodie. Jesus, you'll never get close."

Jack smiled.

Each time the kid did so, Fuller thought the room lit up. He beamed from ear to ear, his eyes no more than slits,

"You're dead funny sometimes, Mr Fuller," said Jack. "And you have a point, like. But you've never been a dipper have yer?"

"A dipper?"

"A pick pocket, a dipper is a pick pocket. There's no violence involved. It's down to sleight of hand and fleet of foot, mate."

"Really?"

"Yeah, look. This fella, Abrahams, he'll have walked that road hundreds of times. He'll take the same route, cross at the same point, see the same faces, probably. But this is London. Like any big city, people are cold, detached. There's no eye contact. I'll take him side on, walk across him and let him knock me over. Human nature takes over then. He'll apologise, even if it ain't his fault, maybe even help me up, that or he'll call me a few names and cause a scene. Either way, he'll be distracted, knocked from his routine. It's like an alter-irritant. Because he's feeling one thing, he doesn't notice the other. I'll get that pen, Mr Fuller."

"What if he doesn't stop, what if avoids you and just walks on? After all, he's an arrogant fucker."

Jack smiled again. It was a different kind of expression, more of a smirk. His eyes stayed wide open with a flat calm to them.

"Then it's plan B," he said, tucking up into his boxing stance. "I'll just take it the old fashioned way."

At that Jack turned and made for the kitchen. Fuller considered the lad never stopped eating. He remembered those days himself. Never counting calories, never reading the fat content on labels. The days when all that mattered was portion size and how often it fell on your plate. Those were his Ireland days, Bogside, The Falls, meeting Des Cogan, killing his first human being.

"You look miles away, Fuller."

It was Casey.

She wore a Ted Baker Leyora Elderflower smock dress and Nelah floral trainers, which kept the whole look as young as she was. She'd tied back her hair and applied just enough makeup to make it noticeable.

"And you look just perfect," he said.

"Why thank you, Fuller. I think that is my first compliment."

He sat back in his chair.

"I suppose I'm not noted for my flattery."

"Agreed," she said. "And I have never made life easy for you, so we're even."

He smiled, nodded.

"What are you thinking of doing once this is over? I mean, I'd understand if you decide to stay here in London. No doubt Longthorn Grey will keep your post open for you… if you wish to take it, that is?"

"I quite like Liverpool, and Manchester for that matter," she said. "And it's cheaper to park."

"Excellent," he said. "I have a feeling that we will have plenty of work pushed our way if we pull this one off."

She checked her watch.

"Speaking of which, have you heard from Cogan yet?"

Rick shook his head.

"No, but he has eyes on the exit that Abrahams usually takes from the SIS building. As soon as he's on the move, we'll take up our positions."

He pulled the small bottle of sesame oil from the pocket of his new Paul Smith suit and handed it to Casey. She took it and examined the clear fluid in the light.

"Who would have thought that something so innocent looking could be so lethal."

Fuller looked her up and down.

"Who indeed."

Des sat on the wall outside Pret a Manger, four lanes of traffic separating him from the exit that Abrahams allegedly always took from his workplace, the Secret Intelligence Service building at Vauxhall Cross. He wondered briefly what kind of day the double agent had had, how many awkward questions there'd been. Maybe none. Perhaps his fellow spies had been given strict instructions to let sleeping dogs lie, allow him enough rope.

The February weather was being kind to him, so at least he was dry. His only concern was that the light was fading, and rush hour was upon him. Hundreds of people a minute passed him by, heads down, hurriedly making their way home, on phones, pushing, bustling, fighting for their square yard of pavement. A man like Abrahams could lose himself in this crowd in seconds and Des knew it. An undertaking like Cogan's, the surveillance of a target, especially one so dangerous as a Mossad trained double agent, would usually take a full team, something they didn't have. However, what they did possess, was their man's destination, and that made life considerably easier.

At exactly 1908hrs, all Cogan's wonderings and concerns evaporated, and the tall dark handsome figure that was Arron Abrahams slipped between the dark green, bombproof, metal gates opposite, and jogged across the road, past the bus station and along Wandsworth Road.

Des was on his comms in an instant.

"Target is on the move, turning left left left onto Parry Street."

Just eight minutes later, Rick, Harriet and Jack were sitting at a window table in the Fentiman's Arms which directly overlooked the entrance to Massimo. Fuller was listening intently to Des' commentary before feeding the information to the others.

"He'll be another ten minutes," he said. "Jack, are you ready for this?"

Shenton took a drink of his Coke, rested his glass on the table and stood.

"Watch and learn," he said, pushing his comms into his ear and pulling his hood over his head.

Rick and Harriet did exactly that. They watched Shenton lope across the street, dodging the crawling traffic as he did so, before finding himself a lamp post to lean against, a spot that gave him a great view up Fentiman Road.

"He's not lacking in bottle, that boy," said Casey.

"I just hope he's as good as he thinks he is," said Rick.

Des was back on.

"Target's on Harleyford Road now. Maybe he's going home… cooking his own supper."

It was a possibility of course. Nothing was certain, and the team knew they may have to repeat this process several times before they got their result.

Rick tapped the table with his fingers, his lack of patience already getting the better of him.

Des helped his mood some.

"No, he's cutting through. Meadow Road, now. ETA five minutes."

"Roger that," said Rick. "Jack's on plot, now."

He watched Shenton rub the top of his head, a sign that he had heard the transmission and that he was ready. Fuller interlocked his fingers and cracked his knuckles. He sniffed and the air seemed cleaner, crisper. He felt the skin tighten on his back causing an involuntary shiver. The atmosphere when a job was in full flow was unlike any other.

Casey eyed him.

"You love this, don't you Fuller?"

"And you don't?"

Harriet flushed slightly and gave him a look that he couldn't quite read.

"Neither of us do it for the money, do we?"

Des again broke the spell.

"Okay, Jacko. You should have eyes on now. He's on your side of the road, thirty metres, camel coat, black umbrella."

Jack rubbed his head again, slipped a glance over towards Rick and Harriet's position then scanned the street for his prey.

He casually left his position and tucked himself up against a black Transit van parked at the kerb. In that one simple movement, he was out of plain sight, but still had a clear view of his quarry.

The action he was about to undertake was something Jack had done dozens of times as a young kid. Rolling rich tourists had been one of the many ways he and his mates had put food on the table back in the day. After all, his mother didn't have a sharing caring kind of nature and the cupboards in his Croxteth flat were invariably bare.

He'd clocked Abrahams the second Des had called his position. A tall, swarthy looking guy that dripped money. He used his umbrella like a walking stick, his overcoat open and flapping in the evening breeze. Underneath that was his suit jacket, buttoned at the waist.

He counted Abrahams' steps as he approached.

The move wasn't unlike any made on a dancefloor. Timing and a light touch were essential. That said, the first contact would not be so gentle.

The spy was ten steps away.

Six, five, four.

Jack stepped away from the van and strode directly across the path of his target. Abrahams had no chance to avoid the collision, he was too focused on making progress of his own. He clattered into the youth, crying out in shock. His natural reaction was to drop his umbrella and raise his hands, first to protect himself from the collision and then to try and keep his stability.

Jack, however, was playing his part to a tee.

As he bounced off Abrahams he reached out and grabbed at his target's coat lapel. Now both men were totally off balance, Jack falling backwards, and the spy with both hands raised with no option but to fall on top of the youth. Jack twisted his lithe frame as he fell, tugging on Abrahams' coat with his left, whilst searching his inside pockets for the pen with his right. At the very last second, just as he was about to hit the pavement, Jack twisted again. He tucked his fists under his chin and his elbows into his gut a split second before he hit the floor with a thump.

Abrahams piled on top of him, cursing and swearing.

"You fucking imbecile," he bawled, rolling off the youth, dragging himself to his knees. "Why don't you watch where you're bloody going?"

Jack stayed where he was a moment, face to the floor as he quietly pushed Abrahams' lifesaving EpiPen into the waistband of his jeans.

Finally, he rolled over, rubbing his elbow.

"Sorry pal," he said. "Didn't see you there. You okay, like."

Abrahams was on his feet. He collected his umbrella and sneered at Jack.

"Should have known. A bloody northerner. Why don't your lot stick to your own dreary cities?"

Jack pulled a face.

"No need for that, like," he said. "Was an accident. No harm done eh?"

"Idiot," spat Abrahams and strode away.

Jack shrugged, pulled himself upright, turned and jogged back to the Fentiman's Arms. Moments later he dropped into his seat opposite Rick.

"Well?" said Fuller.

Jack slid the pen across the table.

"Couldn't happen to a nicer fella," he said.

* * *

Massimo had just eight tables. Guests entered through a revolving door, a modern addition to the property, which took them directly into one modestly sized, but lavishly appointed square room with an open kitchen to the rear.

Casey was instantly greeted by the restaurant manager. He gave her a pleasant smile and checked her reservation. He pointed out that she was somewhat early, but maybe she would care for an aperitif?

Casey returned his beam, apologised for her poor timekeeping and was shown to the cocktail bar that ran along the left hand side of the room.

It was an ornate affair, carved from the darkest wood, and had obviously been imported from a far older building. There were just four ebony stools, and sitting on the first of those, brushing dirt from his camel overcoat, was Arron Abrahams.

As Casey drew closer, he looked up and they locked eyes.

She thought she saw suspicion in there, concern maybe, but it was brief. He stopped his cleaning, examined her from head to toe and broke into a smug smile.

"Well, well," he said, sliding from his perch and handing his coat to the nearest waiter. "What do we have here?"

"Hello, Arron," said Casey with as much modesty and restraint as she could muster.

He gave her bare legs another lingering leer.

"See you topped up your tan... Thailand wasn't it?"

"It's lovely this time of year," she offered, wondering just how much he knew of her recent movements.

"Isn't it just," he said. "Running to your Great Uncle for help was indeed an inspired decision." He gave her the fakest of pained expressions. "A terrible loss to the department by the way, my condolences."

"Thank you," she managed.

"Look," began Abrahams. "I hope there's no hard feelings, Harriet. I mean, I had no choice but to ask you to stay in France another day. Operational reasons, you see? But all's well that ends well." Then turning to the barman. "Maurice, make the lady one of your specials." He gave Harriet another fleeting smile. "They do a wonderful Bellini here. It's up there with Harry's, it truly is."

"Why thank you, Arron."

He patted the stool next to him. "Come and sit with me... are you dining alone?"

She edged closer.

"As a matter of fact, I am."

Abrahams raised his brows. What was this? Rosemary's idea of subterfuge? He'd play along. Why not? It may even work to his advantage.

"In that case I insist you join me... my treat, as by way of an apology for the operational fuck up."

"You are very kind, Arron," she said.

He took a sip of his own cocktail.

"Have you spoken with Rosemary since your return?" he asked.

Harriet looked surprised.

"Didn't you hear? She had me arrested."

Abrahams had spent the day checking the operational bulletins for anything pertaining to his problems. He'd seen that Longthorn Grey had scrambled the CTSFO and that arrests had been made, but on his copy, the detail had been redacted. His security levels had been changed overnight. He was under scrutiny and he knew it.

"Really?" he offered.

"Yes, call me suspicious, but when I got back, I wasn't quite sure who to turn to. I'd intended to hand the package to Uncle Damien, but it seems your… special friend was desperate to get her hands on it. I would have thought you had that information to hand, Arron. You two being… close."

He managed a smile again, but it was pained. "We're keeping a low profile right now."

"Wise," said Casey, sipping her Bellini.

He eyed Harriet closely.

"I hear the compatible computer is circulating too. That it reared its head up north?"

Casey shrugged.

"Couldn't say," she picked up a menu. "But what I can is declare that I'm famished. I believe it's good here."

"The food is quite exquisite," he said, with another leer. "Just like my current company."

Harriet thought she may puke. Instead she released her hair from its fastening, shook her head and allowed her curls to fall.

"I think I'll have the Burrata with marinated Olasagasti anchovies to start," she purred. "And the pumpkin ravioli with sage butter sounds divine."

Arron nodded, turned down his mouth.

"A fine choice," he said, then beckoning the Maître d', "Giuseppe, the Burrata and the pumpkin ravioli for the lady. I'll have my usual, and a nice bottle of your Brunello di Montalcino, Fossacolle."

The head waiter bowed somewhat theatrically.

"Certainly, Sir. May I show you to your table?"

Abrahams gave Casey a knowing look.

"I think that would be acceptable, don't you, Harriet?"

Back in the Fentiman's Arms, Rick, Des and Jack were listening intently to the proceedings.

"Smug fucker," said Des, sipping his Guinness.

"Could have told you that myself," offered Jack.

Rick was looking out of the window, across the street at the entrance to the restaurant. A red Range Rover Sport had pulled up outside and it sat there, idling away, white exhaust fumes billowing from the twin exhausts.

"That's not travelled far," he muttered.

"What?" asked Des.

"The Range Rover that just pulled up, the engine's cold," he replied, trying to get a better look at the driver, who was staying put.

Next, Rick saw the rear door of the car open and a heavy set man step out. He strode from the car, then stood to the left of Massimo's revolving door, back to the wall, hands clasped in front of him, making no attempt to enter.

"Bodyguard," said Des, his attention now drawn to the goings on. "Someone's dropping a VIP off by the looks of it."

The 'VIP' then stepped from the passenger seat.

"Jeezo," said the Scot. "Would ye look at the size of that boy. He must be seven feet tall."

That took Jack's interest. He leaned over Des so he could see the man in question.

"I've seen him before. Couple of years back," he said. "In town, Liverpool, with Nix."

Des frowned.

"Julian Nix, the guy…"

"The guy I took the laptop from, yeah. That massive bloke, he was with Jules one day outside Lime Street. He's a Russian, fer sure. You never forget seeing that fella."

Rick stood.

"Come on," he said. "Let's move."

Anatoly Ivanov pushed at the revolving door. The contraption was simply too small to accommodate someone of his size. Having no choice, he edged his considerable frame into the available space and shuffled his feet awkwardly until finally, he was inside the dining room.

The Maître d' walked over to him somewhat wide eyed but managed his trademark smile, nonetheless.

"Good evening, Sir, may I ask if… "

Ivanov took hold of the man by his throat, one handed, lifted him from his feet and hurled him into the bar. He crashed into the empty stools, his flailing arm sending glasses clattering across the polished surface.

A woman screamed.

Casey and Abrahams were two tables away, on Ivanov's right. Harriet sat with her back to him but had turned to see the source of the commotion. Ivanov thought her pretty, but didn't recognise her as the same woman that had caused so much trouble for him and Honecker in Frankfurt.

Abrahams was already pushing his body away from the table and making to stand. He was reaching inside his jacket. The Russian didn't know if his target would be armed. He considered it unlikely in the current setting, but it would have no consequence either way.

Anatoly Ivanov allowed his coat to fall open to reveal an AK47 with the stock folded under it. The full sized weapon looking almost toylike in his massive grasp. He held it at waist height, calmly cricked his neck, and opened up with the gun set to fully automatic.

The first two rounds hit Casey in the back and shoulder, tearing into her flesh and exiting out of her chest cavity. Ivanov adjusted his feet slightly and the next four rounds struck Abrahams, two in his chest, one in his throat and the last in his cheek.

The deafening sound of the weapon, the screams of the diners, together with the shouts of the kitchen staff caused total panic. One couple in their fifties tried to run by the Russian and make their escape. He pushed both back towards their seats, tossing them like rag dolls, then twisted his frame and for no reason other than it pleased him, shot them both dead.

As Rick, Des and Jack barrelled out of The Fentiman's Arms, Ivanov was climbing back into the Range Rover. The man who had been standing guard outside, calmly walked from his position and joined him, before the car screeched away.

As it did so, a member of the kitchen staff, dressed in chef's whites, ran from the restaurant. He stumbled, then fell, flailing around on the pavement, screaming in Italian for a priest.

Des broke into a sprint, vaulting over the prostrate man and shoving at the still turning door.

Once inside he took in the carnage.

Slaughter had been something he'd seen before. The aftermath of explosions, car bombs, IED's, assassinations. And make no mistake, this had been an assassination.

Most of the remaining customers were strangely silent. They sat in total shock, the remnants of their first courses chilling in front of them.

Rick was in next. Des grabbed at his jacket and pushed him to his right.

"Check them," he shouted, gesturing to the middle aged couple who had been shot last.

Cogan approached the table where Casey had been sitting, took one look at Abrahams and made a simple prognosis. Half his head was missing.

He gently lifted Harriet's body away from the table so he could examine her wounds.

"Come on, hen," he said. "I've got ye the now."

The two entry wounds in her back were clean enough, but the exits were shocking. Jack appeared at his side. He was pale and wide eyed.

"Get me some clean linen, Jacko," barked the Scot. "Napkins, anything."

Des felt for a pulse in Harriet's neck. It was there, barely, but she was haemorrhaging badly.

Rick had checked the middle aged couple.

"Dead," he grimaced. "Both of them."

Des was lying Harriet on the floor. As he did so, she went into spasm, arching her back, gasping for air.

"She's going into arrest," he said, looking at Rick. "How long since you did CPR?"

Rick shook his head.

"Belfast?"

Jack was back with clean napkins.

"Right, son," said the Scot. "Stuff them in the exit wounds. And keep the pressure on."

Rick was clearing Casey's airway, working methodically, calmly. Des grabbed Jack by the wrist, unhappy with his attempts to stem the flow of blood.

"Come away, son. I'll do that. Go get the Disco, we'll take her to St Thomas' ourselves. If we wait for an ambulance, she'll be dead."

Jack didn't move.

"Are ye deaf, son?" bawled the Scot.

The young lad was bright red.

"I don't have a licence," he yelled.

"I don't give a flying fuck, son," shouted Des throwing him the keys. "Go and get it."

Jack sprinted from the restaurant to where the Discovery was parked. He'd driven cars before, stolen cars, him and his mates, down on the docks, doing doughnuts, but he'd never driven on a road, in a city.

He hit the remote and saw the indicators flash. Seconds later, he was in the driver's seat.

"Please God, please God," he hissed, as he pulled out from behind the pub barely missing an oncoming taxi.

He made the few yards to Massimo in seconds. Des and Rick had moved Harriet to the pavement outside. They swiftly lifted her into the back, Des climbing in with her. Rick opened the driver's door, pushed Jack roughly across into the passenger seat and spun the Discovery around.

"How is she?" asked Jack, instantly wishing he'd stayed quiet.

"Talk to her," said Rick, flooring the car.

Jack was open mouthed.

Rick shot him a glance.

"Go on, lad. Talk to her. Tell her she's going to be fine."

Jack nodded, twisted in his seat and looked over the headrest into the back. Des' hands and arms were soaked in Harriet's blood. He gave the young Liverpudlian a nod before turning his attention back to Casey.

"Right, hen," he said. "Jack's here the now, eh? We're all here with ye."

"Hi Harriet," managed Jack, his voice shaking with emotion.

Des glared at him.

He finally got the message.

"Come on Casey," he said. "We need you to help us nail this fucker. You'll be fine, honest you will. We'll be at the hozzi in a few minutes and they'll fix you up good as new."

There was no response.

Des looked over to Rick.

"Come on pal. We're losing her here."

Rick ran a red light. Horns blared, tyres screeched.

"Five minutes tops," he shouted, over the roar of the Discovery's engine.

Des was doing his best to give Casey CPR, but her airway kept filling with blood. He rested her head on his knee, turned her on her side, held her to him and said a silent prayer. There was nothing else he could do.

Four minutes later, they were at St Thomas'.

"Let's go," barked Rick as they screeched to a halt at the entrance to A and E. He ran around to the rear doors and he and Des lifted Casey out. Two paramedics were standing by an ambulance chatting.

"Get us a trolley, pal," shouted Des. "And call a code blue. Gunshot to the chest. She's twenty three, female, unresponsive. No allergies we know of."

Moments later, Casey was on a trolley and the code team were running down the corridor towards her. As each arrived, they called out which task each would perform, taking separate roles, compression, airway, defibrillator, documenter and crash cart manager, the latter in charge of meds. She, a woman who to Des looked no older than Casey herself, was shouting out the drugs to be given, repeating out loud what the doctor was asking for as the trolley was pushed deeper into the hospital, leaving Rick and Des standing in desperation at the door.

Fuller and Cogan stood on the apron, oblivious to the chill of the night. Des used his sweatshirt to wipe blood from his hands, then found his pipe and makings. He pushed the mixture into the bowl and lit up, taking down the smoke into his lungs. Somewhere more sirens wailed.

"You did all you could, pal," said Rick.

The Scot nodded, relit his pipe.

"If we'd waited for the paramedics, we'd still be in the restaurant, I reckon."

Rick frowned.

"Where's the kid?"

Des gave him a worried look.

"The Disco?"

They walked over to the car. As they approached, Cogan could see the forlorn figure of Jack Shenton, still sitting in the passenger seat.

Des pulled open the door. Jack sat motionless, his pale face, illuminated by the streetlights, streaked with tears, he turned his head and looked into the Scot's eyes.

"She's gone ain't she?" he began before breaking down, sobbing into his bloodstained hands, shoulders heaving.

Des reached up and wrapped his arms around the lad.

"Come on son," he soothed. "Come on, let's go see how she's doing eh?"

"She's dead," he cried. "She's fucking dead cos of me. First it was me Mam, now Harriet."

Des turned his head and gave Rick a look.

"Why don't you check on her, pal? I'll move the car away from the apron, and me and Jack here will have a wee blether."

Rick wandered to the main entrance as Des jumped in the driver's seat and edged the car from the half circle of road that fed the A and E.

"Going to be murder finding somewhere to park," he said, just for the sake of having something to say. "I reckon we'll have to pay."

Jack looked vacantly at the road ahead, absently picking dried blood from under his fingernails.

"I think I should go home," he said.

Des shot him a glance.

"To Liverpool? That's where we're going son. That's where that fucker came from. Ye said so yersel."

Jack bit his lip. Tears fell again.

"No, I mean, just go home, like. I'm no good at this kind of stuff."

Des swung the Land Rover into the car park.

"No good at what?"

Jack lay his head back against the headrest, blew out his cheeks and widened his eyes, trying to hide his embarrassment, his distress.

"I dunno, Des. I'm not like yous. I panicked in there, in that restaurant. When I saw Harriet like that. All the screamin' and shoutin'. And the blood… there was so much blood."

Des parked the car and switched off the engine. He turned in his seat, took a deep breath.

"1979… I was seventeen, on patrol in Belfast. A foot patrol, Iveagh Drive, just off the Falls, an area well known for Loyalist attacks. I was in company with a guy called Gary Stevenson. He'd nine years under his belt and had no intention of putting his ticket in. He was a career soldier, a veteran. Tough as they came. Wife, three kids, big rugby fan." Des smiled. "It's all the fucker ever talked about. That and his eldest boy. Anyhow, it was a fine summers' day, not a cloud in the sky, and one of the local girls just came up to us, out of the blue, and gave us an ice lolly each. A big smile and a red lolly. Not the kind ye bought in a shop. But the wee ones ye Mam used to make fe juice, y'know? Gary said no, he didnea want one, but me, being a wee nipper, I took them from her."

Des took a beat.

"Well… we stopped there, on that corner, licking those lollies, when out of that same clear blue sky came a single shot. Now, whoever fired, and we never did find out who it was, used a hi velocity rifle, same as the boy did tonight. He hit Gary in the guts. I heard it punch into him, before I heard the crack of the gun itself. Gary's legs just gave way. He didnea even shout out. He lay there on the pavement holding his stomach with a look in his eye I'd never seen before. That look was fear, Jacko. Y'see he knew. He knew that he would bleed out before we could get him help. I'd never seen a man shot and I'd never seen so much claret. I dragged him into a doorway and pointed my rifle about like a demented duck shooter. Who was I pointing at? Fuck knows, son. I called it in of course, tried to stop the bleeding... but."

Cogan sat back in his seat and blew air down his nose.

"Gary died in my arms. I reckon it took ten minutes, but it felt a lifetime. He never saw the inside of an ambulance. And ye know what son? As he took his last breaths, as he begged me to tell his missus he loved her, to tell his boys he didnea suffer, that same wee lassie walked by us again... and gave me a fucking wink. That wee girl was a killer. Every inch of her. She may as well have pulled the trigger."

"And what did you do?" asked Jack.

Des shook his head.

"What could I do? I played by the rules and watched her walk by."

"Shockin'"

"I blamed myself, son. I was the one who took the lolly ice eh? If we hadnea stopped te eat them, the guy wouldn't have been able to take the shot. See what I'm sayin'?"

"You can't say that for sure though."

"Why?"

Jack frowned.

"Cos, yer can't. Anything could have happened. It wasn't your fault."

Des grabbed Jack by his shoulder.

"And whatever happens to that wee lassie Harriet, isn't yours either, son. But there's a difference."

"What?"

"The difference is, we dinnea have to play by the rules. We don't have to let the bad guys walk by. We see to our own tonight, and tomorrow... we go and kill the fuckers that did this."

TWENTY ONE

St Thomas' Hospital, London

Rick's burner phone vibrated in his pocket. He peered at the screen. Other than Des and Jack who were slumped, sleeping in the chairs opposite, only two other people knew his latest number, and one of those was in theatre.

"Fuller," he said quietly.

"Where the hell are you?" snapped Rosemary Longthorn Grey. "And… why aren't you using the secure phones we sent you?"

"Firstly," he sighed. "I'm at St Thomas' waiting for one of my team to come out of theatre, and second, I prefer not to be a dot on a map in some office in the SIS building right now, as I don't know who the fuck to trust."

"What the hell happened in there?" she asked. "In the restaurant?"

"What happened, is the Russians appear to have decided to cut their losses and show you how pissed off they are."

"Show me?"

"Well, I've left my crystal ball at home so can't be too sure, but as the shooter was seen in the company of one, Julian Nix in Liverpool over two years ago, I'd say the connection is pretty obvious."

"Julian Nix, the guy with the laptop?"

"One and the same, a Brigadier with the Brothers Circle. Answered to Savalovsky himself."

"Shit."

"I take it the cops haven't come up with anything?"

"The Range Rover they used was found burnt out about forty minutes ago in Brixton."

"And what's your security like… Ma'am?"

"I'm the Home Secretary, Richard."

"So two CPO's?"

"Yes."

He lowered his voice.

"Where are you now?"

"The Kensington flat."

"So your only protection has gone to bed for the night and you're alone?"

She didn't answer.

"Rosemary, do me a favour and get the fuck out of there. Call whoever you need to. Just make it happen."

"Richard, I know it doesn't look like it, but this flat is like Fort Knox. Bullet proof glass throughout, steel reinforced exterior doors, CCTV, panic alarms. Honestly, I'll be fine." She softened her tone. "More to the point, how are you, Richard… and young Harriet?"

"Me, I'm even more pissed off than the Russians."

"But Harriet? Tell me, I believe she's very poorly."

"She took two 7.62 rounds almost point blank. One snapped her collar bone, the second has taken part of her left lung with it. Not to sound like Doctor Kildare or anything, but she really is fighting for her life in that operating room right now."

"Oh my, that's awful," said Rosemary. "However, Richard, there's nothing you or any of your boys can do right now. Why don't you get yourself back to the house in Reform Street, or even…"?

"We're okay here, Home Secretary, and as for what you are about to suggest… I wouldn't be good company right now."

"Of course, I understand, but…"

"But what?"

There was an unexpected edge to Longthorn Grey's voice.

"I was scared tonight, Richard. The early reports were of three dead, two men one woman. I know that it's silly of me. I know that we've just, well, only kind of had one…"

She trailed off.

Fuller pinched his lips together, ran his free hand through his hair and had a quick look over towards Cogan and Shenton.

"I'm fine, but I want you to be safe too. Make the call, Rose. Get yourself somewhere safe, and hopefully…"

"Hopefully?"

"One night may turn into more."

He closed the call, stood, stretched himself and walked to the vending machine in the corner of the waiting room. He peered at the menu and felt in his pocket for change.

"Sounded," cosy said Cogan, eyes still closed.

Rick fed the machine.

"I thought you were asleep, you sly fucker."

"Coffee, two," he said, opening his eyes and stretching his back.

The machine whirred and clicked before Rick handed Cogan a plastic cup full of what laughingly passed for coffee.

"Casey's still under the knife," said Rick.

"I gathered, and you sound under the thumb, pal."

"Hardly."

Cogan pretended to put a phone to his ear and produced his best English accent.

"One night…may turn into more."

"Shut the fuck up."

Des smiled, tried his coffee and pulled his face.

"Never gets any better," he said.

"Neither does the waiting," said Rick.

"True, pal. But seriously, do you think Longthorn Grey is a target? You think she may be next?"

Rick shrugged.

"That stick contained information on two people, and as far as I can see, the main party was Longthorn Grey. It was her that would lose her seat, her the Russians wanted gone. Abrahams was merely the love interest. His

phone records, all that JDL business, just muddied the waters. They wanted their own man in Rosemary's seat, and I think Savalovsky, if that's his
real name, is an old fashioned kind of gangster. Now the newfound tools
of the internet and social media have failed him, he'll revert to type… and
slot her."

Des pursed his lips.

"If ye want te go to her, pal, you go. Ye know as well as I do, there ain't
nothing gonna happen here anytime soon. If they've to remove the lung it's
two to six hours, and that's with a fair wind on whatever other shit she's
got going on."

Rick checked his watch; it was just after 0100hrs.

"She's been in there almost four hours now. Longthorn Grey is at her flat
in Kensington. It's three miles away, max. Maybe I'll have a look see. I'll
catch a cab, leave you with the Disco, in case you need to go back to the
house on Reform Street. Call me if you hear anything, pal."

"Fair one," said Des. "But hey, take a Sig and a couple of mags, you never know eh?"

* * *

Rosemary Longthorn Grey had taken Fuller's advice, and, as her two close
protection officers had turned in for the night, she'd called in some extra security. This took the form of a Trojan, or Armed Response Vehicle, which
was now parked outside her front door.

The BMW sat with its engine running. It was crewed by three officers, a
driver, a comms operator and a navigator all armed with Glock 17 pistols.
In a secure safe behind the rear seats were two Heckler & Koch MP5SF
carbines, two G36C's and an L10 projectile launcher, along with various
baton rounds. A Trojan was a serious piece of kit.

Anatoly Ivanov was parked six cars behind the ARV on Queen's Gate.

Alongside him were his handpicked team. The first of these men, a man
by the name of Kutuzov, the same man who had stood guard outside Mas-

simo whilst Anatoly had dispatched Arron Abrahams, sat directly behind him. He was a former member of the 45th Guards Independent Reconnaissance Brigade and a special forces veteran of the first Chechen war.

Ivanov's second player was a man called Chernyshevsky. He had served with the Russian Underwater Diversionary Forces (PDSS), or the Navy Spetsnaz as it is sometimes called. A world class swimmer, Chernyshevsky had been one of the combat divers who, during the Russo-Georgian War successfully demolished Georgian torpedo and missile boats inside Poti harbour. The blond cut an impressive figure, his immense fitness and skills in close quarter combat ensuring his position in the team.

Finally, behind the wheel was Lebedev.

He had never been a soldier in the true sense of the word. A skinny, pocked marked man with small eyes and a birdlike expression, he looked out of place in the same car as three such giants. That said, despite his lack of military background, he too had been involved in the Chechen conflict, notably the Novye Aldi massacre.

He had been one of a number of mercenary-like short-term contract soldiers, known as Kontraktniki. This rag-tag band of fighters worked alongside the OMON detachment, a version of the Russian riot police. He and his comrades had entered Aldi supposedly to check villagers' internal passports, but this simple task, turned into a killing frenzy. Discipline was non-existent and the two sets of para-militaries began a murderous spree that would later cause an international outrage. Between 60 and 80 people died in a three hour rampage of bloodshed. Lebedev's first victim had been sixty six years old. The Russian had blown off the man's head with a grenade from an under-barrel launcher. Most of the fatalities that day were elderly men, pregnant females or infants.

Lebedev was so proud of his efforts, he had the name of the town tattooed on his arm.

He may not have possessed the physical attributes of the other carefully selected players, but he had something that Ivanov needed. He was as cruel and ruthless a man as he had ever met.

All three of the men Anatoly had specially selected for the mission, were armed with PB's or Pistolet Besshumnyy, which literally translated as 'Pistol Silent.' Based on the Makarov SLP and manufactured by Kalashnikov, it had been the preferred suppressed handgun of the KGB since 1967. Ivanov himself had ditched the AK and now carried an M4 carbine. His reason for the change in weaponry was twofold. Firstly he considered it best the AK be burned with the Range Rover, and second, he was about to use an Israeli made device, The SIMON, to gain entry to Longthorn Grey's flat. And that required a 5.56mm rifle to deploy it.

The somewhat innocently named SIMON, was a rifle propelled grenade consisting of a bullet-trap tail section which slides over the muzzle of the weapon, an explosive midsection and a front standoff rod. Simply slide the tail over the end of any 5.56 carbine, aim and fire. The grenade, propelled by the round itself, is detonated by the impact of the standoff rod against the door. There was no need for Ivanov to aim at hinges or locks, the explosive charge would take the whole door and frame down in one fell swoop.

The huge bodyguard slipped out of the black Audi Q7, and waited for his Bratok to do the same. Not a word was needed. Each knew their task down to the finest detail, the rewards for success, and the cost of failure.

The three mercenaries walked briskly towards the police BMW, with Ivanov crossing the road just yards behind. As the paid killers reached the ARV, Chernyshevsky peeled away towards the offside of the car. All arrived on point simultaneously, Lebedev took the driver, Kutuzov the navigator and Chernyshevsky the front passenger and comms operator. As the Bratok drew their silenced weapons and opened fire into the car at point black range, Ivanov knew his first task was complete.

He stood across the road, listening as the windows of the BMW shattered and the numerous dull thuds of his assassins' rounds found their targets. Longthorn Grey would be oblivious to the fact that her security, PC Michael Thomas, PC Helen Woods, and Sgt Dean Vickers, were dead where they sat.

However, she was about to get a rude awakening.

Their targets downed, the three Bratok took cover behind the police vehicle as Ivanov slid the tail section of the grenade over the muzzle of his carbine. He took a deep breath, exhaled down his nose and took aim at the Home Secretary's front door.

The blast from the grenade was devastating. Despite the reinforced steel, the door was blown ten feet down the hallway of the flat. Instantly, alarms sounded along the street, the sonic blast of the grenade not only triggering Longthorn Grey's system, but several other car alarms too.

Ivanov wasn't concerned. As Lebedev ran back to the Audi in preparation for the teams escape, Anatoly strode across the road, up the four steps that led into the flat and fired half a clip into the ornate ceiling above him.

"Find her," he barked.

Kutuzov and Chernyshevsky didn't have far to look.

At that very moment, Rose stepped into the hall boasting Dolce and Gabbana silk pyjamas and a Glock 19.

Longthorn Grey came from money. She spoke and acted as such. She'd attended the best schools before graduating with honours from Cambridge. However, that money, that education came not from inherited wealth, but from honest toil. Yes, her father was what some would describe as a 'property magnet,' but he had begun his business of buying and renovating houses as a one man band. A plasterer by trade, he had slaved every hour God sent to grow his business. He knew the value of hard work and the rewards that came with it, yet also knew the value of family, and doted on his only child. He taught Rose to fish, to shoot, to build walls and to know the worth of education and skill. He had also taught her to fight.

She opened fire instantly. Despite her trembling limbs and inexperience with the weapon, her first efforts were close enough to keep the heads of her attackers down. Rose only had one plan, she simply kept firing until she hit something. That first something, was Kutuzov. He was struck in the hip and thigh, his blood splattering the pure white walls behind him. The formidable ex-soldier fell backwards, screaming in agony.

Now, Ivanov had a problem. His orders were to kidnap Longthorn Grey and take her to his Pakhan alive. That was now proving extremely difficult. He carefully returned fire, keeping his aim low, the 5.56 rounds from his M4 pounding into the solid oak floors of the beautiful Edwardian building, tearing at the Persian rugs, marching ever closer to Rosemary's bare feet.

Despite her fear and the deafening noise of the M4, the Secretary was nimble enough to back away, tucking herself behind the door jamb and firing again, keeping both her remaining assailants momentarily at bay.

Ivanov changed mags, selected single shot on his carbine and began to pepper the doorway where Rosemary was hiding. He gestured for Chernyshevsky to move forwards, to get beyond the opening where their target took refuge. The enormously powerful navy man sprinted down the corridor, firing his silenced pistol as he went. Moments later he reached his goal, but all went quiet.

The former Russian Olympian ducked into the doorway, sweeping his weapon left and right. He instantly saw that the room was empty and that their quarry had exited the fashionable dining room via yet another door, that led to the kitchen.

Ivanov had remained in the hallway. He checked the street behind him, then his watch. It had been three minutes since the alarm had been triggered. The plan had been to be in and out in five. After that, the security services would be enroute. He looked down at the seriously wounded Kutuzov, who was sitting with his back against the wall, doing his best to suppress his own bleeding.

Anatoly briefly caught his eye, sniffed, pulled the trigger on his carbine and shot him in the head.

"Goodbye Comrade," he said.

Inside the dining room, Chernyshevsky flinched as he heard the crack of Ivanov's weapon. He didn't need anyone to tell him what that single shot had meant. Yet he'd known the risks when he agreed to take the job, as did Kutuzov. And to be fair, it was better to die quickly, than as a failure at the hands of the Pakhan. He mentally shrugged off the problem and began to move, keeping his body low, knees bent, tiptoeing his way forwards. The dining room was overly warm, and he was sweating profusely. He wiped his eyes with the back of a gloved hand. The kitchen was dead ahead. He shuffled his feet in an attempt to get a better look at where Longthorn Grey may be hiding. Seconds later, the whole flat was plunged into darkness.

"Fuck," he spat.

As Fuller's taxi pulled into Queen's Gate, he could hear the numerous car alarms sounding. He leaned around the driver so he could get a better look. The screeching sirens came from a line of vehicles parked on the same side of the road as Rosemary's flat, the indicator lights flashing on all except two. A police BMW directly outside, and a black Audi 4 x 4 that was parked some fifty yards further away.

As the cab drew closer, Fuller saw that three of the windows of the BMW were shattered. One officer's head lolled from the front passenger side. Blood dripping from a headwound onto the road below.

Rick tossed the cabbie a tenner.

"Drop me here," he barked. "Get your foot down, pal. And call the cops, tell them there are officers down. Do it now."

As Fuller jumped from the cab, he spotted the devastation to Rosemary's front door for the first time. Pulling his Sig from his belt, he edged his way closer to the police BMW. A quick glance at the three crew told him that there was nothing that could be done for any of them.

"Bastards," he hissed.

Weapon in the aim, he skirted around the front of the car towards the steps of the flat. As he reached the pavement, he heard a small calibre round bury itself into the boot of the Beamer. Rick instinctively ducked down, taking cover behind the engine block. He raised his head for a look-see and was instantly welcomed by a further three rounds, aimed at his position. One found the rear window of the ARV, whilst the other two flew harmlessly over the roof, clattering into vehicles further down the road.

Rick shuffled his body backwards, edging his way around towards the rear of the car for a better angle. He crawled on his belly the last few feet. Finally, he could see the doorways of the neighbouring flats, and there, not twenty yards away, was the shooter.

A weird looking skinny guy with a hook nose and bad skin was kneeling on the steps of the building two doors down, tucked in behind one of the ornate pillars that graced each entrance.

Still prone, Fuller took careful aim, let out a long slow breath and fired.

He saw the puff of concrete as his round hit the pillar just inches from the shooter's head. The man ducked back into darkness for a moment, before pushing his own weapon forwards and letting go with another salvo of wayward fire that rattled around the parked cars close by.

Rick again took aim and fired, but his target was in good cover and the bullet once more struck the pillar that the player hid behind.

"Fuck this for a game of soldiers," he muttered.

Levering himself up on his haunches, Fuller pushed himself forwards and sprinted, head down, ten yards along the street towards the hook nosed Russian's position, staying low, using the parked vehicles as cover.

The skinny shooter tried his luck, firing again at his now moving target. Rick felt one round whizz by his head and saw another kick up sparks as it bounced off the road in front of him. It had been a dangerous move, but worth it, as he too was now in cover and level with his attacker.

Fuller popped up from behind a small yellow Fiat, his speed and instinctive accuracy confusing the pock marked Russian. He squeezed the trigger of his Sig and put two rounds into the guy's midriff.

Rick watched as the player rolled down the four steps onto the footpath, gripping his gut with both hands, groaning with pain.

Fuller casually strode to him, pistol pointing to the floor. He fired once more, and the man went quiet.

"Fucker," he muttered, buttoning his jacket.

Chernyshevsky had found his mini Mag-lite, yet knew it was safer to wait for his eyes to adapt to the darkness than use the torch. As he did so, he heard the shooting outside.

Ivanov had heard it too, and the gunfire could only mean one thing. Time had run out and Savalovsky would just have to be content in the knowledge that his enemy was dead, rather than he himself have the pleasure of her murder.

He called to Chernyshevsky from the hallway.

"You see the bitch?"

"No."

"Then we move. Find her, kill her and leave by the back… on my call."

Anatoly had edged his way to the doorway of the dining room, just as Fuller entered the hall, Sig raised.

"Now," barked Ivanov, firing towards his new enemy as he did so.

Rick threw himself to the floor and took cover behind an obviously dead body crumpled just inside the entrance. The powerful rounds from the Russian's M4 carbine slammed into the plaster above his head, shards of it slicing the skin on his face and covering him in dust.

Rick blinked trying to clear his vision, but the huge Russian had ducked out of sight, the hallway was suddenly empty, and the only sounds were the wail of car alarms in the street and his own breathing.

Fuller tentatively raised his head again, taking a quick look at the corpse he had been using as a shield. He immediately recognised the man as the same player who had stood guard outside Massimo. Rick lifted himself slowly, weapon in the aim.

"Rose," he bellowed. "Rose."

The hall may have been empty, but his huge foe with the M4 was still just inside the doorway to his left. Rick's calls to Longthorn Grey were instantly answered by another salvo of 5.56.

Fuller once again tucked himself behind the dead man. He was pinned down. His opponents were in the dark and he was framed by the streetlights behind him, as precarious a position as could be.

On Ivanov's last command, Chernyshevsky had entered the kitchen, skirting an oblong island of units, his Mag-lite tucked under his handgun. Miraculously, he'd failed to see Longthorn Grey hiding under a small table off to his left. She fired on him instantly, four, five, six rounds, before finally hitting him in the shoulder. An action that left her Glock empty.

The Russian was gravely wounded. He staggered but didn't fall.

Slowly, deliberately, Chernyshevsky raised his Makarov and eyed his motionless, terrified target, illuminating her in the beam of his torch. He was taking huge gulps of air, doing his utmost to block out the pain of his wound.

Even so, despite his agony, the Russian thought he couldn't miss.

Instinctively, Rose threw her empty weapon at her enemy, the Glock sailing harmlessly past Chernyshevsky's head and smashing into a glass cabinet behind him. Instinctively the Russian turned his head away from the flying weapon, and in the split second it took for him to recover his sight picture, Rose had scrabbled to her knees.

Bleeding badly, the former Russian Navy man roared in anger. He blinked feverishly, trying to focus on his target. Feeling suddenly lightheaded, he stumbled as he fired, his solitary round missing Rosemary and burying itself into the tabletop. Rose automatically covered her head with both hands and screamed in panic as she shuffled forwards. Then, twisting her body, she grabbed the edge of a worksurface and pulled herself to her feet. She thought her heart would burst, but she took hold of the nearest kitchen stool, spinning her body again and hurled it in Chernyshevsky's direction.

As her attacker once again ducked away from the flying furniture, Rose managed the four steps to the patio doors, to grip the handle, to tear it open and run out into the small walled garden.

Rick had heard the small arms fire coming from the kitchen. He wiped sweat from his eyes and peered down the darkened corridor towards the dining room doorway, looking for any clue as to the position of the monster of a guy with the M4.

Ivanov had decided that whoever the man was in the hallway, he was alone, and that their female target was of far more importance. He'd backed away from the dining room entrance, covering the opening as he did so. Once he reached the kitchen doorway, he spun his frame and surveyed the scene. Anatoly glared at Chernyshevsky, who was leaning on the edge of a worksurface, blood pouring down his arm, face pale.

"Where the fuck is she, you fool?"

Chernyshevsky didn't have time to answer. Rick had taken full advantage of the unguarded doorway, had stepped silently through the dining room and into the kitchen.

Fuller lifted his SIG and expertly put three rounds into the big blond Navy man, two chest, one head.

Ivanov was just a few feet to his right. Rick spun himself, weapon still raised, as his giant foe lurched forwards bellowing in fury, twisting his body and M4 in Rick's direction.

Fuller grabbed at the muzzle of Ivanov's carbine, pushing the weapon away from danger. The enormous bodyguard pulled the trigger anyway, sending white hot bullets crashing into the kitchen units. Rick knew he needed to put distance between himself and his enemy. Ivanov was too big, too powerful to fight hand to hand with. He also knew he had just one round left in his mag and the chances of finding time to reload would be slim to none. He had to make that one shot count. Rick smashed the butt of his SIG into Ivanov's nose, splattering blood across the Russian's cheek and tried to push him backwards.

It was like trying to move an oak tree. The Russian merely grunted, slammed his left palm under Fuller's chin and tore his M4 from Rick's grasp. Fuller felt like he'd been hit by a train. He staggered off balance and dizzy. Ivanov saw his chance. He lifted his knee and punched out a hugely powerful leg, kicking Rick in the gut, sending him flying backwards.

Fuller couldn't stop himself from falling. He crashed into a dresser, launching pots and pans into the air, before he hit the tiled floor with a thud, cracking the back of his head in the process. He lay on his back covered in shards of glass and pottery, blood streaming from the cut to his scalp. He tried desperately to clear his head as Ivanov took aim with his carbine. Rick had no choice, He punched out his Sig one handed, firing the last round in his mag. But with his vision blurred, his final bullet went astray.

The big Russian sniggered as he saw the SIG's mechanism stay open.

"Time to die," he spat.

Ivanov took a step closer, lifted the M4 to his shoulder, and let fly. Rick rolled to his left, as the barrage of 5.56 rounds pounded the tiled floor just inches from his head. He dropped his useless SLP, grabbed at the leg of a table and dragged himself under it, twisting his body, pulling his knees up under his chin.

As he gasped for air, he heard Ivanov changing magazines. Fuller knew if the Russian completed that task, he was a dead man.

Rick gripped the underside of the table and, using all the strength in his legs, pushed himself upright and launched it in the Russians direction. Ivanov ducked, but couldn't avoid the contact, the edge of the circular wooden top striking him on the cap of his shoulder.

Before Anatoly could recover his composure, Fuller was upon him.

Rick threw himself at Ivanov, landing a massive right hand directly into his face. He followed it with a second and a third.

He'd lacerated the Russians lips. Blood now poured from his enemy's nose and mouth. Any man would have gone down under such punishment, yet Ivanov stood firm. Rick smashed his left elbow upwards under the man's square jaw, grabbing at his M4 again with his right, this time tearing it from the Russian's grasp and hurling the carbine across the kitchen.

Ivanov countered by cuffing Fuller with the full magazine he held in his left. Even though Rick parried most of the blow, the sheer power of the strike sent rivers of pain down his arm.

Ignoring the agony, he rolled his torso and went low, hooking his foe to the body, slamming his fists into his ribs with every ounce of strength he had left.

The giant bodyguard responded by grabbing Fuller by the throat. He first lifted him from his feet, one handed, then with a roar, tossed him across the room just as a petulant toddler would an unwanted toy.

Rick landed on the island in the centre of the kitchen. Something sharp had been on there. Something innocent, a pastry cutter? A corkscrew? Whatever it was, it had buried itself into his lower back.

He went to roll from his position, but Ivanov was on him again, gripping his jacket, lifting him upwards, before slamming him back down again.

Smashing his already damaged skull onto the wooden worktop.

Rick was disorientated and winded. He couldn't breathe. The Russian lifted him again, this time one handed, drew back a huge fist, and hooked Fuller to the head.

It was a sickening blow. Rick was barely conscious. He knew his cheek-bone was fractured, maybe his eye socket too. He turned his head to the side and spat out a tooth.

He could hear sirens, but they were too far away to help him. He had nothing left.

Ivanov straightened himself, wiped blood from his face and strode around the centrepiece of the stunning designer kitchen.

"Who the fuck are you?" he barked.

Rick found it hard to take a breath. Blood filled his mouth.

"I'm the fuckin' Avon lady," he managed.

Ivanov snorted. He walked to the corner of the room and collected his M4, racked the mechanism and inserted the full magazine.

"You joke, but it is you who are about to die, Englishman."

"Not today," coughed Fuller.

"No?" sneered, Ivanov.

Rosemary Longthorn Grey buried the carving knife into the back of Iva-nov's neck with so much force it severed his spinal cord.

Anatoly hadn't seen the Home Secretary creep in from the garden, hadn't seen her select the longest, sharpest knife in the kitchen.

The Russian eyed Fuller a moment, a dumbfounded expression etched on his face.

"You see," said Rick, lifting himself gingerly from the worktop. "I have friends in high places."

Rose ran to him, cradled him in her arms, tears rolling down her beau-tiful face.

"You should have done a runner," he croaked.

"Thank God, I didn't," she whispered. "Thank God."

ROBERT WHITE

TWENTY TWO

St Thomas' Hospital, London.

Des and Jack lolled in a pair of plastic chairs by Fuller's bedside. He'd been three hours in theatre. Two separate procedures had been successfully completed. A repair to his left eye socket to relieve pressure on the eye itself and the removal of a pizza cutter from his lower back.

He had a hairline fracture to his right forearm, and in the coming days, he'd need some dental work, but miraculously he'd be good as new.

Finally, he opened his eyes and looked at Des.

"Well if it isn't Sleeping Beauty," said the Scot. "Not that you look so pretty right now."

"You should see the other guy," croaked Fuller.

"I cannea let you out of my sight for two minutes. Look at the state of ye," smiled Des. Happy to see his friend awake.

"Casey?" asked Fuller.

Des pulled his face.

"Critical. They think they've managed to save her lung, but she'd been oxygen starved. It's a waiting game pal. We're all batting for her. Her old man's with her the now in ICU."

Rick tried to lift himself, winced and gave up.

"You ain't going anywhere for a few days. So ye can stop with that bollocks," said Des.

"Yes Doc," grimaced Rick. "You heard from Rose?"

Des blew out his cheeks.

"I'll tell ye the now, pal. She's a tough one, but. She's been giving interviews all day, looking like a super model, smiling at the camera."

"She saved my life."

"And you hers, I reckon."

Rick closed his eyes and took a deep breath.

"And Savalovsky?"

Des sat forwards in his chair, his expression dark.

"I've been goin' over that file ye had, pal. He lives in what can only be described as a modern fortress with a wife and two kids. And ye know what job that reminds me of."

Rick turned down his mouth, remembering Frankie Green and Tiji.

"So what's the plan, Stan?"

"Your plan is to get yersel right, ye wee jobbie. You leave Mr Savalovsky te me and the boy here."

Jack sat up in his chair.

"Hope you're better soon, Mr Fuller."

Rick eyed the lad.

"And how are you feeling, son?"

Jack's smile was back.

"Good. I know I had a wobble last night, but I'm okay now. Me and Des had a chat, like. He explained it all to me. Made me see sense."

There was a quiet knock on the room door. It slowly opened and Rosemary Longthorn Grey popped her head inside.

"How's the wounded soldier?" she asked.

Des stood.

"Grumpy as ever, Ma'am." He gave Jack a nudge. "We'll leave you two alone eh. Jacko and me are going to have a run back to Reform Street, get a shower and shave. We'll be leaving for Liverpool tonight."

Rose stepped into the room, looking fabulous. No hint that her ordeal had affected her. She gave Des and Jack a beaming smile.

"I'm so grateful to you Desmond. Actually, *we*, are so grateful to you all. I've just got off the phone with the PM and he sends his regards."

Rick snorted in his bed.

Des raised his brows.

"We were never ones for politicking, Ma'am."

"Quite," she smiled.

Des took hold of Jack by the arm, the youngster close to gawping.

"Come on Jacko. Ye look like yer catching flies."

Once they were alone, Rose walked to Rick's bed, leaned over and gently kissed him.

"You okay?" he asked.

"Thanks to you, yes."

"I think I could say the same, don't you?"

"I should have listened to your advice."

Rick shrugged. It hurt and it showed.

"Sorry about the pizza cutter," she said.

"Was that what it was?"

"So the surgeon said."

"I'll never look at a double pepperoni the same again."

She smiled at him and for the first time, he saw a hint of pain in her beautiful face, pain and sorrow.

"I can't stay long. I have appointments with the dead officers' families."

"Goes with the territory."

"Something you've done?"

"Too many times."

Rose bit her lip.

"What in God's name do I say to them, Rick. One of them has three children."

Fuller shook his head.

"It's a shit sandwich. Whatever you say can't bring them back."

Rose nodded.

"I know, it's just…"

"You heard from hubby?" asked Rick, changing the subject.

Rose looked surprised.

"Peter? Erm, well as you ask, yes. He called earlier. He's at a climate change conference in Switzerland."

"Not flying back?"

"No."

Fuller thought on that one.

"Any news on the dead shooters?"

Rose sniffed.

"The big guy, the one I… well, he's definitely connected to the Circle. Interpol have had sightings of him in Germany recently."

"Can't really miss the fucker," said Rick.

"Suppose not… look, I really must be off, my car is waiting."

"You know you won't be safe until Savalovsky is dead?"

"I know. I offered Cogan some help, but…"

"Did you now? He never mentioned that."

She smiled, stroked his bandaged face.

"You're all the same. He wants to do this his way."

"I'll bet he does," said Fuller.

TWENTY THREE

Larkhill Lane, Formby, Liverpool

Jack sat alongside Des in the Discovery as they watched the comings and goings from Semion Savalovsky's palatial home.

"Stevie G lives on this road y'know," he said.

"Do ye ever stop thinking about the football, son?"

"Sorry, Des."

"Ne bother, Jacko," offered the Scot. "I'm just a wee bit frustrated is all. The guy is so well protected. You would think after losing as many men as he has these last few days, he'd be shorthanded eh?"

"I reckon he's got ten guys in there," offered Shenton.

"And I'd say you were right, son. He knows what's coming. Or he thinks he does. Our only chance is taking him when he's out and about. He can't afford to lock himself away for the rest of his life, eh? After all, he has to play his part as the pillar of the community."

Jack was deep in thought.

"You said that Bentley was bulletproof."

"I reckon so, son aye. And there's no way we can use any kind of explosives either. When there are women and kids about, it's a nightmare. Just like Libya was."

"You've been to Libya? That's Africa init?"

"North Africa, aye. It borders Egypt, Tunisia, Chad, that area. Back, before you were born, 1987, me, Rick, Butch and Frankie went out there to slot an arms dealer called Abdallah Al-Mufti."

"Was he a terrorist then?"

"He was actually. An Egyptian by birth, a real nasty piece of work too, but he ran his business from Tiji, a small town in the north-west, in the Nafusa Mountains. Al Mufti and his crew were supplying arms and explosives to the Provisional IRA and the head shed wanted that supply line closed. We had a plan to blow up his house, but when we got there, he had a wife and kid living with him."

"So you didn't do the job?"

"That is a long story, son."

"And what happened to this Butch fella, and Frankie? What happened to them?"

Des swallowed hard.

"Frankie was captured. They nailed him to a tree. Crucified him."

"Fuckin' hell. And Butch?"

Des blew out his cheeks.

"That's an even longer tale, lad. But hey, heads up, our man's on the move."

The pair watched as Savalovsky's Bentley exited via his electric gates. In front of the Continental was a Range Rover and behind a big Merc saloon. All carried bodyguards.

"This is a nonstarter," groaned Des.

"Looks like he's going to play golf," offered Jack. "He's all Pringled up."

Des shrugged.

"Let's have a look eh. What have we got te lose?"

Sure enough, the convoy made steady progress into the City of Liverpool, then through the Birkenhead tunnel, towards the Wirral.

"Wooly country this," said Jack. "Why travel all the way out here when you've got the Royal Birkdale on yer doorstep?"

Des screwed up his nose.

"What in heavens name is a Wooly?"

Jack smiled.

"A Wooly? A Woolyback is someone who isn't from Liverpool but travels into town for work or to watch the footie."

"Where on earth did that come from?"

"Well, according to me Mam… "

Jack's voice trailed off.

Des noticed his pain. He gave the lad's leg a slap.

"Hey, come on the now. We'll sort out a good send-off fer ye old Mam, Jacko. I promised ye, and I keep my word, son… Come on, tell me the tale. I'm interested."

Jack nodded and appeared to recover his composure.

"Well, when the docks were going through the changes and everyone was on strike, like, the ship owners used to bring in scabs from out of town. The story is, that some of these blokes were used to move the wool bales from the ships to the warehouses. They carried them on their backs like and went home covered in scraps. So… Woolybacks."

"Well ye learn somethin' new every day," smiled Des.

"You're right there, mate. Y'know, when we was taken to that house up in Northampton, after the cops lifted us, well, while we were there like, I read a bit of this book that had been left there. All about Russians it was."

"Is that right," said Des, pulling the Discovery over a discreet distance away from where the convoy had pulled into the grounds of Prenton Golf Club.

"Yeah. It were all about this bloke, Georgi Markov. Apparently, he was poisoned by these Russian spies. They used an umbrella to shoot this kind of poison dart into him."

Des nodded.

"I remember it well. I was just about to join the army when it happened."

"So," mused Jack. "I was thinking like. Why don't we do the same with this mush?"

"Poison Savalovsky?"

"Yeah."

"Well, for a start, I'm all out of Ricin, that's the poison they used, and it's a banned substance, so ye cannea just go te Boots and ask fe a bottle. And if I remember rightly, the umbrella gun wasn't a gun at all. They think the wee pellet that they shot into the bloke's leg was delivered by compressed air."

"I bet Mr Fuller's bird could help us out."

Des shook his head.

"The Home Secretary? I think you've lost the plot son."

Jack looked slightly crestfallen.

"All I know is, if you can get me in close to this Savalovsky bloke, out there on that golf course, I can stick a needle in him without him feeling it."

Des snorted.

"How?"

"Same way as I got that EpiPen from yer man Abrahams... An alter-irritant."

Des eyed Shenton for a moment.

"Yer serious eh?"

"As cancer."

The Scot smiled.

"Can ye play Golf?"

Jack tapped his chest with a finger.

"Me? Golf? Listen, mate... anythin' that involves a ball, a bat or a pair of boxing gloves, and I'm yer man."

"Ye've never played in ye life have yees?"

"No, but..."

Shenton could almost see Des' mind at work.

"Alright," said Cogan. "I'll make some calls. That EpiPen gives me an idea."

* * *

It was their fourth night in Liverpool and Des and Jack sat in the downstairs bar of the Holiday Inn, on Albert Dock. It was 2000hrs on the nose.

Des sipped his Guinness, whilst Jack opted for a J2O.

"Still think it looks like an airport lounge," said Des.

Shenton looked around him.

"It's nice. Better than any of the pubs in Crocky."

"I like a wee bit of spit and sawdust, mysel," said the Scot. "We should have a run up to my hometown when this is done. Take in an Old Firm game."

Jack came alive.

"Oh, Des, that would be boss. I used to have a Celtic top, till one of me Mam's punters nicked it."

Des shook his head.

"Ye havenea had the best of upbringings eh, kid?"

Jack shrugged and changed the subject.

"Good to hear about Harriet like."

"Aye, she'll be a fair while in recovery, but all well and good, she's on the mend."

"I like her," said Jack. "She's well fit."

Des smiled, recalling the days when all that mattered was how tidy your girlfriend was.

"She's a bonny wee thing, I'll give ye that… now, are ye hungry, or is that a stupid question?"

"Starvin'"

"Thought so, what d'ye fancy?"

"A Chinese would be boss mate. And I know a top place n'all. We can walk it from here."

The Tai Pan was located in a vast old warehouse building, nestled above a Chinese supermarket, overlooking Liverpool docklands. The main room held two hundred and fifty diners.

Despite the huge numbers of hungry folk, the service was swift, and Des tucked into Dim Sum, fried squid with green pepper and black bean, all washed down with a good few bottles of Tsingtao, a Chinese beer that reminded him of German Pilsner. Jack had sticky ribs, spring rolls, chicken curry and two portions of chips.

"Philistine," said Des.

"I know what I like," offered Shenton, ordering another Coke.

Cogan's phone vibrated in his pocket. He looked at the screen.

"Yes," he answered. "Okay, good, that's fine. Eight it is."

Shenton looked quizzical.

"We're on," said the Scot. "Tomorrow morning we'll have our delivery. MI6's version of an EpiPen. Looks like we need to buy some golfing gear."

By lunchtime, the following day, Des and Jack were, 'lifestyle' members of Prenton Golf Club. This meant that for just £400, a third of the cost of full membership, each could enjoy full use of all club facilities, access to the club professional for lessons, eat in the restaurant, and be entitled to members discounts at the bar.

However, warned the helpful chap on the phone, they would be limited to just 20 rounds of social golf per calendar year and would not be able to enter competitions.

Jack had done some digging to ensure that they didn't come a cropper with the clubs dress code. Prenton didn't care for any visible labels on their members' clothing unless the emblem was golf related. According to their members forum, they'd recently had to warn a member for wearing a Nike waterproof.

This was serious stuff.

So, a visit to American Golf in Aintree was needed. Clothes, shoes, clubs and trolleys, set the boys back just shy of two grand each.

With the Discovery packed with kit, the pair sat in McDonalds, a short hop from the golfing superstore.

Des munched on a double cheeseburger.

"Now I know why I never played golf," he said.

"Sport of the rich and famous," said Jack, squirting ketchup on his fries from a sachet. "Funny how you can learn to box for next to fuck all, init?"

"Ah but," pointed the Scot. "Ye dinnea get punched in the coupon playing golf eh?"

Jack smiled.

"You're funny you Des."

"It's been said before," said Cogan laying down his burger and wiping his hands on a napkin. "But what isnea amusing, is that we have to get ourselves looking like we can at least hit a feckin' golf ball. And then, somehow make sure we're on the course at the exact same time as our man."

Jack's eyes were wide with excitement.

"You mean we can go and have a game now, Des? Practice and that? Oh, that's top that is." He pulled out his phone. "You can book yer tee time online. I'll get on it."

Des sat back and considered just what Jack had told him. He pulled his own mobile from his pocket and dialled. It rang out for what seemed like an age before a croaky voice answered.

"Is that you, Simon?" asked the Scot. "It's Des here, Des Cogan. Rick Fuller's colleague."

"Oh, hello Mr Cogan," rasped Egghead. "Sorry about that, I've just got up. I had a late one y'see. The old crone is away at her sisters and I was up half the night doing a deep dive into Katie Price's Facebook account."

"I'm sure that's fascinating, Simon," offered Des.

"It was actually. Did you know that she…?"

"Simon," snapped, Cogan. "This is a wee bit more urgent than a topless model's sexual predilections. See what I'm sayin' pal?"

Egghead finally got a grasp of the situation.

"Ah yes, sorry Mr Cogan. Of course it is. What can I do for you?"

Des gave a Sigh of relief.

"That's better, son. Right, well, y'see… I've just joined this wee golf club…"

TWENTY FOUR

The Holiday Inn, Liverpool Docklands

Cogan's golfing practice had not gone well. A mixture of embarrassment and frustration had resulted in seven lost golf balls and the Scot being censured twice by the club captain for foul and abusive language.

Jack however, had fared far better and appeared to be improving with every swing of his club.

The light-hearted afternoons on the greens had been in stark contrast to Jack's hours of practice back at the hotel, where, using a modified tailor's dummy, he had worked tirelessly on his technique to deliver the poison into the bloodstream of Semion Savalovsky.

Egghead had easily hacked into Prenton Golf Club's system, allowing Des and Jack to book their games to coincide with the Russian's presence at the course, teeing off just minutes behind him. They had already completed a dry run, watching Savalovsky and his partner play a full round, noting his movements, the positions of his bodyguards and identifying the exact spot to make their move. Now, it was time to complete the mission. The Russian Godfather was due to play at 1400hrs the next day, and the game was finally on.

With the excitement brewing, both men had retired for the night. Des lay on his bed surfing seemingly endless channels but finding little of interest.

Just after midnight, his phone rang. It was Fuller.

"And how are you, pal?" asked Des.

"Not as good as you," he said. "I'm stuck in Reform Street. They say I may need a pin in my arm now."

"That would be shite, but at least you haven't had to flog yer arse up and down a golf course fe the last few days, dressed like Rupert the fuckin' Bear. Who was it said that the game was, 'a good walk spoiled?'"

"Mark Twain, I believe."

"He was right, pal. That said, young Jack is fair getting the hang of it. The Pro has been watching him today, he says he's a natural with a club."

"Is he a natural with a needle?"

Des pondered on that.

"He's a funny old character, pal. He's good at a lot of things. He's had to be I reckon, listening to some of his tales. The kid's had a hard life."

"Ain't we all."

"Aye, some more than others, I suppose. But, changing the subject slightly, this wee job worries me, some. I'd bet a pound to a pinch of shite that these boys have seen pictures of Jacko and me."

"I'd say so. Can't Six sort out some kind of disguise?"

"They could, but I cannae be bothered with that kindae stuff. I've grown a full set, we'll be wearing poncy caps, Jack has some clear glasses. He looks a proper twat. I just hope that they'll be too wound up by the back story to twig."

"I hope so too. The Firm have done some digging on your target since he was put in the frame, and he's a piece of work. Savalovsky, real name Sergei Stefanovic is a Ukrainian Jew who made his name with the Brothers Circle as a leg breaker over in Dubai. His nickname is 'Lezviye' which means blade in Russian. Apparently, he carries a knife wherever he goes, and knows how to use it."

"That's just what we needed. I'll let the kid know, but it won't change his attitude."

"Would it have changed yours?"

Des snorted.

"Would it fuck. Anyway, tell me this, how's the unbelievably delicious Mrs Longthorn Grey?"

"Remarkably resilient."

"I'll bet. I would have thought you'd have been too sore to take advantage of this wee layoff."

"She's very gentle."

"Lucky bastard."

"Listen, Des. Be careful tomorrow. I know the Firm would like this job done all nice and quiet, but don't take any chances with this fucker. His golfing partner is a guy called John Hodiak. He's Savalovsky's right hand. He looks like an accountant because he is one, but he's a vicious bastard with it. His file would make your hair curl."

"If it comes on top, I have a plan B."

"You do?"

"Aye. Slot the lot of 'em."

TWENTY FIVE

Prenton Golf Club, Wirral

The drive from Albert Dock to the Wirral had been a quiet one. Jack had appeared deep in thought. The young man was no longer new to killing, despite his tender years, he'd now dispatched several men. But those killings had all been in the heat of battle, in defence of his own or another's life. This was different. The planning and execution of the murder of another human being was a unique experience few would ever encounter.

Des edged the Discovery into Prenton's car park. They were exactly thirty minutes early.

If Savalovsky stuck to his routine, he would arrive in just fifteen more. He and Hodiak would have a golf buggy waiting for them, they would slip out of the Bentley, pull their golf bags from the boot, jump in the cart and be on the first tee at exactly 1400hrs. They would leave two of their security detail with the vehicles, whilst the second pair walked the course, a discreet distance behind them.

Jack held the modified EpiPen, rolling it around in his hand.

It was far from the standard device.

It had the same cigar tube size and shape, and its internal workings were similar, however, the standard 22 gauge needle had been replaced with a much smaller and stronger 32 gauge, about the size of a strand of hair. There was no need for the thicker needle, essential to deliver the standard dose of ephedrine and saline fluid. No, this barb had to merely break the skin and deliver an amount of poisonous fluid smaller than the head of a pin. Once the Ricin was in the target's bloodstream, there was no going back. With no known antidote, after an hour, the Russian would feel feverish, within two, he would suffer stomach cramps and headaches, his skin would become blotchy and he would undergo severe nausea. At three hours, breathing difficulties would begin and an hour later, he would be dead from pulmonary edema, drowning in his own bodily fluids. Not a nice way to go.

Des was checking and re-checking three SLP's. His own favoured Browning and two Sig's. He handed one of the Swiss-German self-loading pistols to Shenton.

"Insurance," he said.

Jack turned down his mouth.

"Won't need it. This will be a piece of piss, mate."

"You remember what I said about this guy carrying a knife?"

The lad nodded.

"Yeah, but he's a big lump, must be sixteen stone. That makes him slow, cumbersome. And he's old."

The Scot gave Shenton a playful punch in the arm.

"He's the same age as me, ye cheeky wee shite."

Jack took the Sig and smiled.

"Thanks, Des. I know you'll have me back."

Moments later, there was the sound of fat tyres on gravel and the pair's eyes were drawn to the convoy as it rolled into the carpark.

"Here we go," said Des. "Get yer specs on."

The plan was simple enough, just as the best are. After Savalovsky and Hodiak played their ninth hole and turned for home, they would play the shortest fairway on the course. Any decent player would be able to reach the green in a single drive.

No matter how badly Jack, or more likely Des, had played on their own front nine, they would ensure that they'd caught up with their target by that tee shot for the tenth.

Etiquette then demanded that either the players behind waited for the

Russian pairing to clear the tee and be a safe distance away before taking their own approach shot, or an agreement could be struck for the 'faster' players to leapfrog the slower and 'play through.' It would be as the four golfers were all standing together, discussing these options, that the deadly move would be made.

As Des pulled the buggy up to the tenth tee, Savalovsky and Hodiak were still pondering which clubs to use, their two Russian bodyguards lumbering across the course some fifty yards behind.

"Alright chaps," chirped Des.

Savalovsky looked up from the depths of his Ping bag and glowered at the Scot.

"You'll have to wait," he spat, pulling out a nine iron.

"That's no too friendly," said Cogan. "Come on lads, you know the rules. We started fifteen minutes behind yees. We're way faster. Just let us play through."

Hodiak was leaning on a gap wedge like a walking stick.

"And I think you will find that as you are not full members, that you have no standing on this course, and will have to wait."

Feeling confident he hadn't been recognised, Des jutted out his bearded chin and walked closer to the Bookkeeper.

"Is that right, pal. I'm not too sure I like the sound of yer tone eh?"

Even though he should have been, Hodiak wasn't easily scared.

"And you have mistaken me for someone who gives a shit… Jock."

Des got in close.

"Yees have a remarkable command of *my* Queen's English fe a foreigner." He turned to Jack who was standing with a pitching wedge over his shoulder. "What d'ya say eh, son?"

Jack's pre prepared insult, rolled off his tongue.

"Fuckin' Polaks get everywhere," he said, looking more like a high school prefect than an assassin.

Hodiak instantly took the bait and tried to push himself past Des and get at Shenton.

"You call me Polak, you bastard," he bellowed.

Des clocked the security. They'd broken into a jog.

"Who's this ye got comin'?" he asked. "Scared to go out on yer own, boys?"

At that, the Scot felt something hard and cold poke him in the ribs.

Savalovsky had prodded him with his club.

"Back off, Scotsman," he said. "We're playing a game here, not starting a war."

Des did as he was asked, and stepped away, glaring at Hodiak.

"Well get on with it," he snapped. "Play on, or we play through you."

The two brutes charged with protecting the Russians finally made it to the tee, blowing hard. Des gave them a derogatory glance and snorted.

"And what are you two girls going te do, eh?"

Savalovsky looked to his long-time ally, Hodiak.

"Come, John. Play your shot."

Hodiak addressed his ball.

"I've got an idea," shouted Jack.

The bookkeeper stopped his swing, bursting with anger.

"What now?" he bellowed.

Shenton swaggered over to the tee.

"Who's the best player between yous two?" he asked.

Hodiak knew he'd always bested his Pakhan on the Prenton course. However, knowing it and saying it out loud, were two different matters. He faltered.

Jack turned to Savalovsky.

"Yous don't look like you can hit a barn door from ten yards pal." He stuck a thumb in Hodiak's direction. "Your mate just don't want to say it."

The Godfather could barely hold in his rage.

"I'm better than a slip of a boy," he hissed.

Jack gave Savalovsky his best fuck you smile.

"Come on then, nearest the hole plays on. Loser waits here."

There was a momentary stand off as each pair judged the other.

"Deal," said Savalovsky. "And why not make it interesting. A small wager, say a hundred pounds?"

"Why not a grand?" said Des, resting his golf bag on the ground next to him, top open, in readiness for what may be to come.

The Pakhan curled his lip, strode to the tee.

"A thousand it is," he said, shoving Jack in the back. "Come on boy, out of my way."

Savalovsky pushed his tee into the ground and addressed his ball, staring down the fairway at the green. He adjusted his feet, wiggled his hips, looked at the flag again and took his swing.

"Good shot, Pakhan," offered Hodiak as the ball flew straight and true towards the green, landing some fifteen yards from the hole.

Jack, playing his part, sniggered like a petulant schoolboy.

"What's a Pakhan? A wanker?"

Des could see the situation was about to boil over. Shenton had both men where he wanted them.

Savalovsky stood aside, seething in anger as Jack prepared his ball.

Shenton planted his feet, sniffed and took his swing.

All Russian eyes were on the flight of the strike. All British on their prey.

Des knew that wherever the ball landed, win or lose, the outcome would be the same. Turn the screw until all patience was exhausted. As it happened, Jack's shot was a peach.

Shenton threw his club into the air, sending it spinning over his head towards the two bodyguards. They ducked instinctively as Shenton raised his hands in victory.

"Fuckin' told ya," he shouted, turning to the Godfather. "England one, Polaks nil."

That did it.

Savalovsky threw his club to the floor.

"You little shit," he growled.

The Godfather took a mighty swing at Jack, a real haymaker. Shenton read the move instantly, rolling his body at the waist, the punch missing him by almost a foot. Jack continued his move. As he did so he felt for the EpiPen in his right hand back pocket.

Once he held the pen in his fist, Jack stepped in and caught Savalovsky with a snapping left jab, followed by what to all watching was a right hook to the ribs. No one, not even Cogan, saw the EpiPen.

Savalovsky felt the sting of the jab and the punch to his ribs. With his pride hurt more than his body, consumed by rage, he lifted his jacket and went for his knife.

Hodiak grabbed at his boss,

"Pakhan, no. Come on my friend. This is not worth it. He is nothing but a child."

Savalovsky was breathing hard, more from anger than exertion. He shrugged off his bookkeeper, let the hilt of the knife slip from his hand and stepped away.

Jack lowered his guard.

Cogan reapplied the safety to the Browning nestled between his golf clubs.

"Jacko!" he called. "Come on son. Leave it. You beat 'em fair and square."

The two bodyguards were getting closer.

Des gave them the eye and slid a driver from his golf bag.

"If ye dinnea have private healthcare in yer package, boys, I'd stay put."

They took the advice.

Des threw his bag into the buggy, "Come on son, let's go home." He turned to Savalovsky. "And ye can keep yer money, pal. Pickin' on a wee boy like that, Ye should be ashamed of yersel."

Minutes later, Des pulled the golf cart up alongside the Discovery. He turned and gave Jack a pat on the back.

"Ye fuckin' beauty," he said.

TWENTY SIX

Piccadilly Gardens, Manchester

It had been six months since Semion Savalovsky aka Sergei Stefanovic had been poisoned. The press had enjoyed a field day, claiming the country was, once again, crawling with Russian spies. Oblivious to the uproar, the team had enjoyed a bumper payday and a well-deserved holiday in the Caribbean.

There had been sadness too. The funerals of Sadie Shenton and Damien Cartwright had been solemn affairs, and Harriet, despite her rehabilitation would never recover the full use of her left arm again. Deciding that field work would no longer be an option, she had once again joined her brother, Warren, at GCHQ.

Des had travelled to Scotland, to find that Grace had found solace in the arms of a young farmer by the name of Gregory. He had left with a mixture of emotions, and his Collie dog, Bruce.

As the summer reached its height, Rick, Des and Jack spent two weeks clearing out the old offices on Piccadilly Gardens, their intention, to start a new business in private investigations.

A final lick of paint, and they would open their doors.

"Well, I dinnea know about you two," said Des, dropping his sanding block and wiping sweat from his brow. "But I'm ready fe a beer or three. How about a wee run over te the Scholar?"

"I'm up for that," said Jack. "Not a beer, like, just some juice. I'm sparring later."

Rick pushed the lid on his paint.

"I could go a nice cold one." He threw the keys to his brand new Range Rover Autobiography over to Jack.

"Now you've passed your test, you can drive us."

Shenton smiled.

"Really?"

"Really," said Fuller. "Just don't prang it."

The Thirsty Scholar was cool and dark. Rick and Des sat around their usual table, as Jack played on the vintage Space Invaders game.

"Have ye heard fe Rose?" asked Des.

Rick guzzled his bottle of Pils.

"On and off. It's hard, you know, her going through a divorce. Considering her hubby liked to play away, he's making it difficult."

Des felt a tinge of sadness. He never quite got over his own separation.

"Aye, suppose so," he said, picking up a dogeared copy of the Manchester Evening News, flicking absently through the headlines. "Jeezo, see this rag. There's never any good news is there, pal it's …"

Rick saw the Scot tense his body. Grip the paper, eyes wide.

"What?" he asked.

Des slowly lay the paper onto the table. He tapped the story at the top of page three.

The headline read:

'Manchester Murder Cop Freed.'

"Larry fuckin' Simpson." he said. "That's what."

END